FAKING UNDER THE MISTLETOE

ASHLEY SHEPHERD

To Diane

[signature]

Cover Art by: Jasmina Jovanovic

Copyedits by: Riley and Velvet

PREFACE

This novel contains mentions of sexual assault.

To: *Loveridge & McGowan Employee Network*
Cc: *Ana Loveridge-Herrera, River McGowan*
From: *Olivia Langley*
Subject: *12 Days of Holiday Cheer!*

'Twas the night before Thanksgiving when all through the office, not a person was stirring, not even Alba from Human Resources trying to get in the last of her ten thousand steps. The stockings were hung by the water cooler with care, in hopes that St. Nicholas soon would be there!

If the peppermint hot chocolate on tap in the break room and the absurd lines at Macy's (and just about every other store in this city) weren't obvious enough, it's THE MOST WONDERFUL TIME OF THE YEAR! But as far as I'm concerned, it's been Christmas since November 1st and I would like to personally thank all of you for humoring my playlists—even that one person who turned it off on November 11th at 1:49 p.m. when they thought I left the building. I'm not upset. Anymore. Asher.

In the spirit of all things holly and jolly, I've taken it upon myself to plan a few events to get everyone in the holiday spirit!

November 27th: Christmas Kickoff!
Enjoy drinks and appetizers after work while we select Secret Santas.

November 29th: Oh, Christmas Tree!
Bring your family to our special viewing of the Rockefeller Center tree lighting ceremony!

December 1st: Lace Up Those Skates!
Bring your family back to Rockefeller Center for a night of ice skating! Hot chocolate, cookies, and skates will be provided!

December 4th: Holiday Trivia!
Join us down at the Rose Tavern for holiday themed trivia! Winner gets a paid day off for holiday shopping!

December 6th: It's a Pajama Party!
Wear your pajamas to work and enjoy a rooftop viewing of your favorite Christmas movies! Blankets, popcorn, and heating lamps provided!

December 8th: The Christmas Crawl!
Drink around the city! Uber reimbursement will be provided for a safe sleigh ride home!

December 12th: Ugly Sweater Day and Lighting the Menorah!
Wear your ugliest holiday sweater to work! Prizes will be awarded to the most hideous! And don't forget to stay for our menorah lighting ceremony!

December 14th: Cookie Exchange!
Bring in your favorite holiday dessert and a box to take home some extra goodies! Prizes will be awarded to the most delicious!

December 16th: An Afternoon of Giving!
Volunteer your time at the New York Children's Hospital's Christmas Extravaganza!

December 18th: Winter Wonderland Gala!
Enjoy a night at the Metropolitan Museum of Art for our annual holiday soirée! Mingle with coworkers, clients, and history's finest!

December 22nd: Secret Santa Swap!
Enjoy drinks and appetizers after work while we swap gifts!

December 31st: Ring in the New Year!
Say goodbye to 2019 and hello to 2020 at the Gansevoort rooftop park! Open bar and appetizers provided!

The global calendar has been updated with each event! For everyone's convenience! And so that you can't say you forgot! Email reminders will also be sent a business day in advance!

I wish you all a safe and Happy Thanksgiving! Enjoy your extra long weekend! I look forward to Christmas Kickoff on Monday!

Yours truly,
O. Langley
Social Media Intern & Santa's Executive Helper
Loveridge & McGowan International
98 W 52nd St, New York, NY 10019
olivialangley@lmi.com

* * *

"Go home, Livi."

Celeste shoves a plastic bag at me, her dark brown eyes narrowed into a glare that suggests I better do what she says before she gets *real* mad.

I graciously accept her offerings, but sigh reluctantly. "You have a newborn and a husband. You should leave."

"Baby, this is a vacation for me," she says. "You've been here since nine this morning. It's almost midnight. I'm surprised you aren't passed out on the floor."

"I've had three quad shot peppermint lattes today."

My hands are still shaking. I'm wired. I don't think I'll sleep again until the new year, which is perfect because I have too much to do.

"No wonder you've got your crazy eyes on," she laughs. "Go home. Go to bed. You gotta do this all again tomorrow."

It doesn't take any more convincing. I grab my coat from the backroom and wave a quick goodbye as I skirt around the tables of *Porcelain Straw* and exit into the hotel lobby.

It smells like mulled wine and gingerbread cookies. A warmth rushes through me, one that's saved specifically for this time of year. It's happiness and cheer and over-whelming joy all rolled into one perfect little bubble. I'm giddy. Bursting at the seams. Five seconds away from breaking into song and dance. I'm Christmas drunk and not at all ashamed.

"Have a good night, Olivia." Bernard smiles at me as he pulls the door open. "Thanks again for the cookies."

"Make sure some make it home to that wife of yours."

"I can't make any promises."

I laugh. "Goodnight, Bernie!"

I brace for the cold and pull my coat tighter. I'm still smiling.

It's flurrying tonight in New York City and I feel like I'm living in a snow globe. I walk home, despite being numb from head to toe. I can't stand the thought of missing this in favor of the subway. This is the reason I moved to the city. I'm going to soak up every last snowflake.

No one else looks as happy as I do. Their necks are tucked into their scarves and their hands are shoved into their coat pockets. They brush by me without a second glance. Places to go. People to see. Everyone's in a rush.

I'm not.

I take my time. I admire the window displays and the dusting of white that's coating the ground.

When I do get home, my face is chapped and my lips are quivering. I pull off my jacket, scarf, and mittens and change into a pair of flannel pajamas and my bathrobe. Joey's door is closed, like it always is. I know she's home because the TV is on, but it's late, so I don't knock to see if she's awake. Instead, I curl into a spot on the couch and reach for the remote.

My Thanksgivings have never been traditional. There were no fancy dinners or pumpkin pie. No extended family gatherings or football teams to cheer for. Some years I ate day-old pizza. Other years I sat in the nurses' lounge at the hospital while my mom worked. I was alone. *A lot.* Most of the time, I would pretend I wasn't. I'd make the best out of my situation. With stuffed animals and dolls, I'd create my own Christmas stories. And when my mom got done working, I'd reenact all my favorite scenes. I guess it was our own weird tradition.

Tonight I'm sitting on the couch. With restaurant left-overs. Watching a recording of the parade that took place while I was setting tables.

Another holiday alone.

Like always.

2

Levi Booker is ten thousand times hotter when he's standing underneath the mistletoe holding my hand. I am also ten thousand times hotter when Levi Booker is standing underneath the mistletoe holding my hand. I'm dizzy and lightheaded. I think I might pass out.

"You, my dear, are a breath of Christmas cheer." He presses his lips to the whites of my knuckles and I want to bottle up this moment in a snow globe and keep it on my mantel forever.

Me and Levi Booker. Underneath the mistletoe. Like that movie he starred in last year. I'm his leading lady. We're in love. He's going to propose. We'll have a June wedding, and three children with his dreamy blue eyes and my blonde hair. A house in Connecticut. With a white picket fence. And a Range Rover.

Our Christmas cards will be *legendary*.

"Olivia? My bagel?"

My eyes don't leave Levi. I throw the white paper bag at Asher. My lack of hand-eye coordination leaves it landing at his feet. I feel him scowl.

"It better be cinnamon raisin."

"It is."

"Double-toasted?"

"Of course."

"Extra cream cheese?"

"A whole tub."

Levi Booker is still holding my hand. Underneath the mistletoe. Like a freaking romantic comedy. Where is my Oscar for Best Outstanding Actress in a Dream Role?

"From the place—"

"Asher, she's an intern. Not a waitress."

Levi drops my hand and looks over my shoulder at Asher. I feel empty, like a box that was carelessly opened on Christmas morning and cannot be used again. I'm ruined. *Destroyed.* Throw me in a recycling bin.

"I'm aware," Asher snaps. "But if you offer to get my breakfast, I don't expect it to be *thrown* at me and I'd prefer it to be delivered before I *die* of starvation."

"I see someone's brushed up on their acting skills since middle school drama club."

The whole office laughs. Asher doesn't. He slams his door shut and the wreath I hung this morning falls to the floor. What a Grinch.

"I guess some things never change," Levi laughs and glances back at River McGowan, the co-CEO and Asher's father, who is also laughing.

"Let's go to my office," he says.

For one last time, Levi looks down at me and winks. "It was a pleasure standing under the mistletoe with you."

The only thing I can think to say is, "thank you."

He walks away and I don't move for at least forty-five seconds. I keep waiting for him to come back. To get down on one knee and confess his love.

He doesn't.

I sigh wistfully as I search blindly behind me for the doorknob and stumble back first into Asher's office.

"I hope you're here to apologize for assaulting me with a bagel that is neither double-toasted nor slathered in cream cheese."

"Sorry."

"Yeah, you sound it."

Levi Booker held my hand. Underneath the mistletoe. If I had a blog—*which I definitely don't, especially not one about extraterrestrial conspiracy theories that the government might be interested in*—I'd never stop writing about this moment. For the rest of my life. It's all I'm ever going to talk about. I have officially peaked.

"Levi Booker is a fucking toad."

I take a deep breath and count to three, which is how I start every conversation with Asher.

"There's a Prince Charming inside every frog."

"No, he's just a fucking toad," Asher says and he has cream cheese smeared over his lips. "But he sure did charm the panties right off of you."

"That's rude."

He shrugs. "I wouldn't feel too special. He did the same thing to Harriet from accounting and she's, like, sixty-eight."

"Stop trying to ruin my moment."

Asher rolls his eyes. "You're gonna meet a lot of Levi Bookers in this industry and the sooner you realize he's already forgotten your name, the sooner we can move on to more important matters, like this exceptionally *wrong* bagel and the press releases I needed on my desk thirteen minutes ago."

"I was just getting them."

"Were you? Because I think you were drooling over a troll."

"That is so—"

"Time is money, Olivia." Asher clicks his pen and tucks it behind his ear. "And while you were making a fool out of yourself with one *client*, another just gave birth to Nashville's next little country starlet. Ava Mae Rutland. Born at 4:45 a.m. on November twenty-seventh at Vanderbilt University Medical Center. Nine pounds. Six ounces. Twenty-one inches long. Mother and daughter are both happy and healthy. Dad and big sister, Maisie Lane, are smitten with the family's latest addition—why aren't you taking notes?"

"Oh, you want *me* to write this press release?"

"Yes, Olivia. I'm a busy man. You think you can pull yourself away from the North Pole long enough to get some actual work done?"

I take a deep breath and count to three again. "You'll never get off the Naughty List with that attitude."

"That's not really my top priority."

"Well, it should be," I say before grabbing a stack of manilla folders from his desk, and then I leave him alone to eat his *normally toasted* bagel in brooding silence.

* * *

Darius throws back a nip of tequila and chases it with a gingerbread cookie. He smiles at me and shrugs, "'tis the season!"

The break space at Loveridge & McGowan International is shaking to the beat of a Mariah Carey song. I want to start belting out the lyrics, but I bite my tongue. It's too early in the evening for a choreographed performance. I need everyone to be significantly less sober. Not that I'm shy, or anything, but for the sake of my coworkers, my dramatic rendition of *Christmas (Baby Please*

Come Home) must be viewed with vodka-colored glasses. They would thank me later.

"Olivia, you've put together such a lovely evening." Ana Loveridge-Herrera is standing next to me and she's glowing like a Christmas tree that's fitted with thousands of tiny, bright white lights. If I hadn't walked into the bathroom at the same time her pregnancy test returned a faint positive sign, I would assume her glow was holiday related. Turns out she likes Christmas a normal amount and is just hyped up on all those blissful baby pheromones.

"Thank you for humoring me," I say, replenishing a tray of peppermint hot chocolate cupcakes. "I know it's a lot, but I just really love this time of year."

"You don't need to thank me," she laughs. "It's about time someone got this office into the holiday spirit. Keep up this enthusiasm and after your internship is over, we might have ourselves a permanent holiday coordinator."

"Really?"

"Really," she says. "I'll have my assistant email you about getting involved with the winter gala. I think you deserve a spot on that team."

I wait until Ana walks away before I squeal. It's not every day that you practically get a job offer from the most *badass* publicist in New York City. She once stormed onto a set of a live morning talk show because the host asked a question they weren't supposed to. It was the most streamed video on YouTube for three months.

"Are you having a seizure? Should I call an ambulance?"

Asher blinks at me before his eyes shift into a glare. He lives in a perpetual bad mood, which I think is a shame. Life is too short to be unhappy all the time. And he's too cute for frown lines.

Also, he has a penthouse apartment in SoHo and his girlfriend is a freaking Rockette. He hit the life lottery.

"Of course I'm not having a seizure," I say. "And I would hope you'd have a bit more urgency if I was."

"There's fifty other people here," he says. "I'm sure someone knows how to dial 911."

"Wow, you're definitely the person I'd want to be around during an emergency."

"Speaking of," he says as he reaches for a cupcake. He takes a bite and puckers his face in disgust. I'm offended. "I need you to moderate a book signing tomorrow in Union Square."

"You consider that an emergency?"

"Not really, but I was tired of the small talk and it was the reason I came over here, so… be at *Barnes & Noble* at four o'clock. It's for Emmy Raynard. Her book is about nail polish, so it'll be a bunch of tween girls asking for makeup tips. You'll fit right in."

"I'm sorry, Asher, but I can't."

"You can't?" Now he looks offended, like I just insulted his very expensive Gucci boots or ran over his grandmother's dog.

"When I got the internship, I told HR that I couldn't do late nights on Tuesdays, Thursdays, and Fridays. They said it wouldn't be an issue."

"Of course it's an issue," he huffs and takes another bite of a peppermint hot chocolate cupcake. His face puckers again. "Because if you don't do it, then I have to do it, and I would much rather get my wisdom teeth extracted without anesthesia than moderate a reading about nail polish."

"I'm really sorry."

"You don't sound really sorry," he says. "What could you be doing that's more important than this? Are you singing Christmas carols to homeless people in Central Park?"

"No, that's not until December tenth."

"Of course." He rolls his eyes. "I'm very upset."

"You look very upset. Especially with all that chocolate all over your mouth."

His face turns a funny shade of red as he reaches for a napkin to wipe his mouth.

I feel bad because, well, I always feel bad when I disappoint people, which is why I try very hard not to do it. But I can't skip a shift at the restaurant. I make more in tips in one night than I make here in a week. I don't have a trust fund or a wealthy great aunt to fall back on. I have rent and student loans that aren't going to pay themselves.

"Will it be over by seven?"

"I would hope so," he says. "How long can teen girls talk about makeup?"

"Hours. Days. Months, really."

"Then it'll probably go all night."

I sigh. "I can stay until seven."

I'd only be a half hour late for my shift. I could make it up after hours. Staying at the restaurant until one in the morning won't be fun, especially when I have to get up four hours later to make it here by eight, but I knew this wasn't going to be easy and I'm prepared to lose sleep in order to achieve my goals.

And there is a light at the end of the tunnel. Ana said that if I continue to do a good job, they'd take me on permanently. It's probably not in my best interest to blow off this book signing.

"Fine," he says. "Seven it is. I'm sure her manager can *manage* after that."

"Perfect."

I'm daydreaming about the four crème brûlée lattes

I'm going to need to drink tomorrow when the Secret Santa hat comes around to me and Asher. He snarls at it like the Ebenezer Scrooge he is.

"I'm not participating," he says.

"Yes, you are," I tell him. "Your name is in there. You have to."

"I didn't put it in there."

"I did."

"That's forgery. It's illegal."

"As if I could forge your terrible penmanship," I say. "Please stop trying to ruin the spirit of this. Pick a name and then buy a twenty-five dollar present. But not a gift card! That's thoughtless and impersonal. And I think everyone deserves a little time and effort and not something that's bought ten minutes before the party at *Duane Reade*."

He glares at me as he shoves his hand into the Santa hat that Alba from HR is holding. When he reads the name written on the tiny piece of folded paper, his face stiffens.

"Wow, someone's gonna be *real* happy when they find out you got them."

He crumples the paper in his hand before he stomps off towards his office. I sigh and pick a name.

Eleanor McMannis.

A copywriter on a visa from Ireland.

She just became the luckiest person in the office.

3

_____

"Wʜᴀᴛ's your _second_ favorite lipstick color?"

I glance at my watch and then back to the three pages of makeup tips I've acquired over the last two hours. It's 6:58 p.m. Emmy's momager has been on her phone in the War History section for the past forty-three minutes. I've developed a nervous twitch, which may or may not be due to ridiculously high amounts of caffeine consumption.

"Can you recommend me a good palette? And, like, what's your favorite foundation blending technique? Because, like, whenever I use a stippling brush it looks cakey, but like, I watched this video on beauty blenders and they're, like, really unhygienic."

My watch ticks to 7:03 p.m. and I get out of my chair. I'm not supposed to leave the talent unattended, but the most controversial question that had been asked tonight was which One Direction member she preferred, which sparked a heated debate that I wasn't prepared to referee. I figure Emmy will be fine on her own for a few minutes.

"Excuse me, Mrs. Raynard?"

Elizabeth Raynard is leaning against a shelf of World War II books and she waves me off with the back of her hand.

"Like I was saying," she cackles. "They tried to put me in business class. Like, hello! Do you know who I am?"

"I'm sorry, Mrs. Raynard?"

Her eyes narrow like daggers to mine. Her glare sends a chill through me. "I'm on the phone."

"I know," I say. "But Asher told you I have to leave by seven."

"He told me no such thing."

I wrote the email.

"I'm sorry that he didn't make it clear," I start, "but I have a prior engagement that requires me to leave now."

"And what do you suggest I do with this room full of bumbling tweens?"

"They're asking harmless questions. I haven't had to divert any topics. The store manager says the curfew is eight, so it won't go much longer."

"That's an hour away," she huffs into her phone. "Kathy, I'll have to call you back… I know… It's ridiculous. I'm arguing with some airhead of an intern."

I glance at my feet. "I'm really sorry about this—"

"I'm not paying Asher to work ninety percent of the time." She steps closer to me, her lanky figure looming over mine. It's hard not to be intimidated by a woman who carries five phones and is ten inches taller than me. "If this sort of behavior continues, I'll consider finding more professional representation."

"It won't happen again," I say. "I can assure you that, Mrs. Raynard."

"Don't make me promises you can't keep," she snarls. "I'll be speaking to Asher about this."

I try to apologize again, but she holds her hand up to shush me. When she walks over to the stage where Emmy is answering a question about lip stains versus lipsticks, I make my escape through the front door.

It's bitterly cold. The sidewalks are crowded with too many people with too many bags. I weave between them, apologies trembling off my lips. I can't hear my thoughts over the incessant ringing of bells. I'm so late. *So so so late.* Tonight can't get worse.

My heel breaks on E 15th Street. I hobble down the stairs of the 14th Street subway station and limp onto the platform. I wait sixteen minutes because of a technical difficulty and get up to 77th Street just before eight o'clock. I run three blocks and rip holes in the bottom of my tights. When I run through the service entrance of the hotel, I'm already stripped out of my sweater. Elliot from maintenance blushes when he sees my bright blue bra.

Celeste comes running towards me with a pair of heels she bummed off the girl working check-in and it's a joint effort buttoning my white shirt and tucking it into my skirt.

"I'm so late," I say. "Has he realized?"

"Yes."

"He's going to fire me."

"No, he's not. He likes staring at your tits too much."

"Great."

My phone buzzes in my bag. It's Asher. He's called me eight times.

You seriously left?

Do you have any idea what I'm dealing with right now?

A menopausal momager from the seventh circle of hell.

I'm trying to watch Hamilton!

"Olivia." Ivan is standing in the doorway tapping his foot. He looks at me and then at the top button of my shirt that's undone. "Do you know where we keep our schedule?"

"Yes."

"Do you know how to tell time?"

"Yes."

"Then I suggest you put both talents together and arrive when your shift starts."

"I'm sorry," I say. "It won't happen again."

"Let's hope not."

I don't have time to run to the bathroom to cry. I greet my first table and take their drink order. For the next four hours, I play the role of dutiful server.

When I get home, just shy of two, I search tirelessly for my keys, and when they turn up missing, I knock on the door twelve times, but Joey doesn't answer. I slide onto the floor, too exhausted to cry.

* * *

To: *Loveridge & McGowan Employee Network*
Cc: *Ana Loveridge-Herrera, River McGowan*
From: *Olivia Langley*
Subject: *Christmas Tree Lighting!*

Tonight is the annual lighting of the Christmas tree in *Rockefeller Center*! Loveridge & McGowan has reserved a special viewing space for you and your family to enjoy the festivities! Dress warmly and enjoy a night of holiday cheer! The show starts promptly at 8:00 p.m.!

Yours truly,

O. Langley

Social Media Intern & Santa's Executive Helper

Loveridge & McGowan International

98 W 52nd St, New York, NY 10019

olivialangley@lmi.com

* * *

My paper cup of hot chocolate has an Instagram worthy red lipstick kiss around the rim. I pucker my lips and widen my eyes, posing for Bree next to a perfectly lit white tree. I'm going to hashtag the hell out of it and get a thousand likes.

Rockefeller Center is packed tightly with crowds of chattering teeth, bobble hats, and complaints about the windchill. Midtown Manhattan is *freezing*. I lost the feeling in my toes fifteen minutes ago, but I'm trying to remain positive. There are gingerbread *and* snickerdoodle cookies—*I've eaten seven*—and even though my lips are numb and my fingers are tingling, I look *really* cute. I'm wearing high-waisted black disco pants, a cream-colored cropped sweater, and a faux-fur jacket I found at a thrift store for seven dollars. It's hard to be upset about the weather when I'm still buzzing from the deal I got.

And possibly all the coffee I've consumed.

I really need to cut back.

"Did you finish those press releases for Asher?" Bree asks.

"Of course I did," I say. "I need to get back in his good graces."

"What he needs is a good punch in the face."

"Violence is never the answer," I say. "He's just very… particular."

"He's a giant dickhead with a freaking degree in dramatic literature. He only got this job because Daddy handed it to him."

"He's not *that* bad."

She rolls her eyes. "All I'm saying is that he has you running around the city getting bagels and doing all of his grunt work while he sits at his desk and... I don't know... writes passive-aggressive poetry on his secret blog."

"I keep my passive-aggressive poetry in much more private places, Ms. Truong."

Asher has his hands shoved into the pockets of his double-breasted navy coat. He's glaring at Bree, which is a nice break from all the soul-sucking that's usually directed towards me. It's hard to take him seriously when his cheeks and nose are adorably red. I want to pinch them.

I don't.

"Well then." Bree widens her eyes at me. "This just got a whole lot less merry. I'm gonna go find a drink."

I watch Bree run into the bar across the street and I take a sip of my now *cold* chocolate before turning to Asher. I smile. He doesn't.

He's not as annoyed with me as he was last night. I think it has something to do with the fact that his morning bagel was definitely double-toasted and slathered in cream cheese. I also sent Elizabeth "Menopausal Momager" Raynard a wine and cheese basket, which had to have eased the pain a little.

"You look like a poodle that stuck its tongue into an electrical socket."

"How descriptive."

"I'm a passive-aggressive poet."

"And you didn't even know it."

Asher rolls his eyes. "This is a piss-poor turnout."

Bree and I are the only ones here from the office. The sixty percent chance of snow was enough for everyone to mumble apologies to me while they hurried out the door to their much warmer homes. Bree only came because I promised to buy her coffee for a week.

"More cookies for us," I say. "I'm glad you came, but I have a sneaking suspicion it's not for the *epic* hot chocolate and Snapchat filters."

"I'm here because my father insisted the company be represented by someone who doesn't look and act like a deranged elf."

"Oh," I say. "I figured you were here for Francesca."

"What?"

"Your girlfriend? She's performing tonight."

Asher's face turns stone-cold and he snarls down at the crowd below, which isn't a reaction I expect to get from someone who's dating an Italian mega babe who has a law degree and legs for days. He should be beaming like the sun.

"We're not together anymore."

"Since when?"

"A few months ago."

"Why?"

"Apparently I have the emotional capacity of a rock."

That's why he's been more grouchy than usual. It all makes sense. No one wants to face the holidays as a newly-single person, fending off all the when and why and how questions. It must be so depressing having to rehash all the gory details. And then to see all the happy couples living in jingle bell bliss while you're nursing a broken heart? I would be a little grinchy too.

"I'm sorry—"

"Don't be," he says. "And I'd rather not discuss my

personal life with you. I don't even like you. You're shrill and annoying and you write in purple ink."

"I like purple ink."

"It's tacky."

A hum trickles off my lips and I look away from Asher as the lights dim and the live performances begin.

There has to be something I can do to make his holiday a little brighter. The last thing I want anyone to feel is sad around Christmas, when everything is supposed to be holly and jolly and gingerbread-flavored. I could take him to the holiday market at Bryant Park. Or sign him up for a cookie baking class. Something to get him out and doing something festive. I bet he doesn't even have a tree, which is a shame because he has a gorgeous window that's just calling for a Fraser Fir. I'm going to have one sent there tomorrow.

And a wreath.

And a dozen boxes of string lights.

He's going to be living in a winter wonderland.

Francesca comes on after an R&B singer finishes her version of *Last Christmas*. Asher looks unfazed. His lips are set in a pointed frown and he's glowering the same way he does when I enter his office without knocking.

He's hiding it well. To any passerby, he's just here for the show, but I can see his eyes shift as Francesca moves across the stage like some sort of whimsical gazelle. His jaw and fists clench. He looks angry. Though, I'm not sure if it's with her or himself.

I wonder what would happen if I talked to her.

Try to explain that Asher's under a lot of pressure at work.

Maybe she'd give him another chance.

"She's beautiful." I'm in awe of her.

"She's heartless."

He must still be in his angry phase. I wonder if he's already gone through his eat-three-pints-of-ice-cream-and-not-get-out-of-bed phase. I need to know these things so I can gage how far along he is in his recovery. Because if he hasn't cried yet, then we have a very long road ahead of us.

It's when the first snowflake falls and the countdown begins that I realize what I'm actually up against. Because Francesca is on stage cuddled up next to a guy with a ginger beard and Asher is shaking next to me. It's not just snow in the air, but jealousy is rearing its ugly head too.

This changes everything.

She can't see Asher like this—sad and angry and lonely —not when she's already moved on and looks smitten and in love. He's one forehead wrinkle away from losing his mind.

So I think fast, because I'm good at it. I know how to improvise and make do with what I have. The things I can do with a tube of glue and some popsicle sticks.

When I see Francesca turn towards the area Asher and I are standing in, I make a very rash decision.

"Trust me," I say to him.

"What? Why? More importantly: no!"

But I'm already grabbing onto the lapels of his jacket, yanking him down to my level because even in three inch heels, I'm barely five-four. I watch his eyes go wide before I close mine.

We're kissing.

Or, at least, I'm kissing.

Asher needs some serious direction, but that's a lesson for another day.

It's sickeningly sweet and innocent. I giggle into his mouth and my lips part into a smile against his. I've always wanted to do this—kiss someone in front of a Christmas tree in the middle of New York City. I just didn't expect it to be under these circumstances, and I definitely didn't expect it would be with Asher McGowan.

When I pull away, there are snowflakes on his eyelashes. I laugh and brush them off with the pad of my thumb. I wait for a response, but he's frozen. Shocked. Maybe mesmerized? I'm a fantastic kisser. He's definitely savoring the moment. I bet he's going to send me a wine and cheese basket tomorrow.

"What the hell—"

"Asher?"

Francesca is standing next to us, hand in hand with Ginger Beard. I grab Asher's hand, tucking myself next to him. He stiffens.

"Frankie… Brent…" he slowly states. "Hey."

"Hey yourself," she laughs. "How've you been?"

"Good. I've been—"

"I'm Olivia," I say and shove my free hand at her. "Your performance was stunning."

Francesca looks down at me the way most people do—like I'm an alien from some far off planet. I'm not offended. I like being different.

"Thanks," she says slowly.

She's giving me a once over. From the points of my boots to the bobble of my hat, she takes in all five feet and one inch of me. It reads so clearly over her face. She's wondering how Asher went from her to me. We're exact opposites. We have nothing in common. Physically. Intellectually. Spiritually. Emotionally. Mentally. We're *so* different.

"I didn't know you were seeing someone," she says to Asher, practically disregarding my entire existence.

"I'm—"

"It's still new," I tell her. "We just started telling people."

"I see," she says. "Where did you meet?"

"Work."

"Interesting," she says and tugs on Brent's hand, which is code for *I'm happy and in love and not crying over you either.* "If you two don't have plans, there's an after party at the *Rose Tavern* across the street. It's an open bar."

"Yeah, we—"

"We'd love to!" I say and tug on Asher's hand, which is my code for *you better start playing along before we both end up looking like fools.*

* * *

We get all the way to the bar before Asher even says a word to me.

"What the hell do you think you're doing?"

I take my hat off and shake out my blonde hair that has gone all frizzy from the snow. A chill runs through me as I start to unthaw. I shiver when I slip my arms out of my jacket.

"I'm going to order a drink," I say and wave over the bartender. "Can I get a glass of your cheapest red wine?"

"It's an open bar…"

"I don't like to live above my means."

He furrows his brows at me and then looks at Asher. "And for you?"

"Do you have Stella on tap?"

"No, but I have a craft that's fairly similar."

Asher frowns. "Grey Goose and soda with lime."

He waits until the bartender is making our drinks before he starts glaring at me again.

"As I was saying," he says. "What the hell was that?"

"Was what?"

"*Olivia.*"

"I was trying to help!"

"By creating some elaborate scheme about how we're *dating*? As if I would ever date someone who I'm fairly certain has escaped a mental facility."

"That's rude," I say. "Mental illness shouldn't dictate whether or not someone can be in a romantic relationship. Not that I'm mentally ill, but if I was, I'd still be deserving of love and affection and—"

"Olivia!"

"What was I supposed to do? You were standing there pining over her!"

"I was not *pining*. I was telepathically trying to break her leg."

"That's awful."

"She's awful."

"Says the emotionally inept rock."

We get our drinks and Asher downs his before I even take a sip.

"You have no idea what you've just done," he says.

"A thank you would be nice."

"You want me to thank you?"

"It would be greatly appreciated."

He scoffs and slams his empty glass onto the counter. "*Thank you*, Olivia. For fucking up yet another aspect of my life. You really outdid yourself this time. Cheers!"

Before I can say anything, I see Francesca out of the corner of my eye.

"Laugh at me."

"You are a joke."

I frown. "*Laugh.*"

"No, I'm annoyed with you."

"I don't care," I say. "Laugh!"

"No!"

I jam my foot down on his.

He grunts.

I laugh.

And Francesca walks over to us just in time for me to nuzzle into Asher's chest.

4

———

JOEY IS ten chapters deep in a novel with a shirtless pirate on the cover and silences me with a finger whenever I try to speak. She must be at a *really* good part.

We're sharing a car, which is relatively normal for most, but by far the strangest thing ever for us. In the past eleven months that we've been living together, I can count on one hand how many conversations we've had that were more than one word answers. Joey doesn't like to talk. I thought it was just a me thing, but on the rare occasion she brings people over, she's short with them too. Not in a rude way. Just in a Joey way. Some people like to listen. That's okay.

I like to talk.

My gift of gab is documented on every report card I've ever received.

Punctual and well prepared, but does not give other students a chance to speak—does not give me a chance to speak.

Olivia does exemplary work and works to her full potential, but she is a bit chatty.

Olivia enjoys talking. A lot.

A man asked to be moved on an airplane because I was talking too much. He wasn't even sitting next to me. I pretended I wasn't offended, but it still bothers me.

"Thank you," I manage to say before Joey can shush me. "It was very nice of you to stop the car for me."

It's sleeting out and I'm not wearing tights. It would have been a very cold and wet walk to the subway and then to the office. The three dozen donuts on my lap would have suffered the consequences of an almost New York winter. It would have been a very soggy tragedy.

"We're going to the same place." Joey flips the page of her book. "I'm not a complete dickhead."

"I don't think you're a dickhead at all."

It's true. I don't. I wish we had a better relationship and sat up on the couch all night and binge-watched TV shows while eating ice cream straight out of the carton as we cry about our romantic woes and the current state of our government, but I learned a long time ago that life doesn't always look the way it does in the movies.

"Can I have a donut?" Joey says after a moment. "I figure my money partially pays for them. I think I'm entitled to a strawberry frosted."

"Go for it," I say. "I had two before I got out of the shop."

They were delicious. I can already feel them on my hips. And trust me, my hips have already suffered the consequences of a dozen gingerbread cookies and a container of peppermint bark.

Joey's a model with much more discipline than me. She

does double SoulCycle classes on the weekend and she just killed it at the biggest lingerie fashion show of the year. She deserves all the donuts and a nap.

We get to the office after forty minutes of bumper to bumper traffic. It's a good thing Asher is used to me being late, which is usually his fault. The donuts, however, were requested by Ana, and I'm not one to deny a pregnant lady what she wants.

"You're going up to Ana's office, right?" I ask as we wait for the elevator.

"She is my publicist…"

"Then you won't mind bringing this box with you." I nudge a dozen donuts into her hands before she even agrees.

"Are you trying to give her gestational diabetes?"

"I'm sure she's not going to eat the whole box."

"You underestimate the power of a dozen donuts."

We laugh. For the first time ever, Joey and I exchange normal human emotion. It's a Christmas miracle.

The elevator dings and the doors part and our moment is ruined by something equally miraculous.

Levi Booker looks like a vision straight out of an erotic dream. Black jeans. White t-shirt. Perfectly fitted leather jacket. I want him to destroy me.

"Christmas morning came early," he says as he steps out of the elevator with River and Alexander, Asher's brother, following closely behind. "Though I did imagine you'd be wrapped up in pretty red ribbon underneath my tree."

I blush.

"I suppose there's still a chance," he says. "I've been a very good boy this year."

Joey scoffs.

"Josephine," he drawls. "It's been a while."

"Not long enough," she says and steps into the elevator.

"So I shouldn't expect a Christmas card from you?"

"I'd much sooner mail you a dead rat," she says. "Olivia, let's go."

I force a smile at Levi. "It was nice seeing you."

"Always a pleasure, Livi."

Livi.

Livi.

Livi.

Levi and Livi.

My knees go weak.

I'm designing our wedding invitations as the elevator zips up to the fourth floor. I'm so distracted I don't hear it ding.

"Isn't this you?" Joey asks.

"Right," I say and I'm in a Levi induced daze. I practically fall into the hallway, but catch myself before I lose any donuts.

"Olivia?"

I turn around when I hear Joey's voice.

"Yeah?"

"Don't be charmed by him."

How can I not be? He calls me Livi and makes me want to rip my clothes off. Charmed is an understatement.

I'm floating through the office. I hum along to the Christmas song on the radio and I hand out donuts and I don't even get mad when I see the tinsel I hung around Asher's door has been torn down. I'm blissed out on Levi. I can't wait to tell our two daughters and son about this moment.

"Liv!" Bree shoves her hand into my box of donuts before saying anything else. She takes the last chocolate glazed, smells it, and then puts it back. "You... you've got that glow."

"The I-forgot-to-use-powder-on-my-forehead glow?"

"No, the I-just-had-an-earth-shattering-orgasm glow."

"I mean, I did run into Levi Booker and his face is sort of like an orgasm."

"I heard he's pretty one-and-done."

"I doubt he's that selfish, Bree."

She shrugs. "Anyway, Satan has summoned you to his lair."

"What?"

"Asher."

"He's not in until this afternoon."

"He has a car waiting for you."

"Seriously?" Asher doesn't send cars. He just tells me to be somewhere and I find my own mode of transportation. This must be serious. It's probably about Francesca.

"Are you sleeping with him?" Bree opens the box to smell the donuts again.

"What? He doesn't even like me."

She shrugs. "You don't have to like someone to have sex with them. You just have to want to get laid."

"I'm not sleeping with him. He's my boss."

That I've kissed.

"Is he really a boss, though?"

"I report to him, so he's my supervisor at the very least," I tell her. "And we are not sleeping together."

But his ex-girlfriend definitely thinks we are.

I don't need to tell Bree that, though. This is Asher's and my little secret. One he probably doesn't want the whole office to know about. We're probably breaking a lot of rules. Fraternizing with the interns is frowned upon.

"I'll take these." Bree grabs the donuts from me. "And

you go tie Asher's shoelaces before he gets another wrinkle on his forehead."

I take a sour cream glazed for the road and turn back to the elevator.

* * *

Asher is shoveling Lucky Charms into his mouth when he opens the door. He's chewing with such vigor that I have to wonder if he has any teeth left.

"There's a Christmas tree in my living room," he says after swallowing.

"It came?!"

"*Why* is there a Christmas tree in my living room?"

"Because I ordered one."

"I don't recall asking you to order a Christmas tree or five wreaths or an animatronic reindeer that I have absolutely no place for."

"Of course you have a place for it," I say, pushing past him. "You have a veranda."

"I'm not putting an animatronic reindeer on the veranda of my three million dollar apartment."

"That makes you sound very pretentious."

"I've been called worse."

"Okay, Ebenezer."

I follow the scent of coffee through his apartment that feels as cold as it does outside and drop the bagel I brought as a peace offering onto his table next to today's *New York Post*.

He lives in an old industrial building with exposed brick walls and wooden beams lining the ceiling. It's an open floor plan. A countertop bar with four metal chairs divides the kitchen and living room. His computer is set up at the very end where a crumpled up napkin and an abandoned plate of toast lies. There's a coffee stain on the marble top.

His couch is plush and white and marshmallow-like and sits in front of a small oriental rug —the light glaring in from the floor to ceiling windows makes it glow. I want to sink into it with a mug of hot chocolate and a fleece blanket while watching *Hallmark Channel* movies on his TV that's bigger than my entire apartment.

But what strikes me most whenever I come here— which isn't very often—is that the only form of life in this place is the leafy green plant that sits on top of his coffee table. There are no pictures or paintings or small personal touches. It's empty.

Which is why he needs these Christmas decorations— to breathe some life into this place.

"They sent over the Fraser Fir," I squeal, and bend down to run my fingers over the prickly green needles. The scent of pine slowly perfumes the area. It already feels more like Christmas here. "I was so worried they'd send the wrong one and then I'd have to call them back and have them deliver a new one—"

"You do have to call them back," Asher says. "I want them to remove it."

"You're telling me that you've never had a Christmas tree before?"

"Of course I've had a Christmas tree," he says and spoons another scoop of cereal into his mouth. "When I was a child."

"I… didn't realize there was an age restriction on Christmas trees."

"There isn't," he says. "I just don't care to have one in my home."

"That makes me really sad."

"I'm sorry that my lack of enthusiasm surrounding Christmas festivities makes you sad, Olivia."

I take a deep breath and count to three before I walk over to the table and unwrap the bagel.

"Is that for me?" he asks.

"It was," I say. "But you're already eating."

I've already had three donuts, but arguing with Asher really works up an appetite.

"That doesn't mean I can't eat a bagel," he says as I pull the top and bottom apart. "What are you doing? That's not how you eat a bagel. Are you some kind of savage?"

"I don't think there's a right or wrong way to eat a bagel, Asher."

"Of course there is and that's definitely the *wrong* way."

I roll my eyes. "Which is your favorite half?"

"Both."

"I like the bottom," I tell him before taking a bite. "It has more of a chew."

He's glaring at me as I sweep leftover cream cheese off the corner of my mouth with my tongue.

"It's rude to eat a bagel that you bought for someone else."

"It's rude to not thank someone for ordering you a Christmas tree."

"It was an unsolicited Christmas tree."

"This is an unsolicited bagel." I grin. "Besides, you're already ruining your workout with a bowl of sugar. You don't need more carbs."

He's wearing fitted track pants and a gray hoodie, his hair hidden beneath a beanie. He runs. He also does pilates, but his masculinity is too fragile for him to admit that.

"Are you the carbohydrate police?"

"Of course not," I say. "I had three donuts before I got here."

"Then why are you eating my bagel?"

"Because I'm an emotional eater and your lack of Christmas cheer is making me very sad."

Asher closes his eyes and pinches his forehead. I'm aggravating him, which is something I've grown good at without even trying.

"Uncle Asher!"

The door to his apartment flies open and a tiny ball of pink tulle and glitter launches herself at him. He barely has a chance to put his bowl of milk on the table before he has no choice but to scoop her up in his arms. He glares at the woman who walks in behind her.

"I see we've got the knocking thing down," he says.

"Mommy says that if you leave your door unlocked, it's your own fault."

"Mommy's full of sage wisdom, isn't she?"

"She says you need an attitude adjustment and a haircut."

"Chloe, you're not supposed to tell all of Mommy's secrets!" the woman says.

"I didn't tell Mama that you broke her favorite wine glasses."

"Oh, but I might," Asher says. He blows a raspberry on Chloe's cheek until she squeals and wiggles out of his arms.

I'm speechless. It doesn't happen very often, but on a rare occasion something can shock me into silence. This is one of those moments. Asher has a heart. I mean, I knew he did, but I wasn't sure at what capacity he allowed himself to feel things. His niece seems to be the key.

"Are you another one of Uncle Asher's special friends?" Chloe asks me.

"Special friend?" I look at Chloe and then to Asher, who seems seconds away from an aneurysm.

"Like a girlfriend," Chloe clarifies. "But Mommy calls them special friends because Uncle Asher is committed to problems—oh, is that a Christmas tree?!"

Chloe loses interest in us as quickly as I lose interest in baseball games.

"Uncle Asher has commitment problems?" Asher runs his hand over his jaw and looks over at Chloe's mother. "Seriously, Morgan?"

"That girl... the ears on her."

"The mouth on you," Asher says.

Morgan grabs Asher's chin and kisses his cheeks. "I've been intent on ruining your life since the day you came into mine."

"Well done. You've succeeded."

Morgan wrinkles her nose at him before turning to me. "Are you one of Asher's special friends? Because you look much too sweet and wholesome to have to deal with his sour attitude."

"I'm his intern."

A smirk lingers on her lips. "Interns make house calls?"

"They do when they charge Christmas trees to my credit card without my consent."

"He has no holiday spirit," I tell her.

"Believe me, I know," she says. "I swear he woke up one morning and decided to be a little prick."

"Are you here for a reason?" Asher finally asks. "Or did you come over just to insult me?"

"I'll have you know that we're here on official business."

"Which is?"

"You're coming to my Christmas pageant, right?" Chloe asks.

She's sitting on the animatronic reindeer Asher hates so much.

"When is it?"

"December twenty-second," Morgan says.

"He'll be there," I say.

He glares at me. "Thank you, Olivia."

"You're very welcome, Asher."

Morgan wrangles Chloe off the reindeer and the two smile identically at Asher. "We'll see you on Saturday for dinner."

"Maybe," he says.

"Bring me a bottle of something red," she says.

"And don't forget to bring me daisies," Chloe says. "And chocolates! Filled with caramel!"

"A girl after my own heart," I say.

They leave and Asher takes off his beanie and runs his fingers through his hair. He looks exhausted. A brief encounter with his sister requires a recovery nap.

"I didn't know you had a sister."

"Because I never told you," he says and grabs the other half of the bagel.

"But I've been in your dad's office," I say. "He doesn't have a picture of her—just you and your three brothers."

"Morgan and I have the same mother," he tells me.

"What about your brothers?"

"We all have different mothers," he says. "My father's nothing if not consistent."

"It must be nice having a big family."

"Nice is one word for it," he says. "I prefer dysfunctional."

"It's a group of people that love you."

"Tolerate me," he scoffs and bites off another piece of bagel. "And most of the time they barely do that."

"You still have a family. Whether you like them or not."

"What are you? Some kind of orphan?" He glowers at me. "Anyway, thanks to your little stunt the other day, Francesca has invited us to a dinner party at her place on Friday and she refuses to take no for an answer."

"We have the ice skating event at *Rockefeller Center* on Friday."

"I don't ice skate."

"You will on Friday."

He glares at me and I glare at him. We stay like that for a minute before he rolls his eyes.

"Can you drop off my dry cleaning before you go back to the office?"

"Does that mean you're keeping the tree?"

"It means I have a stain on my favorite purple shirt and I need it removed."

He stomps up the stairs to his loft and I lean back against his table. I wait and wait and wait and eventually my eyes drift to the front page of the *New York Post* that is now dusted with bagel crumbs.

DIRTY MONEY: WHY TALENT AGENCIES ARE THREATENING TOP MODELS INTO SILENCE

5

To: *Loveridge & McGowan Employee Network*
Cc: *Ana Loveridge-Herrera, River McGowan*
From: *Olivia Langley*
Subject: *Lace Up Those Skates!*

Don't forget to bring your family down to *Rockefeller Center* for a night of ice skating! The festivities begin at 7:00 p.m. sharp! Enjoy your favorite holiday songs, an endless supply of cookies and hot chocolate, and the chance to watch your coworkers embarrass themselves!

Yours truly,
O. Langley
Social Media Intern & Santa's Executive Helper
Loveridge & McGowan International
98 W 52nd St, New York, NY 10019
olivialangley@lmi.com

P.S.: We have a supply room for a reason. Please stop leaving the staplers empty.

* * *

BREE PULLS the paper towel away from my lip and tilts her head. I feel like a puzzle she's trying to solve.

"Honestly," she starts, "it's not that bad."

I'm a glass-half-full kind of girl, so it pains me to admit that this isn't very good. I'm a shining example of why ice skating should be left to the professionals. I'm also a shining example of why you shouldn't claim to be a professional.

"She's drooling blood, Bree." Emanuel blinks. "It looks like she got into a fist fight and forgot to punch back."

"In my defense, I did hit the ice pretty hard," I say. "I'm sure it felt something."

"Just the crushing irony of you announcing your bid for the Winter Olympics seconds before your grand finale," he says.

I frown. "Someone's going to put that on YouTube, aren't they?"

"I mean, it's already on my Snap, so..." Bree says.

She also put me vomiting into trashcan after too much to drink on her Snapchat. Bree is a great friend.

"How will I ever repay you?"

"Book me a spa day at the Ritz on Asher's card."

"You know I'm only supposed to use it for qualifying purchases now."

"So just Christmas trees, coasters, and PornHub Unlimited?"

"I got him dish towels with snowmen on them and oven mitts to match."

"I feel like those probably weren't on *The List*."

"They weren't, but I couldn't resist."

"I'm sure he'll be thrilled when he opens the box," Bree says and takes the plastic baggie of ice Emanuel hands to her and presses it to my lip. I shiver. "When I said this wasn't bad, I really meant you might need stitches."

"Yeah, I don't have time for that."

"I don't think you have much of a choice," Emanuel says. "You look like *Nightmare at Rockefeller Center*."

My fourth favorite Christmas sweater, which has a Christmas tree with semi-working lights on it—a two dollar *GoodWill* find—is covered in blood. I look like the aftermath of a horror movie. A bad one. With a low budget. And D-List actors. A horror movie with a serial killer who slashes victims with gardening shears.

It wouldn't be an issue if I was going home, but I'm meeting Asher at Francesca's at nine. It's an hour past being fashionably late, but we both had prior engagements. I'm here and Asher, well, he had to floss.

He must have no cavities. His dentist probably has his picture on the wall.

"I need to borrow your sweater," I say to Bree. She's six inches taller and two cup sizes smaller than me, but I can squeeze myself into her gray turtleneck. I'll shrink it back in the dryer.

"What for?"

"I'm going to a dinner party."

"Where?"

"Williamsburg."

"With who?"

Definitely not Asher.

"My college roommate."

"Why are you interrogating her?" Emanuel asks. "Are you her mother?"

Bree side eyes him. "When the police show up to the office on Monday because she's missing, at least I can tell them the culprit is probably some microbrewery-owning hipster with a music complex."

I have an emergency whistle. And pepper spray. I've also been told my voice can wake the dead. She doesn't need to worry about me. I'm good at taking care of myself. I've been doing it for a long time.

"So I'm supposed to go home in your crime scene cardigan? What if the police take me in for questioning when you go missing? How will I explain this?"

"You have video evidence."

"What if it's not admissible in court?"

"*Bree*," I cry. "It's an emergency."

"Fine, but you owe me."

"My life."

I pay fifty cents for us to switch shirts in the bathroom of a *Dunkin Donuts* across the street. When we emerge— casually, like nothing happened—Ana is standing there with her husband and twenty-year-old daughter, Willa, who's home from college for winter break.

"Do I want to know?" Ana asks us.

"No," we say at the same time.

Asher is leaning back against a glass window, blocking a gingerbread house display with his rather sour expression. A little girl walks by—her mitten clad hand tucked into her mother's— and she sneers at him for obstructing her view of the sugar-sweet wonderland. He doesn't notice. He's too busy glaring twelve stories up into an office building while white-knuckling the neck of a bottle of wine. I'm pretending he's annoyed with someone up there and not with me for being six minutes late.

"Sorry." I'm out of breath when I get to him. For someone who runs across the city—definitely not recre-ationally—on the regular, I should be in better shape. It's probably the donuts. And the fact that I consider taking the stairs a high intensity workout.

Asher takes one look at me and glares back up at the sky. This time he pinches the bridge of his nose. I want to ask him if it's because of my bloody lip or the fact that my boobs are trying to escape the hell I've encaged them in.

"Were you assaulted?"

"Sort of."

"By a person?"

"Well... kinda."

"*Olivia.*" He loses his patience so quickly. "When I said I wanted an excuse not to come, I didn't want that excuse to involve a police report. Do you know how long they take? We'll be there all night."

I frown. A little empathy wouldn't kill him. I know he's capable of it. Everyone else may think his heart is twenty sizes too small, but I've witnessed a brief moment with his niece. He can feel things.

"I would hope that if I was assaulted, which I wasn't, you'd be a little more concerned about my well-being and less about whatever inconveniences I may have caused you."

"Olivia, our entire relationship is one giant inconvenience that you've caused me."

"Well it wouldn't hurt for you to pretend to care about my current state of distress."

"When aren't you in a state of distress? You almost started crying this afternoon when you couldn't find staples."

"Maybe I wouldn't be so distressed if you actually filled staplers and showed me a little compassion. I am the woman you're supposed to be in love with."

"You're pushing it," he says as he launches himself off the wall. His Chelsea boots click along the sidewalk in long strides that I struggle to keep up with. "You're the one who started this whole charade."

"To help you," I say as I follow him into the building. I'm so surprised when he opens the door for me that I almost fall and bust open the other side of my lip.

"I don't recall asking for help," he utters, pushing the button for the elevator. "Just like I don't recall asking you to order me oven mitts and coasters and candles that smell like Christmas cookies."

"I'm trying to make your house a home."

"My house is a home. *My home*. And my preferred scent is English Pear and Freesia. Not Sugar Cookie."

"That's very specific."

"I'm a very specific man."

"I'm aware. I order your coffee every day."

"And someday, I hope you'll finally get it right."

I ignore the comment as we step into the elevator. The doors close and we're in comfortable silence. It only lasts a second. I don't like when things are quiet.

"Do you have very specific tastes in decorative pillows?"

"Just that you specifically don't buy them."

I'm sure he'll change his mind when they're delivered on Tuesday.

There's another drum of silence as we're lifted to the second and then to the third floor. I love elevators. We've established my feelings about stairs, and escalators kill thirty people every year, so elevators have always been my preferred mode of vertical transportation. When I was little, I'd press every button to every floor, which was always followed by a very heavy sigh from my mother. When I was twenty and visiting her at the hospital, I'd press every button to give myself more time before the doors parted to reality.

"So what happened?"

I look over at Asher. He has his head tilted back against the wall. He's studying the lines on the ceiling.

"To your face," he clarifies. "I'd like to be on the same page when someone inevitably asks why you look like you got mauled by a raccoon."

The elevator dings and the doors open on the fourth floor. Asher waits for me to step out first. I bet he's going to press the ground floor button and make his escape. Otherwise he's just being a gentleman, which would be shocking behavior from the man who, earlier today, saw me running towards the elevator at work and immediately closed the doors before I could get in.

He steps out behind me.

I think I'm going into cardiac arrest. Maybe when I get rushed to the hospital, they'll stitch up my lip.

"I didn't stick the landing," I say and then I watch his eyebrow quirk up. "Turns out I'm not a professional ice skater."

Asher bites his bottom lip to stifle a laugh. His smiles are so few and far between that I've never noticed the dimples in his cheeks until this very moment. I swear my heart flutters.

"You must be devastated."

"It was a sobering moment," I say. "You can follow Bree's Snapchat if you're interested in the visual recap."

"I'd rather not know what Bree gets up to when she's not at work."

"It's a lot of dramatic commentary while she watches *Jeopardy*. And her dancing on tables."

"Well if dancing on tables is involved..." he says once we stop in front of apartment 401. He pauses and turns to me before he knocks. "Unfortunately, I think I've already surpassed my quota for unethical workplace relationships."

"It's hardly unethical for two consenting adults to be involved."

"I don't recall consenting to being involved with you."

"I don't recall consenting to being your personal bagel delivery girl and yet, here we are."

His nostrils flare and he gives the door three hard raps before it swings open. I quickly grab his hand and lean into him. We reek of being in love.

"You made it!" Francesca's hair falls in dark waves over her shoulders and she's wearing a long-sleeved black dress that shows off what my legs would look like if I was ten inches taller and did five thousand high-kicks before breakfast.

"We wouldn't miss it for the world," I say and I'm beaming. The human embodiment of the sun. I'm responsible for global warming. I could melt glaciers. I look up at Asher and I'm completely enamored. I should have gone into acting. I'm killing this whole pretending-to-be-in-love thing. The hearts in my eyes are going to explode.

And when Francesca leans in to kiss Asher on the cheek, I feel a pang of jealousy twist in my stomach. Even my emotions deserve an Oscar. We're so good at faking it.

"Olivia, oh my God." Francesca is horrified when she sees my face. I was too when I saw my reflection in the train's window. "What happened?"

"Oh, I—"

"This little show off." Asher squeezes my hand so hard that my fingers quiver in pain. "She got a little too confident on the ice."

"A little confidence never hurt anybody," I say.

"Are you sure about that, darling?" Asher replies tightly.

"It does look like it hurts. Are you sure you're okay?"

Francesca asks. "Why didn't you take her to the hospital, Asher?"

"I'm fine." I laugh it off. "I was an Olympic gold medalist in a past life. I just had an off night."

"If that's what you need to tell yourself to get to sleep at night," Asher says.

"Usually all I need is the lull of your heavy breathing."

"Awful, isn't it?" Francesca laughs and steps aside. "And when he sleeps on his back? And grinds his teeth?"

"It's the worst. I'm looking into getting him a mouthguard."

"Are you two done?"

"We're just comparing notes, sweetheart." I rise onto the tips of my toes and plant a kiss on his cheek. "It's all in good fun."

"I'm not having any fun."

"You never do."

Asher glares down at me and then slips his hand out of mine in order to press it to the small of my back, urging me through the door with more force than necessary. I nearly roll my ankle.

Francesca's apartment is sleek, white and minimalist, but everything blends together fluidly, like a well-choreographed dance. The position of the couch against the window. The angle in which the dining room table rests at. The bouquet of white lilies on the counter. The flickering candelabra on the mantle of the fireplace. It all melts into the perfect performance. Crisp lines. Straight edges. Style and grace.

Asher greets everyone with either a kiss on the cheek or a handshake. Despite his total disregard for common courtesy and well, *smiling*, he knows how to work a room. He's charming when he wants to be, which isn't very often, so I have to take advantage of any moment when he's not snarling down at a bagel. Or screaming at someone on the phone. I like this Asher. No wonder we're in a blissfully happy relationship. How could he not be this way when he has me on his arm?

"You're coming up to East Hampton next weekend, right?" Francesca asks. "Costa said he invited you."

"I don't think so," Asher says.

"What's in East Hampton?" I ask.

"Every December there's an event at the Ragnar Estate," she explains. "All the industry types get together and mingle over expensive liquor and fancy appetizers. It sounds ragingly boring, but it's actually a great time. They have sleigh rides and fake snow and carolers."

I gasp.

Sleigh rides and fake snow and carolers.

I feel faint.

"We have plans—"

"We can change them!"

Asher's face pales. Sleigh rides must make him feel faint too. Probably for very different reasons.

"I'm so excited," I say, clutching Asher's arm. My eyes twinkle up at him adoringly. "I've never been to East Hampton. Or any Hampton, for that matter."

"You're gonna love it," Francesca says.

It's all I can think about for the rest of the party. I've long forgotten about my busted lip and *busty* shirt. I'm sleigh-riding through fake snow in East Hampton while carolers serenade me with Mariah Carey classics. I'm sipping gourmet hot chocolate with fancy industry people at an estate.

I need to go shopping.

"Have you seen Asher's new girlfriend?"

I'm looking for the bathroom when I overhear two girls

that I don't know talking in the kitchen. About me, apparently.

"I can't believe Frankie invited them," one says.

"Why wouldn't she?" the other scoffs. "There's no bigger 'fuck you' than looking better than your ex's new bed-warmer. She wants him to see what he's missing."

"Didn't she break up with him?"

"Yeah, because he was miserable. If I were her, I'd be doing the same thing. Show him what he could have had."

Someone hums. "He does look happy. I don't think I've ever seen him smile before."

"Because he has some naive little plaything with pouty lips, big boobs, and no brains that he's nailing on the regular."

"Have you seen how clingy she is?"

"Yeah, she must be young."

They laugh into their champagne flutes.

"She's definitely, like, twenty-one."

"Fresh off that internship," one scoffs.

"Asher's not *that* stupid."

"Please," the other says. "Do you know who his father is? I wouldn't be surprised if River screwed her first."

They're quiet for a moment.

"Can you imagine having a six-figure job handed to you and still be so fucking wretched and ungrateful all the time?"

"It must be so tiring," one says. "I almost feel bad for the girl. I hope she's not banking on him falling in love."

"She's in for a rude awakening."

"That's for sure."

I never find the bathroom, but I do find Asher standing by the window in the living room. He's alone. In every sense of the word. And maybe even a little lost. I watch his eyes fall on Francesca, who is planted on Brent's lap and giggling something soft into his ear, as she nuzzles against him. Asher shifts his eyes back to the Brooklyn skyline and raises his glass to his lips, gulping down something strong to numb whatever it is that he let himself feel for that short moment.

My heart breaks a little. Not for the reasons those girls seem to think—not because I'm dumb or naive or blinded by love. Not because they think my looks somehow dictate how intelligent I am. That doesn't bother me. I've dealt with that my whole life. I know that my 3.92 grade point average had nothing to do with the fact that I can fill out a bra nicely. I earned it. It was not given to me because I batted my eyelashes and giggled. I don't need to defend myself to them and I definitely don't need their approval. I know who I am. That's all that matters.

But they don't know Asher. And frankly, I don't either. But I know there's more to him than what he shows people. He built up his walls and hardened his shell for a reason. And maybe I'll never know why, but I'll sure as hell be by his side whether he wants me there or not. He deserves to know that there's someone on his team.

So I slip my hand seamlessly into his. We don't look at each other. We're trapped in silence. And I meet his gaze out the window and into the city.

We're alone together.

6

To: *Loveridge & McGowan Employee Network*
Cc: *Ana Loveridge-Herrera, River McGowan*
From: *Olivia Langley*
Subject: *Holiday Trivia & Pajama Day!*

Friendly reminder that tonight is holiday trivia at *Rose Tavern*! Winner gets a paid day off!

On Wednesday, don't forget to wear your pajamas to work! And snuggle up under a blanket for our rooftop viewing of *The Santa Clause!* Popcorn and heating lamps will be provided!

Also, I find it very offensive that someone would eat all the chocolate out of my advent calendar.

Yours truly,
O. Langley
Social Media Intern & Santa's Executive Helper
Loveridge & McGowan International

98 W 52nd St, New York, NY 10019
olivialangley@lmi.com

P.S.: Asher, I know it was you.

* * *

CELESTE CALLS out sick on Sunday.

"It's your lucky day, Olivia." Ivan comes up behind me and slides his hands up and over my shoulders, giving me an unsettling squeeze as he lowers his mouth against my ear. "You get to close tonight."

"Okay." I hope that my quick response will get him away from me, but he lingers, thumbing over the faint outline of my bra strap. He smells like expensive cologne and stale cigarettes. I hold my breath until he leaves. I can feel his hands on me for the rest of my sixteen hour shift.

I'm a zombie come Monday morning. And Monday afternoon. And straight through to Monday night. I spill Asher's coffee. I forget his bagel. And if he wasn't already annoyed with me, he definitely is when he finds me half asleep under his desk, which isn't until he's already on a very important conference call with a tennis star who has just been caught doping.

"You are in so much trouble," he says once his call ends.

He never gets a chance to tell me what *so much trouble* entails because Morgan and Chloe come bursting through the door before I can crawl out from under the desk, which leaves me unintentionally eavesdropping on a highly confidential conversation.

"Nanny says you ignore her phone calls," Chloe says. "And Mama says you're having a quarter-life crisis…whatever that is."

"I'm not ignoring anyone's phone calls and I'm not having a quarter-life crisis," Asher says. "And do you all just sit around gossiping about me all day?"

"No one's gossiping. We're just worried, Ash. You've been so withdrawn."

"We should not be having this conversation around a six-year-old."

"I'm six and three quarters," Chloe says. "Nanny says I'm an old soul, but not too old 'cause I can't cross the street by myself and I don't have taxes and I still can't write my *J*s the right way."

"We just want you to be happy," Morgan says.

"I'd be much happier if everyone stopped meddling in my life. I'm twenty-six years old. Contrary to popular belief, I can take care of myself."

"But it's okay to ask for help." I immediately slap my hand over my mouth, and no sooner than the words leave my lips, Chloe's face pops into view. She gives me a lopsided smile.

"Olivia, why are you under Uncle Asher's desk?"

"Yes, Asher, why *is* Olivia underneath your desk?" Morgan asks.

"That's a good question," Asher says. "One I would also like the answer to."

No one gets their answer and I don't get my sleep, which is why I'm currently sitting on a barstool at *Rose Tavern* drinking Irish coffees like they're going out of style.

"Hanukkah is the festival of..."

Emanuel jingles his bell. "What is lights?"

"During which Hebrew month is Hanukkah celebrated?"

Emanuel jingles his bell again. "What is Kislev?"

"For the hundredth time, we're not playing *Jeopardy*!" Bree snaps. "Alba! Tell him we're not playing *Jeopardy*. And threaten to fire him if he keeps answering questions with questions."

"Loveridge & McGowan intern with a perpetually bad attitude and last season's Gucci loafers? Who is Bree Danchev-Truong?" Emanuel tips his glass to her.

"Loveridge & McGowan intern with spinach in his teeth and an irrational fear of ladybugs. Who is Emanuel Rivera?" Bree tips her glass back at him.

"Enough you two," Alba says and guzzles the rest of her wine.

I should have explained to Asher that I was sleeping under his desk because these two made it impossible for me to sleep under mine. Their constant arguing—while amusing most days—just adds to my pounding headache. They both belong on the Naughty List.

And I belong on the Sleepiest Girl Ever List.

My eyes shut for a moment and I almost tumble off of my stool. Thankfully, my phone buzzes on the counter and I jolt awake, which, in turn, also makes me almost fall off my stool again.

It's Asher, who conveniently had to miss tonight's festivities because his favorite episode of *Friends* was on. When I told him he could watch it on Netflix, he told me it wasn't the same.

Asher
Did you send Trent Costner's statement to media outlets?

Olivia
Of course I did. You sent me 17 reminders.

Asher
Calvin from ESPN said he never received a packet. They get the exclusive.

Olivia
Which is why I emailed him and hand-delivered one to each of his assistants.

Asher
Then why is he telling me he doesn't have anything?

Olivia
Because his assistants are grossly incompetent and he doesn't know how to open his email, so he'd rather blame me than admit that his team didn't follow through.

I lock my phone and throw back the rest of my coffee. Buzzed and tired isn't a good combination. I order black coffee and mix in six packets of sugar. That should be enough to get me home.

"Why's Asher texting you?" Bree asks when my phone buzzes again. "Does he need you to read him a bedtime story?"

"Probably," I say.

Asher
You're in a mood.
Did you wake up on the wrong side of my desk?

Olivia
Someone ate all the chocolate out of my advent calendar.
Which is an offense punishable by death in all 50 states and 5 major self-governing territories.

Asher
I should probably contact my lawyer.

Olivia
I think that's a good idea.

Asher
I should probably mention to her that someone has stolen my identity and my credit card and has ordered me a collection of holiday decorative pillows and a robotic vacuum that chases me around the house.

Olivia
It has 4.5 stars on Amazon.

Asher
It has 4.5 demons living inside it.

"Is that still Asher?" Bree asks, glancing at my phone. She scowls. "Why are you smiling?"

"Delirium is setting in," I say. "I'm running on two hours of sleep."

"What did you get up to last night?" she asks.

"Not nearly as much as you did at that strip club."

"The preferred term is *gentlemen's club*."

"And she'd prefer it if you didn't mention that she got kicked out of VIP for being sloppy," Emanuel adds.

"Remember when you weren't an asshole?" Bree snarls at him.

He thinks for a moment. "No."

Bree scoffs and grabs her rum and Diet Coke before she turns to watch another intern and Helen from accounting duke it out in the final round of trivia.

"Please be careful," Emanuel says.

"With what?"

"Yourself," he says. "I'd hate to see you get hurt because you trusted the wrong person. You're a good girl, Liv. People will take advantage of that."

My phone buzzes, but I don't look down at it.

"Thank you for looking out for me," I say. "But I promise I know what I'm doing."

He takes a deep breath through his nose. He doesn't believe me, but he doesn't push it, for which I'm grateful.

"You wanna share an Uber?"

"Yeah," I say. "I'll meet you outside."

I wait until Emanuel walks out the door before reading the message.

Asher

My lawyer says you have no case.

Olivia

Your lawyer clearly didn't pass the bar.

Asher

My lawyer says your *Legally Blonde* version of law isn't admissible in court.

Olivia

I'm offended that your lawyer thinks Elle Woods, a Harvard graduate, isn't a legitimate lawyer.
She owes me a box of milk chocolate sea salt caramels for all this pain and suffering.

Asher

And what do I get for all my pain and suffering?

Olivia

A collection of holiday decorative pillows and a robotic
vacuum that chases you around the house.
You also get me as a fake girlfriend.
Which is a gift in and of itself.

Asher
I want a refund.

Olivia
I'm nonrefundable.

*　*　*

There's a box of milk chocolate sea salt caramels on my
desk.

I eat three before I see the note, and then I almost
choke when I read it.

For all your pain and suffering.

He probably laced them with arsenic.

I pop another into my mouth and decide that death by
expensive poisoned chocolate is a noble way to go.

"Oh, what are we eating?" Emanuel peeks over my
shoulder and snatches one before I can tell him they might
be deadly. "Who sent you a box of eighty dollar caramels?"

"A client." This lying thing is getting really easy.

"They must really like you."

"Honestly," I laugh. "I'm pretty sure they don't."

"Damn, I wish more clients didn't like me."

I close the box and Emanuel flicks one of the bells on
my reindeer antler headband before he falls into his chair
and pops the tab on his energy drink. He's wearing actual

pajamas and not gym clothes like everyone else in the office. I'm glad I'm not the only one who got into the spirit, but had I known Ana would be going through a pregnancy-induced hot flash and insisting we keep the air-conditioner on, I would have worn something warmer than a pair of candy cane striped shorts and a gray henley. My saving grace is my padded bra. And the cable knit socks that go over my knees. I'm practically wearing pants.

"Bree called out," he tells me.

"I know. She said she caught the flu."

"Yeah, the vodka flu."

"I'm still gonna send her over some soup for lunch."

"Remember what I said about being too nice?" He looks at me over his computer monitor.

I shrug. "I have to order lunch for a meeting. What's an extra sandwich and a bowl of soup?"

"What's two extra sandwiches and a bag of salt and vinegar chips?"

"That depends on how you feel about making twelve copies of this contract for me."

His eyes narrow. Mine narrow back. We sit like that for a few moments before he lets out an exasperated sigh and stands up, taking the papers I'm holding out to him.

"There better be a pickle involved."

When I boot up my laptop, I have over one hundred emails, half of which were forwarded from Asher, and the other half being flash sales from all my favorite stores. I order him a new silverware set and three English Pear and Freesia candles that cost forty dollars each. Specific *and* expensive taste. I'm not at all surprised.

I pick at another caramel and write a non-apology statement for an actress who was criticized for posting a picture on Instagram of her breastfeeding. It ends up being much more eloquent than I planned because I'm sure

Asher would have had an issue with me writing #fuckyou and #mindyabusiness.

He's not in until this afternoon, or else I would have already marched into his office and thanked him for the caramels. Luckily for him, this just means my long list of questions is only going to get longer. Why did you send them? What does it mean? Am I no longer a giant inconvenience? Have I graduated to just a small inconvenience? Am I melting your iceberg of a heart? Does this chocolatier also make coconut patties? What about white chocolate truffles?

I eat another caramel.

"Oh my God, Ollie, you're driving me crazy."

Willa Loveridge is standing halfway between my desk and the door that leads to Asher's office. The grim frown she's totting suggests she's not having a very good day. And when she ends her call without a goodbye, my suspicion is confirmed.

"Boys are so needy." She shoves her phone into the pocket of her coat and crosses her arms.

"That's the understatement of the year," I say.

Willa laughs. I'm happy to see her frown waver into a smile.

"How is the mega-famous Ollie Dunbar doing? I haven't heard Asher screaming at him about his drunken Twitter escapades in a while, which is probably a good thing."

"Currently accusing me of smuggling his lucky hoodie out of the United Kingdom."

"*Did* you smuggle his lucky hoodie out of the United Kingdom?"

"Yes, but that's beside the point," she says. "He shouldn't have left it at my apartment. It's only lucky now that I washed it with my laundry and he didn't have to."

I've never had a serious relationship, only semester long flings that lasted as long as my class schedule did. I found it hard to commit to anything that wasn't maintaining my GPA. I had a scholarship I needed to worry about, romantic entanglements always came second. My fake relationship with Asher is the most committed I've ever been to anyone besides Betsy, who I keep in my bedside table for those particularly lonely nights.

"Does Ollie ever send you chocolates?"

"No."

"Flowers?"

"He writes songs for me," she says. "Sometimes they're sweet. Most of them are about how bad my feet smell and the hair I leave in the shower drain."

"Charming."

"Yeah, he's got the romance thing down," she laughs. "Have you seen my mom?"

"I believe she moved her office to the roof," I tell her. "Because even with the air-conditioning on, it's still too hot in here."

Willa begrudgingly takes the elevator to the roof and I glance down at the clock. It's after eleven. Sighing, I pick up the phone.

"Hi, this is going to sound like a silly question," I say when they answer. "But do you use Bolero carrots in your carrot and ginger soup?"

* * *

Levi is in the conference room when I get there with lunch. He has his hands shoved into the pockets of his leather jacket and there's a pen in his mouth. He's leaning back in his chair, looking like he wants to be anywhere but here. He's not paying attention to a word Alexander is saying, but when he sees me, his lips curve into a devilish smile.

I almost drop scalding hot soup onto my feet.

"Jesus Christ." Asher all but slams his head onto the table. He's clearly upset that he forgot about Pajama Day.

I reminded him.

Twice.

"Olivia, why didn't I receive an invitation to your little pajama soiree?" Levi's eyes trail all the way up from my cable knit socks to the tips of my antlers. I think he might be undressing me.

My knees buckle.

"I'm very good at pillow fights *and* pillow talk," he says. "Imagine all the other fun things we can do with pillows."

"Like smothering you in your sleep?" Asher says.

"I don't think there would be a whole lot of sleep happening, Ash."

"I mean, I don't think anyone's opposed to smothering you while you're awake."

"Enough, boys," River says. "We're here for a reason and Ms. Langley is just delivering lunch."

"Right," I say and place the box on the table. I turn to Asher, who is trying to murder Levi with his eyes. "They couldn't confirm if they use Bolero carrots in their soup, so I got you the roasted tomato because—"

"Do they use—"

"—they could confirm that they use San Marzano," I say. "They could also confirm that I'm the only person to ever question their carrots. The things I do for you, Asher McGowan."

"The list of things you don't do is much longer."

I resist pinching the miserable look off his face.

"You didn't happen to get me the corn chowder, did you?"

Levi slides his chair over to me and he's so close that I can feel the warmth radiating off him.

"Of course I did."

"That's my girl," he says and when I feel his hand slide over my lower back, my mouth goes dry.

I don't know a girl who wouldn't want to be in my position—up close and personal with Levi Booker—but the butterflies that typically fill my stomach suddenly sting like bees. I'm hot, but for all the wrong reasons.

There's a soft thud behind me. It's Levi's pen. He's grinning.

"I'm so clumsy," he says. "Livi, would you be a doll and pick that up for me?"

"Oh, um, sure—"

"That's not necessary." Asher is half out of his chair and leaning over the table. He slams the pen he always keeps behind his ear onto the table. "Use mine."

Levi laughs under his breath as Asher settles back into his chair.

"You're ruining all the fun, Ash. Just like old times."

"That's my job," he says. "Olivia, can you please contact Emmy Raynard's manager and let her know we're all set for the *Good Morning Chicago* interview?"

"But I thought—"

"I need it done right now, please."

"Okay."

"Oh, and Olivia?" River says and I turn to look at him. "Can you send Bree up to my office?"

"She called out," I tell him, and in return he glowers at me, like I'm the one that was pouring shots down her throat last night.

When I'm downstairs, I head to Asher's office and for twenty minutes, I listen to the Menopausal Momager from the Seventh Circle of Hell go off on me for sending her a wine and cheese basket when she's lactose intolerant. I try to apologize, but she goes on and on and on, until I consider strangling myself with the phone cord. When Ana and Willa walk by, all I manage to do is smile weakly at them as they walk hand-in-hand into the elevator. I don't hear anything else Elizabeth says after that. I'm consumed by a pang of jealousy.

I don't see Asher again until after five and the office is empty. No one stays for movie night. Not even Emanuel. I have no idea what I'm going to do with an entire trolley of popcorn and thirteen bags of Twizzlers and M&Ms, but I have a feeling I'm going to be on a sugar high for the rest of the year.

"Hey." I peek my head into his office and he glances up at me briefly. "Are you staying for the movie?"

"No, I'm staying to finish work."

"Can it wait until tomorrow?"

"I don't think Ellen Thompson would appreciate me putting off her mother's death announcement until tomorrow."

I swallow. "I'm sorry. I didn't—"

"Do you need something, Olivia? My breakfast order for tomorrow? Some work to take home? Levi Booker's phone number?"

His jaw is clenched so tightly that I worry for his teeth. I can't read his expression, just that he's staring straight through me and he looks angry. And I've seen Asher angry, but never quite like this. He's a ticking time bomb.

"Thank you," I say. "For the chocolates."

He looks back at his computer screen. "They weren't from me.'

"Right," I say and shrink back through the door frame. "They were from your lawyer."

I take the elevator to the roof and bundle up beneath a

blanket and a heating lamp. After too much popcorn and a bag of Twizzlers, I feel sick.

* * *

The light in Asher's office is still on, which might be the least shocking thing *ever*. Energy conservation is clearly not one of his top priorities. I'm going to add motion detecting lights to our suggestion box *again*.

I flick the light switch in his office off after I pull on my jacket. My candy cane striped shorts are barely covered, and I'm still shivering from my rooftop rager for one, so I decide to treat myself to an UberPool. Riding the subway in my pajamas this morning was enough for me.

The elevator dings just as I hit the button, and when the doors part, I'm greeted by Alexander McGowan.

Asher and Alexander are alike in last name only. I would have never guessed they were brothers. Asher is lean and gangly with striking features that sort of take your breath away. Alexander is… shorter and muscly in a way that suggests he takes arm day a little too seriously. He's not unattractive. The McGowans are pretty fortunate on the genetic spectrum, but it's clear that Asher hit the DNA lottery.

At least where his face is concerned.

His attitude could use an adjustment.

"Olivia." Alexander steps out of the elevator and smiles. "Good, you're still here. I need you to order dinner. That sushi place on West 55th. The usual order."

"It's almost nine o'clock," I say. "You're never here this late."

What I want to say is: *"You're here this late and you didn't come to movie night?"*

Not that Alexander is the McGowan I'd want to cozy

up with under a heating lamp.

"Roman Rafferty was arrested in Australia."

"The minister that runs that big church in Tennessee?"

"Apparently prostitution is not a sin in God's eyes," he says. "The Australian government, however, are not as forgiving."

"Yikes."

"So sushi?" he says. "Enough for six. My team is on their way in."

"Of course."

"And I'll need you to stay and work on some press releases." He pauses for a moment to glance down at my exposed legs and knee-length socks. "You do know how to write them, right?"

"I do."

"Good, I was worried all you do is run around the city getting Asher's muffins."

"Bagels," I say.

"What?"

"Asher doesn't eat muffins," I say. "He eats bagels."

"Right," he says. "Sushi?"

"I don't think I've ever ordered him sushi," I say. "But judging by his cream cheese consumption, he probably likes a Philadelphia roll."

"*My* sushi, Olivia."

"Oh, right," I laugh. "I'll get on it."

Alexander turns into a conference room, leaving me alone to order two hundred dollars worth of sushi. At nine o'clock at night. When I want to be ordering a seven dollar Uber to go home. So I can eat stale cereal on my couch.

I order myself three spicy tuna rolls and a slice of cheesecake (with extra strawberries) from the deli next door.

Alexander's team arrives after I drop all my things off

at my desk. While I'm normally comfortable in my own skin, there's something about being in a room with six guys while I'm in my pajamas that makes me feel like *hired* help. Their sly smiles and wandering eyes don't help matters. I'm going to get whatever work they want me to do and lock myself in Asher's office.

"Do you have a media list for me?" I ask.

"It should be in your email," Rajiv, a junior associate, tells me.

"Great," I say. "The food should be here in five minutes. I'll be at my desk if you need me."

"You're more than welcome to work here with us," Alexander says. "There's plenty of room."

"I wouldn't want to get in the way." I force a smile.

"Aw, c'mon." He leans back in his chair. "We'll work quickly and then you can come to a party with us. It's definitely tiny pajama shorts casual."

"A party?"

"You were personally requested."

"Requested?" The only person I want *requesting* my presence at a party is Harry Styles.

Or Beyoncé.

Or Jonathan Van Ness.

And the only reason they should be *requesting* me is because they saw one of my legendary karaoke performances on my Instastories.

"Levi's having a holiday party at his place in Tribeca," Alexander says. "He told me that I'm not allowed to come unless I bring you wearing that festive little getup…"

"Most people just bring a bottle of wine," says a voice.

Asher is standing behind me. He looks cold and miserable with wind-chapped cheeks and a Rudolph-red nose. He's holding two paper bags and a cup of coffee.

"Ash, you're still here," Alexander says. "What a

surprise."

"Funny, I was thinking the same thing."

"Roman Rafferty got arrested," Alexander explains.

"I mean, it was only a matter of time," Asher says. "Did someone order food?"

"I did," I say, taking the bags from him. I set them on the round table and begin to unpack. I make sure to keep my three rolls in the bag along with my cheesecake. If I've learned anything over the past eleven months of this internship, it's that any food on the table is fair game.

And I'd sooner die before watching someone else eat my cheesecake.

"The offer still stands, Liv," Alexander says. "We can finish here quickly, and then head to the party."

"I think I'll pass," I say, clutching the paper bag to my chest. "I'll be at my desk if you need me."

I don't go to my desk. I sneak into Asher's office and sit down at his desk like I own the place. And boy, if I owned this place it would be a much less hostile environment. Asher treats his office like an extension of his apartment—cold, bare, and lifeless. It's just a desk, a few chairs, and a coat rack.

He needs a mini Christmas tree.

And tinsel.

And an animatronic snowman that dances to *Jingle Bell Rock*.

I resist the urge to bypass my email inbox and go straight to Amazon. I have press releases to write before I can next-day-delivery Asher some Christmas spirit.

"You better not be getting soy sauce all over my desk." Asher's scowling at me while I try to simultaneously chew and smile at him. He does not find it endearing.

"Oh, I'm getting it everywhere," I tell him. "I think there are sesame seeds in every crevice of your laptop."

He's still scowling at me as he moves deeper into his office. He sits down in the chair opposite of me. I'm surprised he doesn't tell me to move, because by bureaucratic practices, I'm in charge. I'm the one behind the desk.

My power senses are tingling.

"I thought you left for the night," I say, picking up another piece of sushi.

"I went to get coffee."

"I was under the impression you couldn't do that on your own."

"I was under the impression that this was *my* office."

"And yet I'm the one sitting behind the desk." I try to chew and smile again. Asher rolls his eyes. "I'm sorry, Mr. McGowan, it's not working out. I'm going to have to let you go."

"We'll see who's getting let go if there isn't a Philadelphia roll in this bag, Ms. Langley."

"Why would there be a Philadelphia roll in there?"

"Why wouldn't there be?" His frown softens when he pulls out *my* slice of cheesecake.

"Don't you dare."

"Consider it my severance." One of his elusive smiles sneaks onto his lips as he opens the plastic container.

"That's just *rude*." I watch him take a bite. "Eating your intern's cheesecake while she writes press releases at ten o'clock at night…"

"You should have told Alex to fuck off," Asher says. "His clients aren't your responsibility."

"Dude, I need a job when this internship is over," I laugh. "I'm not about to insult your brother."

Asher shrugs. "I insult him daily. I still have a job."

"Yeah, funny how nepotism works," I say. "I don't have the luxury."

"If it's any consolation, I'd do just about anything not to be genetically related to him."

"And I'd do just about anything to have a full-time job next year."

"Even if that means going to Levi's party?"

The thought of a party in Tribeca is kind of thrilling. But it's a weeknight and I'm already in my pajamas and I don't like being treated like a consolation prize.

"You'll be happy to know that I've turned down his very informal invitation."

"You mean you don't like it when men treat you like a Yankee Swap present?"

"Shocking, isn't it?"

We fall into a comfortable silence. I finish my sushi. Asher finishes *my* cheesecake. I get three press releases done by the time eleven o'clock rolls around.

"You should head out," Asher says. "It's late. I'll order you a car."

"I still have like ten of these to send out." I appreciate his offer, but at this point I'm probably just going to curl up under my desk tonight.

"I can finish them," he says. "I have to make a call into *The Post* anyway."

"You're making calls this late?"

"The media never sleeps," he says.

"That's a damn shame," I say. "Sleeping is the best. I don't do it enough."

"That's why you should go home and get a few hours."

I decide to take this rare moment of compassion and run with it. "Don't you dare think about calling me back here after I leave."

"I wouldn't dream of it," he says as I put on my jacket. "Goodnight, Ms. Langley."

"Sleep tight, Mr. McGowan."

7

To: *Loveridge & McGowan Employee Network*
Cc: *Ana Loveridge-Herrera, River McGowan*
From: *Olivia Langley*
Subject: *Christmas Crawl!*

Gas up those sleighs for our first annual Christmas Crawl!
Drink around the city tonight with your favorite—and least
favorite—colleagues! Come for one stop or all five! It starts
at 7:00 p.m. at *Baker Street Lounge*.

Yours truly,
O. Langley
Social Media Intern & Santa's Executive Helper
Loveridge & McGowan International
98 W 52nd St, New York, NY 10019
olivialangley@lmi.com

* * *

THREE LINGERIE MODELS are pregaming a club opening with *Shake Shack* in my living room. They offer me cheesy fries and sips of their milkshakes. I'm living a fantasy I never realized I had.

"Have you guys ever been to the Ragnar Estate?"

"In East Hampton?" Paloma drags a fry through a glob of ketchup. "That place makes *SoHo House* look like a *Comfort Inn*."

"It's ridiculously exclusive," Natasha adds. "You need, like, three recommendation letters, a DNA sample, and a background check to get on the property."

"I worked with a photographer who said they confiscated her phone before she was allowed inside," Anouk says.

Asher mentioned none of this.

"Okay, so I'm going there tomorrow," I say.

Natasha chokes on her frozen hot chocolate. "Who are you sleeping with?"

"No one." It comes out with an air of frustration that I didn't know I felt. "It's for work. I'm an intern at a publicity firm. I was invited by a client."

And by *client* I mean I was invited by my boss's ex-girlfriend who we're trying to make jealous. We're obviously not doing a very good job. She keeps inviting us places and hasn't done anything in retaliation, like seductively brushing up against Asher or trying to lure him away from me. I really have to step up my clingy girlfriend game.

"I don't know what to wear," I tell them. "Because it's formal, but not black-tie formal. And I don't want to be underdressed, but I also don't want to be overdressed. It's all very stressful. I shouldn't have agreed to go."

"You never say no to the Ragnar Estate!" Paloma says. "Show me your closet."

The thing about my closet is that my room is the size

of a closet. I barely fit in it, so imagine cramming four girls in there—three of which are the height of Amazonians and have long, gangly limbs. I have to dodge Natasha's wayward elbow.

"This is cozy," Anouk says.

She must mean small because my room is not cozy warm. It's a glorified walk-in freezer. There are no heating vents and my window is drafty. Most nights, I fall asleep to the sound of my teeth chattering.

And the downstairs neighbor screaming at the TV in German.

But if we're speaking figuratively, my room is very cozy and warm and inviting. Not that I'm inviting many people into my tiny bedroom Or, really, *any* people, for that matter. But I've worked really hard to make the little space I have feel like a home. A sheet of pastel florals on the wall. A string of fairy lights along my headboard. A fluffy white duvet with a mountain of pillows and a heating blanket. An apple cinnamon candle that smells like my childhood home.

"This is your closet?" Natasha stares at the clothing rack in disbelief—the same way I did when I saw it sitting on the sidewalk with a FREE sign taped to it.

"There's more stuff in my dresser, but I don't think disco pants and leggings are appropriate for the Ragnar Estate."

"You would be correct," Paloma says before they start picking apart my small wardrobe, like this is an episode of *What The Hell Was She Thinking: Fashion Edition*. And while I'm sure someone thinks that twenty Christmas sweaters is excessive, I am definitely not that person.

"You love an a-line skirt," Anouk says.

"And a chunky heel," Paloma adds.

"Which isn't bad," Natasha says.

"But it's nice to have a few different things to shake it up."

They're trying to be helpful, but that doesn't mean the comment doesn't sting. I don't have access to designer clothes and I'm not gifted free samples. I'm limited to what I can find secondhand at thrift stores, which is hit or miss.

"This." Natasha holds up a black dress with a high neckline. I don't wear it often. I only got it because there's this belief that every girl should own a little black dress.

"No." Joey's voice sends a chill through my already ice-cold room. She pushes herself through what little space is left. I dodge another elbow and a leg. I swear they're trying to box me out of my own bedroom. "She's going to a Christmas party, not a funeral."

It stings.

I'm not sure it'll ever stop.

"This," Joey finally says.

It's a long-sleeved, asymmetrical wrap dress in a shade of burgundy that is dripping with holiday cheer. It's a little short and bares a lot of cleavage, but I can pull it off. Even the shortest dresses look long on my stubby legs.

"I have a pair of heels that'll go with it," she says. "They might be a little big on you. They're a size nine."

"I can work with that."

"'But bring another dress just in case," Paloma says. "Life is about choices."

"You also don't want to be the girl wearing the same thing as someone else."

They throw more pieces onto my bed that they deem "Ragnar Estate approved" and leave me to finish packing my bag while they get ready for their club opening.

Asher is picking me up tomorrow morning at nine *sharp*. He has reminded me twenty-seven times. I'm not exaggerating. I have nineteen text messages, five emails, and three voicemails. He even told the building's doorman to remind me as I was leaving today. It's like I have a reputation for being late.

But it's usually because I'm waiting for something to be double-toasted and slathered in cream cheese.

I zip my bag and place it next to my door before I coat my lips in bright red lipstick and glance in the mirror for a final check before I leave for the Christmas Crawl. I'm wearing a flouncy camisole that leaves little to the imagination and a green leather skirt.

My boobs look *great*.

I look *hot*.

I'm definitely *not* trying to hook up with anyone.

At all.

"Can you believe Levi had the fucking balls to threaten Alice with Fashion Week?" I hear Natasha's voice when I step out of my room.

"What?" Paloma asks.

"Told her she'd get pulled from Paris if she talked," Anouk says.

"I saw him at my PR office the other day," Joey says. "He's lucky there were witnesses around."

"I don't think I would care," Natasha says. "Actually, I'd prefer an audience. God knows he'd love one."

I'm standing in the conference room again and I see Asher's face, grim and unwavering, which isn't much different than his normal face, but there was something in his eyes. Sharp and cold and glaring. I hear it in Natasha's voice.

What do they know that I don't?

* * *

Bree has a lot of rules.

We have to sit facing the door. Our drinks always have to be half full. We have to be engaged in conversation. We can't eat. We don't initiate. We can laugh, but not too much. They can't be wearing sneakers. Or bootcut jeans. And they have to be at least six feet tall.

The thing about rules is that I'm really good at breaking them.

My shirt is thin and my bra isn't padded, so facing the door is a problem when it's thirty degrees outside. My drink is most likely always empty. Is the conversation really engaging when she's just telling me who not to look at? I'm *starving* and this lounge has truffle mac and cheese. I'm very good at unintentionally initiating conversations. I'm always laughing. Too much. And what's wrong with sneakers? And bootcut jeans? And as a woman of just barely five feet, I don't discriminate against my height bracket.

"You looked!" Bree kicks my shin with the point of her shoe.

"I'm sorry I have eyes!"

"Now they're coming over," she whispers. "Do you see the jeans he's wearing? They're from 2009. Is this a *Jersey Shore* reunion?"

"Oh, for fuck's sake, Bree." Emanuel throws back the rest of his drink. "Get over yourself. They're fucking jeans, not lycra shorts."

"No one asked for your opinion."

"I don't think anyone asked for yours either."

"I have ten thousand followers on Twitter who prove otherwise."

"I have a hard time believing that ten thousand *real* people want to follow you."

"Are you suggesting I buy bots?"

"I mean, who else wants to see you bitching at various companies about their customer service not meeting your tip-top standards?" he asks. "*Seriously, @sephora, Kimberly at your 555 Broadway location suggested I try a FULL COVERAGE foundation and I'm OFFENDED she thinks I need one! #awful #offensive #bbcreamforlife.*"

"You're such a stalker."

"Says the girl who routinely googles every high level exec that walks onto our floor."

"I'm trying to network!"

"Yeah, into someone's bed!"

Bree shrinks back. "I don't like what you're insinuating."

"I'm insinuating that you stop googling men who are married with children!"

"I'm not a mind reader."

"He was wearing a *fucking* ring."

I finish my drink and take a shot. These two are much easier to tolerate with a buzz. I should keep a bottle of vodka under my desk.

"Hey, what's your sign?"

I look up at the guy whose eyes I caught from across the bar. He has messy blonde hair and week old scruff. He's definitely not bad to look at. Definitely not six feet either. But that opening line… does he deserve a chance?

"Really? That's what you're going with?"

A blush runs from his neck up to his cheeks. "Pretty girls make me nervous."

"Guess," I muse.

"I'm sorry?"

"Guess my sign," I say. "And if you're right, you can buy me a drink."

"Give me a hint."

"Nope."

He purses his lips and taps his index finger against

them, like I'm an equation he's trying to solve. Jokes on him. I'm not that easy to crack.

"Cancer."

I frown.

"I'm right, aren't I?"

"I'm drinking cosmos tonight."

He's grinning as he walks over to the bar.

I'm not sure why I'm upset. The goal was for him to guess right. Maybe I just want to retain a little mystery. It keeps things interesting.

"Olivia!"

I don't hear my name until someone throws their arms around me. I'm being hugged to death by my fake boyfriend's real ex-girlfriend. This must have been her plan all along.

Kill me with kindness.

Literally.

"Francesca, hey!"

I've been caught. She's going to tell Asher she saw me flirting with a man who used a terrible pick up line on me. Our little charade is over. I bet she wants to mend his broken heart and slander me on the internet.

"Is Ash here?"

I'm vaguely aware that Bree and Emanuel are in earshot. "He insisted that a Christmas Crawl was not his thing."

"Of course," she laughs. "Doesn't know how to have fun, does he?"

"All work and no play."

"Makes Ash a very dull boy."

I can *feel* Bree's eyes on me. They're burning holes into the back of my head. I'm torched. I don't know how I'm going to talk myself out of this one.

"A cosmo for the Cancer."

There is a pink drink in my hand. A man that is not my fake boyfriend is undressing me with his eyes. And everyone is looking at me like they're waiting for an answer.

"Who's your friend?" Francesca asks.

"Yeah, Liv, who's your friend?" Bree says.

Get. It. Together. Olivia.

"This is my old floormate from college…"

"Deacon," he finishes and holds his hand out to Francesca. "Liv and I used to get up to a lot of trouble in our…"

"City College days," I say. "It's such a coincidence we ran into each other tonight. Who knew Christmas Crawls were so popular?"

"Where are you going next?" Francesca asks.

"Atlas."

"Down in SoHo?" Francesca asks. "Brent and I were thinking of checking it out."

"You should come," Bree says. "The more the merrier!"

I gulp down my cosmo. I'm lightheaded. I'm not sure if it's from the booze or the fact that the web of lies I'm weaving is making my brain malfunction.

"I need to pee!" I announce.

"I'll come," Bree says, glaring at me. "We need to discuss some *very* important matters."

"No, I need to pee alone. I get nervous when there's an audience."

"Last week, I literally stood in a stall with you *while* you peed."

"It's a newly developed issue. Don't judge me."

I'm pushing my way to the bathroom before Bree gets a chance to respond. Three cosmos and a shot ago, I would have been able to think of a plan. Now, I just want to cry.

So I call Asher.

Because that seems like the only logical thing to do when I'm about to have a breakdown in the men's bathroom because I walked through the wrong door.

It takes four calls for him to pick up.

"For the love of God, Olivia, I'm trying to watch *Good Morning America*."

"But it's not morning."

"I record it."

"Oh."

There's a beat of silence.

"Is there something you needed?"

"Yeah."

"And that is?"

I take a deep breath, count to three, and then burst into tears.

"My boobs look *really* great in this shirt and this guy guessed I'm a Cancer and he bought me a drink and he definitely wants to sleep with me, which is fantastic because that was the point of putting my lady business on full display. But then *Francesca* shows up and asks about *you* and suddenly I look like the shady fake girlfriend who's trying to cheat on her fake boyfriend with a guy who's wearing jeans from 2009 and who is not six feet tall and I broke all of Bree's rules and I think she suspects something and I don't know what to do. And I'm very upset and there's a man using a urinal next to me and he's looking at me like I'm crazy, but I'm not crazy—I'm just a little drunk and—"

"Jesus, Olivia, where are you?"

"The men's room."

"*Where?*"

"*Baker Street Lounge*," I say. "We're going to *Atlas* next."

The phone call ends and I smile weakly at the man zipping his pants before I leave the bathroom.

Tonight, I decide, can't get much worse.

* * *

Francesca and her friends are getting their drinks when Deacon comes back with mine. It barely grazes my hand when it's ripped away, like stealing candy from a baby. If that baby was twenty-two and the candy was, well, alcohol. I let out a soft sob.

"Hey, thanks!" Asher chugs down my drink and cringes when he finishes. "That was possibly the cheapest vodka I've ever had the displeasure of tasting."

"That was also possibly the rudest thing I've ever had the displeasure of witnessing."

"The night is still young, Olivia."

I don't know who to avoid first—Deacon, who is confused and rightfully offended by Asher's brash manner; Bree, who is in mid-conversation with Deacon's friend Felix, but is still watching this mess unfold; or Emanuel, who is buzzed and amused by the current situation. Even Javon from Marketing has taken an interest.

"Is this guy bothering you, Liv?" Deacon asks.

"Am *I* bothering *her*?" Asher says. "You must not have spent enough time with her if *she* isn't bothering *you*."

"I don't like your attitude."

"Most people don't."

This is not going to end well.

"Asher." Bree slides up next to me and sips slowly on her rum and Diet Coke. "What are you doing here?"

"This is the company Christmas Crawl," he says. "I believe I was invited."

"It was really just a formality."

"Some would say the same thing about your internship."

"And your career."

"It would be wise to remember who you *work* for, Ms. Truong."

"Your father?"

I need a drink.

I find my way to the bar before Asher and Bree get into a fist fight. I can't see tonight ending well, which means I won't be going to the Ragnar Estate tomorrow and I definitely won't be listening to carolers or going on a sleigh ride through the snow. All the more reason to drink. Heavily.

"Do you have Stella on tap?"

I think the bartender is looking at me, but then his eyes shift up. Asher is pressed against my back.

"Yeah, but we also have this craft—"

"Stella," he says. "And a cosmopolitan. With Grey Goose."

I turn to face Asher as he reaches into his back pocket for his wallet.

"I was very comfortable on my couch," he says tightly.

"I seem to have made a little bit of a mess."

"A little bit of a mess? Olivia, this is a disaster," he says. "I have to spend an evening with Bree. I would rather surgically remove my own kidneys."

"That's a little dramatic," I say. "I have a plan."

"You don't have a great track record with plans," he says. "The last one ended with me in a fake relationship with you."

"Listen, you should be honored to be in any kind of relationship with me," I say. "Have you seen my boobs in this shirt?"

"I believe the whole bar has."

"Then you agree I'm a fucking catch."

"You have a filthy mouth when you're drunk."

"If you think I'm drunk now just wait until we're at the karaoke bar later."

He looks terrified. Rightfully so.

"Now my plan," I hiccup. "You distract Francesca while I schmooze with Bree and our new friends."

"Yes, that's exactly what I want to do on a Friday night —mingle with my ex and her God awful friends while you go off and try to hook-up with some low-level stockbroker."

"Deacon's a stockbroker?" We haven't gotten down to the specifics. All I know is that he's cute.

"For Christ's sake, Olivia. Do you even know this guy?"

"Don't give me that!" I scoff. "Do you get all the credentials for the girls you hook-up with?"

"No."

"Then why should I?"

Asher suddenly doesn't know how to speak.

"Is it because you care about me?"

"No."

"Then it must be because you're jealous that your fake girlfriend is going to have some very real sex tonight."

I hear two glasses hit the counter behind me and when Asher slams his credit card down next to them, he pauses to whisper into my ear.

"We both know you're not having sex with him tonight."

That feels like a challenge.

* * *

Asher is doing a fantastic job of looking like the most miserable person on the planet, but he's keeping Francesca occupied and always has a drink waiting for me when I make my rounds over there, so the only thing I can really complain about is the fact that my drinks have become increasingly less alcoholic.

And by less alcoholic, I mean he's ordering me cranberry and sodas, which is killing my buzz, so I order a couple of rounds of shots that Deacon helps me with.

He's a little self-involved. And when I say a little, I mean a lot. But the more I drink, the less I care. I'm just looking for some fun. And my only standard for fun is consensual. I don't need more than that.

Well.

Maybe an orgasm or two.

"I'm so hungry."

We're walking down West Broadway and my face is squished against the window of a pizza shop. I whimper and paw at the glass. It's so close yet so far away.

"Get a grip, Liv," Bree says.

"I'm *starving*."

"You're not going to wither away."

"I might."

"She has had a lot to drink, *Cruella*," Emanuel says. "Not everyone is a super demon like you. Us mortals need sustenance that's not puppy tails and kitten tears."

"Why are you still here?"

I want to ask Asher the same question. Francesca declined the invitation to karaoke because they're getting up early to get on the road. Asher really has no reason to be here. He's off the hook. He can go back to his couch and finish watching *Good Morning America*. He played his part.

"Just because I don't enjoy your company doesn't mean

I don't enjoy the company of our coworkers," Emanuel answers.

"If you haven't noticed, most of our coworkers have jumped ship."

"Olivia is still here. Blasted out of her mind, but still here." He shrugs. "And honestly, Asher isn't as bad as you two make him out to be."

"Thanks, man."

"I would also like a job after this internship," he says. "So please keep that in mind."

"Noted."

"Is that all it really takes for a guy to get a job after an internship?" Bree asks. *"You're not that bad of a person, bro! Thanks, dude! You're hired!"*

"Generally, you just have to do a good job and earn it," Asher says as he pries me off the window that I almost consider licking. "Tell me, Bree, what exactly do you do in my father's office all day long?"

Bree shoots Asher a cold glare. "Let's go. There's food at the bar."

"But not pizza," I cry.

"You'll survive."

I don't think I will. Pizza is my only life source. I feel like I'm drowning, which makes no sense, but the world is spinning and I'm hungry.

We cross the street and I only realize how dizzy I am when headlights reflect in my eyes in all the wrong ways. I'm seeing spots. I stumble.

"Jesus." Asher has a grip around my arm. "You need to go home."

"I have a date with a karaoke machine," I say. "And Deacon. Where's Deacon? We have a lot of naked business to tend to."

"With that sort of bedside manner? No wonder he ran."

"My bedside manner is fan-fucking-tastic," I say. "My in-the-bed manner is also fantastic. I'm a very generous lover."

"Whatever you say, Olivia."

We cross another street and Asher is still holding onto me. I almost roll my ankle, but I manage to retain what little grace I have left. It's a Christmas miracle that I haven't face planted yet.

"Liv!"

This is my drunken version of a romantic comedy. Deacon is running through traffic. Arms flailing in the winter wind, trying to grab my attention. We're star-crossed lovers the world is trying to keep apart. But we keep fighting it. And he hands me his heart in the form of a greasy slice on a white paper plate.

I'm in love.

"Here's your pizza." He's out of breath but smiling. I'm pretty sure Asher is having an aneurysm.

I also might be having an aneurysm.

"This is so sexy." I have pizza sauce and cheese dripping down my chin. I look so attractive. I'm turning everyone on.

"Liv, please stop making those sounds," Emanuel says. "You're scarring me for life."

"It's so good," I say. "I think I'm having an orgasm."

"It sure does sound like you are," Bree says.

I inhale the pizza in seconds and when I finish, I throw my arms around Deacon and kiss his cheek.

"You are such a gentleman."

"Right," Asher says as he pulls open the door to the bar. "Cheap vodka and greasy pizza. Those are some standards."

"What can I say? I'm easy to please."

The bar is so crowded that I'm up close and personal with every single person I try to pass. It's hot and musty, which doesn't help the fact that I already feel lightheaded. I rip off my coat and shove it at whoever is next to me. Thank God it's Emanuel. I can't afford to lose that jacket.

"I need a drink." I throw myself over the bar, which scares the tender. "Something pink!"

I get my pink drink and I knock it back so fast that I think I might be sick, but the microphone is free and the stage is mine. I'm a star in the making. Someone is going to film me and I'll be viral in two hours.

Asher will be watching me on *Good Morning America* tomorrow.

"I'm Olivia," I scream into the microphone. "I can't feel my toes. Jellybeans are disgusting. I don't understand statistics. And I'm gonna sing you a song!"

When the first line of *Santa Baby* leaves my lips, I lose all inhibitions. I'm on a high. I'm electric and alive, and everyone is watching me shimmy and shake through each note of the song. I'm amazing. I was made for this. Deacon is a lucky man. He gets to take home the hottest girl in the room. I bet there's going to be a fight. Over me. I'm such a commodity. *Sports Illustrated* is going to put me on their swimsuit issue. Ashley Graham who?

I almost tumble off the stage.

The mic cord is tangled around my legs and Asher is pinching the bridge of his nose and I'm definitely going to be sick.

The mic drops with a loud screech and I somehow manage to get off the stage without falling on my face. I stumble over my feet and I'm hanging onto the wall, but I get to the bathroom.

The women's room.

I make sure this time.

I puke in the sink and on my shoes and then I fall against the wall and then onto the floor.

I don't cry.

I don't feel anything.

It's what I like most about drinking. It's all giggles and confidence and fun. Until it's not. Until you're sitting on the bathroom floor and you can't feel anything and you haven't felt anything in years. And you're just existing. And you want to cry, but you can't.

So I sit and wonder what life would have been like if I hadn't been dealt such a shitty hand.

"Olivia?" There's a knock on the door and then it opens. "O?"

I look up at Asher, whose face sinks when he sees the pathetic mess that's me crumpled on the floor covered in vomit.

"Jesus," he says and he bends down to my level and brushes a piece of hair out of my face. "I'm taking you home."

"Can you take my shoes off first?" I ask. "Looking at them makes me sad."

"We don't want that," he says and takes each boot off. "Am I trashing them?"

"I think I already did that."

He helps me onto my feet and wraps an arm securely around my waist. He reminds me that I smell like puke and rancid pizza as we walk through the bar.

"You're so charming," I tell him.

"And you smell like the bottom of a toilet."

"And yet you're leaving the bar with this toilet."

"I'm a lucky man."

"Liv!" We're halfway out the door when I hear Bree. Asher turns us around.

"Where are you going?" she asks. "The guys are getting us a car to their place."

"She can barely stand up, Bree," Asher says. "She's not going anywhere with them."

"You're her boss, not her boyfriend, Asher."

"And you're supposed to be her friend," he says. "And the fact that you would put her in a situation like that when she's not in the right state of mind just goes to show what a shitty friend you actually are."

"Please," she scoffs. "She was looking for someone to go home with."

"She's allowed to change her mind." It's Emanuel who's holding the door open for us. "She lives on East 17th by Stuyvesant Square. There's a purple car that's always parked in front of her building."

Asher mutters a thank you before he puts us into a car.

* * *

Turns out that it's not easy getting up three flights of stairs when you're half unconscious and drunk.

"You're absolutely no help," Asher curses under his breath.

"Sorry."

"Where's your key?"

"Dunno."

"*Olivia.*"

"My bag, probably."

He leans me against the wall and tears into my purse. He drops a pack of gum, an emergency tampon, and a hair clip before my keys jingle in his hands.

"Why do you have three locks?"

"Because not everyone has an around-the-clock security officer in their building."

"He's not very good," Asher says. "Lets you in."

"I bring him chocolates and coffee."

"Do you get his right?"

"Of course I do," I say. "You're just nitpicky."

He rolls his eyes and pushes me through the door.

My apartment is a mess. I would be more embarrassed if I could stand up straight. I might even try to hide the bras that are drying on my dish rack.

"Where's your room?"

"Only door on the right," I say.

We maneuver around the couch and the table that houses my mini Christmas tree. Asher almost trips over a pair of Joey's shoes and then he stumbles into a floor lamp. He's grunting and groaning as we fall into my room, which is pitch black until I somehow manage to turn on the fairy lights.

"Do you not have heat?"

"In most rooms," I say. "Just not this one."

"How is that not a code violation?"

"I'm illegally subletting this room," I say. "I can't complain."

"Of course you can't. You're probably in hypothermic shock."

"Do you care?" I ask.

"Not really," he says. "Get into bed."

"Not in this," I say and I'm ripping off my shirt before he can stop me.

"*Olivia.*"

"I smell like pizza." I'm trying to wiggle out of my skirt, but I lose my balance and fall onto my bed. "Everything is so hard."

"You're a mess." Asher is wrestling to pull down my blankets and sheets.

"I know," I cry. "Take off my skirt."

"No," he says.

"C'mon, someone has to see my sexy underwear. I don't want them to go to waste."

"No," he repeats.

"Fine," I say. "At least get my chapstick. My lips are so dry. They hurt. I can't have my lips cracking, Asher. I'll look—"

"Oh my God, you're giving me a headache," he snaps. "Where is it?"

"Where's what?"

"The chapstick, Olivia!"

"Oh," I laugh. "It's on my nightstand."

I'm buried in my mountain of pillows and I'm so comfortable and I'm so sleepy that I'm not even bothered that Asher is knocking pens and hair ties and bottles of water onto the floor. He looks so bemused. So out of his element. I giggle.

Until he pulls open the drawer.

"No! Betsy!"

The tips of his ears are turning red and he's staring at her and all I can think to do is slam the drawer shut. Right on his fingers.

"Oh, fuck!" he screams. "Fucking fuck fuck *fuck*!"

He's cradling his hand to his chest as he falls onto the bed next to me, wailing like he's just been shot.

"Shhh," I hiss.

"You broke my finger."

"I did not," I giggle.

"I think I'm dying."

"You're so dramatic."

"This isn't funny, Olivia, I'm in pain."

"Of course," I say. "Would you like me to kiss it better?"

"What I want is for you to lie down and stop making my life so—"

"What are you doing to her?" Joey is standing in my bedroom with a broom in her hand.

"What am I doing to her? The better question is what is she doing to *me*?"

Joey swats his leg with the handle.

"*Ow!*" he cries. "Why am I being attacked?"

"Why are you trying to take advantage of a drunk girl?"

"I'm *not*."

"Sure looks like you are." She hits him again. "Get out of here before I get my mace."

"Joey." I'm trying very hard not to laugh. "He's not. It's Asher. You know Asher. He's a… he's a good person. Not always nice and he doesn't smile a lot but, y'know, still cute. Like a grumpy cat."

I don't think she believes me, so she hits him again.

"Stop."

"Leave."

"With pleasure!"

Joey keeps a watchful eye as Asher stumbles out of our apartment. I fall asleep before I hear the door close.

8

Asher does not look happy to see me.

But in his defense, when I looked into the mirror this morning, I wasn't very happy to see me either.

I look like a trainwreck—if the train reversed over me at least twelve times and then once more for good luck. I'm pretty sure I'm dead.

"You're late," he says when I open the door.

I check my watch. "It's 9:03."

"Which is not nine o'clock."

I sigh and launch my overnight bag into the backseat of his Range Rover and then myself into the front, which was definitely not made for people with stubby legs. I didn't even know he owned a car, but the least surprising thing ever is that the car is a Range Rover.

Asher is nothing if not predictable.

I have him down to a science.

That's why I'm not surprised to see a half-eaten bagel unwrapped on his lap. There are crumbs scattered over his thighs and cream cheese smudged into the corners of his mouth. He looks over at me mid-chew and adjusts his grip on the steering wheel. His glare is shielded by a pair of wayfarers.

"Here." He tosses a bagel at me, which would have been a sweet gesture if he didn't, y'know, throw it at me.

"I certainly hope this is bacon, egg, and cheese on an untoasted everything."

It *is* a bacon, egg, and cheese on an untoasted everything.

"How did you know?" I ask.

"There are always two bagels in the bag," he says. "I assume the other atrocity is yours."

"I'm offended."

"Your untoasted bagel is what's offensive."

I'm starving, so I'm not about to get into the Bagel Debate of the Century with the Double-Toasted Weirdo. I unwrap the rest of the parchment and take a bite. My head hits the back of the seat as I let out a long sigh.

Nothing has ever tasted this good.

"Drink this." This time it's a lemon-lime sports drink that he flings at me.

"Asher, I'm starting to think you like me."

"The thought of driving two hours with you complaining about a hangover is literally my worst night-mare," he says. "I'm trying to save us both a headache."

"Joke's on you because my head literally feels like someone took a sledgehammer to it."

He lifts a cup of coffee out of the cup holder. Thank-fully, he doesn't share his usual careless whimsy with scalding hot beverages and hands it to me like a civilized human being.

"You really know the way to a girl's heart."

He scoffs.

"Honestly, Asher," I say, looking over at him as he checks his sideview mirrors before pulling out. "You didn't have to do what you did for me last night. I hope you know how much I appreciate it."

He takes this opportunity to bite into his bagel. "So, you're not upset I ruined all the sexcapades you had planned with your boy toy?"

"I believe I ruined that when I puked on my shoes," I laugh, "All you did was take me out of a situation that probably would have ended badly."

"Contrary to popular belief, I can be a decent person."

"I've never doubted that."

"Just don't get used to it," he says. "I have a reputation to uphold."

And believe me, he upholds that reputation the entire drive to East Hampton. He swats my hand away from the radio. He puts the child lock on the window. He makes me wait forty-five minutes for a bathroom break. And then locks the door and pretends he doesn't hear me banging on the window.

His worst offense? Not the raging control issues or how he rolls through stop signs or the soft rock he insists on listening to.

Asher McGowan is a serial hummer.

Which might be endearing if my head wasn't ready to explode.

Throwing myself out the window might hurt less.

Unfortunately, it's locked because I'm a child who can't be trusted with those sort of privileges, so we'll never know exactly how much it would hurt.

"Are you about done?"

I'm puking on the side of the road, somewhere between exit fifty-nine and sixty, because Asher kept insisting I was fine and that all I needed was to drink more water. A publicist and a medical professional. His parents must be so proud.

I wipe my mouth with a paper napkin. "Remember when you said you're capable of being a decent human being?"

"I filled my quota for the day," he says. "Now will you please hurry up?"

I glare at him for ten very long seconds before I realize it's freezing and I can't feel my fingers.

"I'm *so* sorry," I say as I slam my door. "Did I interrupt the humming of *another* John Mellencamp song?"

"Actually, I've moved on to Phil Collins."

"I'm *so* excited," I say. "Please, serenade me."

He takes his eyes off the road for a millisecond to glance at me. "Are you gonna make it?"

"Two more miles before I cut all the wires to your speakers with a plastic knife? Probably not."

"Because I can turn around," he continues. "We don't have to go."

"Of course we do. It's not every day you get invited to the Ragnar Estate. This is a life changing moment. Besides, we have a fake relationship to uphold. I'll be fine once I take a nap and another shower," I tell him. "But do I really need those three letters of recommendation? And when does the DNA test happen? Did they already do my background check?"

"What?" Asher's face has turned sour. "What the hell are you talking about? Why would you need a DNA test? I already know you're a fucking space cadet."

I frown, "I was told there are certain steps one must go through to be let on property."

"Yes, you go through a security gate and show them your ID."

"That's it?"

"Yes! It's a members only club! Not the goddamn *Pentagon!*"

I'm going to kill Natasha.

Right after I kill Asher.

Who has added some light finger tapping to his current jam session.

* * *

I'm dipping gingerbread cookies into peppermint hot chocolate and living my best life on a couch that overlooks sandy white beaches. I don't know how long this little facade with Asher is going to last, but I can only hope to be back here in July. On the beach. In a lounge chair. Wearing a bikini. And a floppy hat. With a fruity drink in my hand.

All this luxury is really going to my head.

I'll get a nice reality check when I'm eating instant noodles and boxed macaroni and cheese for the rest of the year.

"Olivia!"

Francesca falls onto the couch next to me and jostles me enough to make the contents in my stomach shake. I cannot vomit in the lobby of this bougie hotel. Asher will kill me.

I have so many cookies in my mouth that the, "hey," I mutter doesn't translate to English.

"Isn't this place a dream?"

It is. I feel like I stepped inside a snow globe. There are snow covered trees and a grand staircase wrapped in garland. Everything smells like the warmth of gingerbread and cinnamon and molasses. Michael Bublé classics filter the room. People look happy in a way they don't when they're shoving me out of their way at the *Macy's* in Herald Square.

"I've been in fancy hotels in the city, but they don't compare to this," I say.

"Just wait until the Fourth of July party."

I'm pretty sure she can see the fireworks light off in my eyes.

I'm also pretty sure she's drooling over my plate of cookies. That's when I realize I should probably offer her some because that sort of thing is polite. Even though I would rather get a pap smear than share my food with anybody, which is clearly evident by all the soft and squishy bits on my body.

"They're delicious." I nudge my plate towards her and I feel my heart break a little.

"No, I can't."

Thank God.

"I can't eat dairy until December twenty-fourth at 10:01 p.m."

"That's very specific."

No wonder she dated Asher. They probably did weirdly specific things together at weirdly specific times. Coffee at exactly 7:03 a.m. Double-toasted cinnamon raisin bagels with extra cream cheese at 8:26 a.m. Hot yoga at 10:17 a.m. Avocado toast and arugula salad at 1:34 p.m. Dinner at that vegan place down the street at 7:35 p.m. Sex at 9:48 p.m. Everyone loves a well-planned kink, right?

I'm scheduling you at eleven o'clock, baby. You know what happens if you're late.

"It's my last night of production," she clarifies. "They have us on a really strict diet, which blows but, y'know, anything for the craft. Except I refuse to give up carbs."

"And why should you?"

I love carbs the way most people love their children.

Possibly more.

I would take a bullet for a quality baguette.

"Your outfit is really cute," she tells me. "I can't find a pair of overalls that fit me right."

"I found these in a thrift store in Queens."

"Really? I never think to go thrifting."

"I'll take you some time." It just slips out. "I'm a fantastic barterer."

"Really? I'd love that."

I realize, after downing the last of my peppermint hot chocolate, that this is a little strange. What ex-girlfriend wants to go thrifting with the current girlfriend? Are we going to compare notes on Asher over racks of vintage t-shirts? Laugh over lunch about his laundry list of weird habits? Why is she so nice to me? She's supposed to be ragingly jealous because we're so happy and in love.

And FYI, I've been ragingly jealous in the past and this is not how a normal person acts. She should already have a detailed plan of my well-executed disappearance.

Unless her plan all along has been to get me alone, so me offering to take her thrifting just makes her plan to discard my body in a dumpster in south Jersey a whole lot easier.

"Olivia, our room is ready."

"Thank *God*." I'm hungover and cookie drunk. It will be a Christmas miracle if I'm conscious for the party tonight. "I'm going to sleep for the next twelve years."

"I'm surprised you're alive today," Francesca laughs. "You can really throw back a drink."

"It was my minor in college."

Francesca laughs, but Asher doesn't. When Brent joins us, we all end up walking to the elevator together. Asher looks like he wants to die when he and Brent both reach to press the number two.

"Same floor," I say because we're all thinking it.

"Small hotel," Francesca says.

We realize just how small when we turn right and walk

to the end of the hall. Asher and I stop at 203 and Francesca and Brent at 201.

"Hopefully the walls are thick," I say and slap Asher's back. "Teeth grinder over here."

Asher is shooting laser beams at me as he slides the keycard into the door. It clicks. He opens the door and I hurry in before he can slam it in my face.

The first thing I see is the ocean, waves lapping against the sandy shore. There's a balcony outside the window that the gray sky is pouring through. There's a king-sized bed with a navy blue upholstered headboard. And just two steps down is a small sitting area with a couch and two chairs.

"They didn't have another room available," Asher says as he tosses his keys and wallet onto the dresser. "But I think you'll find the couch comfortable."

"You're going to make me sleep on the couch?" I ask. "Is that really the gentlemanly thing to do?"

"This gentleman just paid five hundred dollars to stay here for the night."

"Seriously?"

"Yes, Olivia, these things aren't free."

I never considered that this might be expensive. I shouldn't have accepted the invitation.

"I can pay half."

I really can't. I'd have to pick up extra shifts at the restaurant and pay him in installments.

"I don't want your money," he says as he kicks off his shoes and shrugs out of his coat. "I would just like you to stop cackling and ordering bed linen. I'm an adult. I don't need snowman sheets."

"But they're flannel," I say. "And I don't cackle!"

"You sound like Ursula in that scene in *The Little Mermaid* when she steals Ariel's voice."

I blink at him.

"I have a niece."

"I'm offended that, out of all the Disney characters you could compare me to, you pick Ursula and not Tinker Bell."

Asher rolls his eyes as he collapses onto the bed. I'm ready to tell him just how *mean* and *grinchy* he's being, but when the headboard hits the wall in a rather suggestive way, a light bulb goes off in my head.

"*Yes.*" It growls up from my throat and startles Asher's eyes wide. They only seem to grow when I jump on the bed. There's another thump. I grin. "*Yes.*"

"What are you doing?" he hisses.

"We're having sex," I whisper. "*God, Ash.*"

His entire body tenses.

"You belong in a mental institution," he says. "It's not even noon!"

"We can't have fake sex before noon?"

What kind of fake relationship am I in?

"Oh my God, do you really have a scheduling kink?"

"Do I have a what? You just told her you were going to sleep for the next twelve years."

"You persuaded me otherwise." I shrug against the pillow. "That look of absolute misery really turns me on. I'm practically falling out of my clothes right now."

"Well, fall back into them," he says and turns onto his side. "And get out of my bed. You smell like the everything bagel you vomited up on the side of the road."

"Wow, you sound so sexy right now."

"It'll give you something to think about when you're alone with Betsy at night."

"Oh, I have plenty of things to think about when I'm alone with Betsy and none of them are you."

"Let me guess, they're all Levi Booker?"

I sit up and throw my legs over the side of the bed. "Why are you so interested in what I think about when I'm alone at night?"

"I'm not."

I'm grinning because we both know he's lying.

"Okay," I say. "Maybe you've crossed my mind once or twice or a dozen times."

I let him marinate on that while I escape to the bathroom to soak out last night's mistakes in the claw foot tub.

It takes four hours and a room service burger, but I feel human again, which is more than I can say for Asher, who has morphed into the Most Annoying Person Ever. He has spent the last five minutes knocking on the bathroom door.

"Olivia, we need to *go*."

I don't have the heart to tell him that we're not going anywhere for at least thirty minutes. I'm still curling my hair. My makeup is only half done. I still haven't decided what dress I'm wearing.

"Give me a minute." Or twenty-nine.

"I've given you too many minutes," he says. "You've been in there for three hours!"

He's not exaggerating, but I don't like his tone. It takes a lot of work to make me look like I schmooze with the elite on the regular. I had to break out the good tweezers.

"*Olivia.*"

I'm certain it's his head that hits the door and not his fist.

I take a deep breath and count to three. I'm not into making deals with the devil, but I should at least be a little accommodating to the guy who spent five hundred bucks for us to be here.

So I set my curling iron down and try on the red dress and then the black and then the red again.

And then the black.

I spin around, checking myself in the mirror at different angles.

I sigh.

"Ash?" I pull open the door and he's hunched over, gripping the doorframe.

"What?" He lifts his eyes slowly to mine.

"Can I ask a favor?"

"I feel like that's all you ask me."

I turn around. "Can you see my panty lines?"

"I'm sorry?" His voice hits an octave I didn't know it could reach.

"On my dress," I say. "Can you see panty lines?"

There's a long pause.

Probably too long.

I should feel uncomfortable, but I don't.

"Yep," he says. "They're… there."

"Honestly," I huff and spin back to face him. "You pay all this extra money for seamless thongs and for what! Panty lines!"

"Right." He swallows. "So I'll see you downstairs."

"Wait! I have another dress to try on!"

He's gone. He doesn't even thank me for allowing him to stare at my butt for ten uninterrupted seconds.

It takes me twenty more minutes, but I follow the ghosts of Asher's footsteps down to the lobby. I take the stairs because who doesn't love a dramatic entrance? And I've watched this scene in every romantic comedy in existence. Jaws drop, the room gasps, and people are stunned by my beauty and grace.

"*Olivia.*"

His voice sends a chill up my spine, but not in a good way.

"Do you have any idea what you do to a man?"

Levi is taking my hand as I hit the final step. Without another choice, I allow him and scan the room for Asher.

"You are a vision in red." He kisses my knuckle.

A week ago, my dress would have already been pooled around my ankles. Levi Booker. In a perfectly fitted blazer. With purposely messy hair. Smelling of Tom Ford and pure sin. Looking at me like I'm the hottest woman he's ever seen. Like he wants to take me to his room and destroy me.

But there's something in the way that he holds my hand. It's careful control. Subtle demand. Just enough force to make my mouth dry.

"I didn't expect to see you here tonight," I say.

"I can say the same thing about you," he says. "I had already written this whole night off, but then I get hand-delivered the most gorgeous Christmas present *ever*? I'm the luckiest man in the room."

I'm not sure he sees me as anything more than a prize to be won. I'm a body to him. Someone who fits a mold that he's deemed fuckable. I've never felt less sexy.

"I have a house not too far from here."

"That's nice."

He laughs and squeezes my hand. "It's right on the beach. It's very romantic."

"I'm not looking to be romanced," I lie. I'm always looking to be romanced. Just not by Levi Booker, who is not well-liked in my small and strange group of friends.

"Then it's all very repulsive," he laughs. "Awful. A complete waste of four million dollars."

"When you put it that way…"

"Does that mean you're interested?"

"I'm sorry," I say and try to pull my hand away. "I'm here for work."

"Aw, c'mon." He squeezes my hand harder. "When Asher's away, Livi should play."

To a room full of people, this looks harmless. It's Levi Booker charming another girl out of her dress. It's a page six write-up. An *E!News* exclusive. A blurry photo passed around Twitter. I'm another notch on his bedpost.

"O?"

When I see Asher, I'm the human equivalent of a sigh of relief. He's standing by the stairs with two drinks in his hands. He's wearing a pale blue shirt (with far too many buttons undone) underneath a fitted black jacket. He looks soft yet professional, like he's about to fire someone but still extend an invitation to the office Christmas party.

"I got you a drink." His voice is low, and his eyes cut sharply to Levi and then to his hand that's still wrapped around mine.

"What is it?" I ask. It's a martini glass filled with something bright red and rimmed with green sugar.

"Jingle juice."

I snort. "I really wish I could have been there to hear you order this."

"It was a low point in my life," he says. "I hope Levi's not bothering you."

"Bothering her?" Levi says. "I was simply inviting her to the real party."

"And how is that working out for you?"

"Not well. Olivia is a perfect employee. Very committed to her work," he says. "But I'm sure you already knew that."

"I'm not sure what you're inferring."

Levi hums. "You don't really see a lot of interns at these shindigs."

"We're networking," I say.

"Networking." Levi licks his bottom lip and smiles. "Is that what you're calling it these days, Ash?"

His jaw clenches. "Let go of her hand."

"If it's bothering her, she just has to tell me."

"It's bothering me."

Levi's response isn't instant. It's slow. Like honey. One finger at a time.

"Livi, the invitation still stands," he says. "We can have a *repulsive* time in my hot tub."

"Yeah, she's good."

Asher's hand is on the small of my back and he's urging me away from Levi and into the party.

"You look handsome," I tell him because he does. Who doesn't love a broody man in a suit?

"Thanks," he says and glances down at me. I'm ready for him to tell me I look drop-dead gorgeous. "Did you… solve your… *problem*?"

"Oh." I take a sip of my drink. "Yeah, I'm just not wearing any."

"Right." I can hear him swallow.

We mingle with the crowd, and a switch flips deep inside of Asher. Gone is the scowling man who called room service three times because his burger wasn't brought to him deconstructed—the bun gets soggy otherwise—and in his place is the bright and charismatic man whose smile could rival the brightness of a thousand twinkling lights on a Christmas tree.

There may or may not be butterflies fluttering in my stomach.

He introduces me as Olivia, an associate at the firm. We're colleagues. But there's never a moment when he's not touching me. His hand has made a home on the small of my back. He laughs at the outlandish things that come out of my mouth and I look up at him with hearts bursting out of my eyes. Are we or aren't we? The question lingers over the room.

"It's flurrying."

We're standing by a large window that overlooks a patio that's sparkling with tiny lights. I sip my jingle juice slowly. Tonight, my limit is one. It's ill-advised to get sloppy when you're not wearing panties.

"I don't think it'll stick," Asher says. "But there's supposed to be a storm coming in at the beginning of the week."

"Maybe we'll have a white Christmas."

"I imagine it'll be covered in dirt by then."

"You love to bring the mood down, don't you?" I laugh.

"What can I say? It's part of my charm."

I take another sip of my drink and glance across the room. I see Francesca. She's glowing. I've never seen someone look so happy. Asher called her cold-hearted once, but I don't see it. She looks like she's so full of love.

When I look up at him, he looks heartbroken, which defeats the whole purpose of this. We're supposed to be suffocating Francesca with our happiness.

"We're standing underneath the mistletoe," I tell him.

He glances up. "How trite."

I live and breathe clichés. I want to bathe in them. I'm *that* girl. I'm every meme you've ever seen.

I kiss Asher. I'm standing on the tips of my toes and I have my hand on his neck and I'm kissing him. There's no urgency. It's soft and sweet. *Romantic.* It takes him a second, but when my finger twirls around a wispy curl tickling the nape of his neck, his lips part against mine. I'm still in control. He follows *my* lead, and pulls me closer.

I forgot how much I love kissing. And never in my

wildest dreams—and trust me, they get pretty wild—did I think I would love kissing Asher as much as I do. He's not brash or demanding or cocky. His rigid personality shifts into something subtle and demure. He might boss me around the office, but I have all the power here.

My eyes are still closed when I pull away, my teeth grazing over his lower lip in one final attempt to prolong this moment. I'm lightheaded and dizzy and he's looking at me like I'm the eighth wonder of the world. Or maybe that's just me hoping. Because I'm not sure how we go back to being what we were after a kiss like that.

Or, at least, *I* don't know how to go back to what we were before.

Because there's nothing fake about my sudden need to kiss him again.

There's also nothing fake about the fact that Francesca is watching.

And so is Levi.

Whoops.

"You really went heavy on the onions on that burger," Asher says.

I frown. "I brushed my teeth three times!"

"You should have brushed harder."

I don't get a chance to stomp on his foot.

"We've been looking all over for you two," Francesca says.

"Here we are," Asher replies.

"I trapped him under the mistletoe."

"You sure did," Brent laughs.

"Do you two want to grab another drink?" Francesca asks.

"Actually," I say and smile up at Asher oh so lovingly. "We were just about to take that sleigh ride."

"We were?"

"Don't be silly, Ash," I laugh. "You were just saying how romantic it's going to be."

"That doesn't sound like something I would say."

"I promise wanting to take a sleigh ride doesn't emasculate you." I kiss his cheek. "We'll catch up with you two when we get back."

I take Asher's hand and drag him through the crowd of people. He's not kicking and screaming like a child, but I can tell he wants to. He's not taking this from me. If I had to listen to the *Best of Phil Collins* on the drive here, he can take a quick sleigh ride around town.

"Where are you two off to in such a hurry?" Levi is standing by the door with a girl who barely looks old enough to drive. "More networking?"

"I really don't think it's any of your business," Asher says as he pulls open the door, a blast of cool air chilling me.

"We're not too different, are we, Ash?"

"Levi, we're not even in the same realm."

Levi chuckles softly and brushes his thumb over his lower lip. His eyes catch mine and I'm left with an unsettling feeling in the pit of my stomach. "Be careful with this one, Livi. He's always up to no good."

I squeeze Asher's hand tighter and pull him right out the door. Someone is up to no good, but it's not Asher.

"On the off chance this sounds like I care," Asher says when we're outside and the wind is blowing soft flurries around us. "I would like to preface it by saying I don't."

"Wow, I can't wait to see where this is going."

"If you ever find yourself alone with Levi, please call me."

"Why?"

"I just need you to trust me."

"I'm going to need more of an explanation than that,"

I tell him. "Especially when you've told me never to call you unless we're under nuclear attack."

"Olivia."

"Asher."

We're having a staring contest and he's going to lose. If there's one thing I'm good at, it's standing my ground. I once stood in a professor's office for forty-five minutes until he gave me the same grade as a male student who put no effort in our group project and only got an A because he needed to maintain his GPA for the basketball team.

"You're difficult."

"Thank you."

The sounds of soft trotting fills the air. I watch the horse drawn sleigh glide over a blanket of man-made snow. I'm covered in goosebumps.

Which may have everything to do with the fact that it's freezing and I don't have a jacket.

"I can't believe this is my life right now," Asher says.

"A romantic sleigh ride with me? Your hot as hell fake girlfriend? You must have been a really good boy this year."

"Do you think if I throw myself in front of the horse, it will trample me?"

"I feel like that would be a very painful death."

"I feel like this is going to be a very painful twenty minutes."

He's not wrong. The seats in the sleigh are painful, but I'm pretty much numb from head to toe, so I'm not bothered.

I'm in a *sleigh*. Under a blanket. With flurries dancing around me. Pine trees are covered in *snow*. The moon is glowing. The stars are shining. I'm living and breathing a *Hallmark Channel* movie.

"Can you stop shivering? You're giving me a headache."

I deadpan.

He rolls his eyes. And in the most shocking event of the night, Asher shrugs off his jacket and throws it around my shoulders.

"That was almost sweet," I laugh.

"A thank you would suffice."

"Thank you *so* much, Asher. What would I do without such a *generous* and *thoughtful* man by my side?"

"Smartass."

I grin and slide closer to him for the sole purpose of jacking all his body heat.

"I know what you're doing."

"I have no idea what you're talking about."

He glares at me, but I smile in return, which makes him shake his head and look away. I'm wearing him down. He's going to be able to tolerate me soon.

"Tell me about your favorite Christmas."

"Why?"

"Because I feel like I don't know you."

"You know my credit card number very well."

"I do." I smile. "And I think you're going to love the heated throw blanket you'll be receiving this week."

He glances at me out of the corner of his eye and then focuses his attention back on the lush grove of trees we're riding by. He always looks so serious. Even with a pink nose and rosy cheeks. It's like he's trying so hard not to enjoy himself. Like showing one ounce of joy would be the be-all end-all. Life's too short to pretend to hate everything.

"I was ten," he tells me. "Morgan was about fifteen, I think. And we went to our grandparents' house in Connecticut. It was the first Christmas that ever felt normal. We didn't have this stuffy black tie dinner. It wasn't catered. There weren't servers. It was my mom in the kitchen making French toast. And she looked happy and relaxed and it was real. We felt like any other family. We watched movies and ate cookies and opened presents. And no one told me to smile or straighten my tie. I got to be a kid on Christmas morning. My dad didn't even call. I think that was the best part."

"Have you two ever had a relationship?"

"I mean, I have a trust fund and a job, so I'd say our relationship is strictly monetary."

"Does it make you sad?"

"Not really." He shrugs and his knee brushes against mine. "I have my mom and Morgan and Chloe."

"But it's okay to want a relationship with your dad."

"I'm the product of an affair, so it's hard to want a relationship with a man who didn't want me in the first place."

When he looks at me, I see the pain in his eyes that he tries so hard to conceal.

"Ash—"

"This is all very merry," he laughs. "Tell me about your favorite Christmas. I'm sure it involved gingerbread houses and dramatic retellings of *How the Grinch Stole Christmas*."

I pull the blanket higher and let out a quiet shiver.

"My mom was a nurse, so she worked every year," I say. "I spent most Christmases alone."

He looks puzzled. How could I—a living, breathing Christmas card—have a long history of sad holiday memories?

"Really?"

"Yeah," I say. "But when she did get off shift, the only places that were open were a Thai restaurant and a *Dunkin Donuts*, so we would sit on the couch with Tom Yum soup and green curry and then gorge ourselves with donuts.

Glazed and strawberry frosted because those were my favorite. And we'd watch those old claymation movies until we fell asleep on the couch."

"You do that every year?"

"Yeah, I did." I nod. "There was one year that she didn't work, but… it was usually just Thai food and donuts."

I glance to the sky. Not because I want to admire the moon and the stars and the falling snow, but because it's the only way I can stop myself from crying. Deep breath in and out. Count to three.

"Are you going home this year?" he asks.

"No, I'll be in the city."

"Alone?"

"Yeah."

"Is your mom working?"

"No."

"Then why—"

"Look!" I point out a deer that's quivering near a brush of trees. The conversation is dropped. Either he forgets, or he's smart enough not to pry.

We get back to the hotel and it's after eleven, but the party's still going strong. Asher heads straight for the stairs and I follow closely behind. I'm frozen solid and exhausted. I need a hot shower and sleep, preferably for twenty hours.

"Ash!" Francesca's voice slurs over the jazz cover of *Last Christmas* filtering through the lobby. "Olivia!"

Asher's glaring down at his feet, like they've somehow betrayed him by not moving fast enough.

I've exfoliated you. I've moisturized you. I've treated you to hot stone spa pedicures twice a month. And this is how you repay me?

"Pretend you don't hear her," he whispers.

"Yeah, I don't think that's going to work."

"Not with that attitude."

"Are you really going to lecture *me* on *my* attitude, Ebenezer?"

"This Scrooge gave you his jacket when you were shivering."

"I'll alert the Ghost of Christmas Present."

He barely gets to glare at me before Francesca is pulling me by my arm down the few steps I managed to climb. Asher grabs my hand and suddenly it's tug-Olivia-war.

On one *literal* hand, it's drunk Christmas shenanigans that probably also include gingerbread cookies and spiked hot chocolate.

On the other *literal* hand, it's me and Asher alone in a hotel room, which could potentially involve naked shenanigans.

Both sound equally satisfying.

"There are reindeer outside!" Francesca is practically vibrating, which is a level of enthusiasm that I appreciate.

Also *reindeer*? Frolicking in the snow? Like the whimsical creatures they are? That's a big jingle bell hell yes from me!

"You've really done it now," Asher mumbles to Francesca.

"Done what?" Francesca asks. "Given your girlfriend the best Christmas gift she never had to ask for?"

"Ah, yes, rabies," Asher mutters. "The gift that keeps on giving."

"What kind of random reindeer do you think they got?" I ask. "I'm sure they're very reputable. I bet they're verified on Twitter."

"Right," he says. "But just so you know, when you start hallucinating and foaming at the mouth, I'm going to tell the doctors to put you down."

"That's fine," I say. "But good luck trying to find

another woman who'll embarrass herself on your behalf at every food establishment in the greater Manhattan area."

"I'll manage."

"Seriously," Francesca says as she grabs Asher's hand, pulling him off the stairs. He stumbles into the spot next to me. "You two are perfect for each other. Ash, you did good."

On our way through the lobby, I steal a snickerdoodle off a tray by the Christmas tree. They're soft and chewy and sugary sweet. I kick myself for not grabbing another.

Francesca, on the other hand, *pas de bourrees* and *chasses* through creative directors and executive producers, completely bypassing the dessert table. She smiles and waves, owning the room and making it her stage. I'm about to give her a standing ovation.

"You're looking at her like you just realized you picked the wrong ex to fake date," Asher says.

"She's hot as hell," I say. "I wouldn't kick her out of bed."

"*Olivia.*"

"What? You must agree on some level. You *real* dated her."

"Yeah," he coughs lowly as we cross onto the patio, a blast of cold air greeting us. "I'm not sure that she'd agree that it was real."

I frown, looking up at him. His nose is the same shade of pink as his cheeks and he's biting his lips to keep his teeth from chattering.

"I don't think that's true."

I saw the look on his face the night of the tree lighting. Whatever feelings Asher had for Francesca, they were real. There are some things in life that you just can't fake— knowing calculus, liking tequila, and the complete devastation of watching someone you love move on with someone else.

But, for now, I leave Asher's buttons unpushed. We have more pressing matters to tend to, like a bucket of carrots and a reindeer named Prancer.

"Look at them!" I take Asher's hand and drag him towards the crowd. We leave hurried footprints in the dusting of snow, and I grab a handful of carrots before stopping in front of a reindeer that looks Vitamin A drunk. "Aren't you just the cutest?"

"His breath smells worse than yours," Asher says.

"You can insult me all you want," I say, scratching Prancer under his ear. "But leave him out of it."

Asher snarls at the animal, who has started nudging his hand for any carrots that he might be holding out on.

"He likes you!"

"He has a poor judge of character," Asher mumbles.

"*Stop,*" I laugh as Prancer licks Asher's hand. "Have you thought about getting a pet? I think you'd really benefit from the companionship."

"I like being alone," he says. "So don't get any ideas. I'm fairly certain you can't Amazon Prime a puppy."

"Oh, c'mon," I laugh. "Even the Grinch had a dog."

"I like living my life without having to worry about someone else's needs."

I hum. "You seemed pretty worried about me last night."

"Because you were drunk out of your mind at a company event," he says. "Your death would have been an HR nightmare."

"Sure." I nod. "If that's what you need to believe."

I feed Prancer one last carrot before his caretaker insists it's time for them to go back to the North Pole. I refrain from asking if I can go with them. Mostly because

I'm fairly certain Asher would have jumped at the opportunity to get rid of me.

"You *guys!*" Francesca throws her arms around me and Asher, and because of the height difference, I almost end the night with a black eye. "I'm just so *happy* that we're all *happy.* Doesn't it feel nice to be *this* happy *and* in love? Because I was *soooo* worried about you, Ash. I'm so glad everyone was wrong about you. You *can* feel things! You have a *heart!* Love is *soooo* beautiful and everything is spinning! Merry Christmas!"

"Yeah," Asher mumbles. "Think it's time for you to go to bed, Frankie."

"Noooo, I think there's another glass of mulled wine calling my name!"

We watch her stumble and stagger through the crowds of people. She finds Brent talking to a few acquaintances and lunges at him in a fit of drunken giggles. It's not long after that when Asher ducks inside, and I follow him through the hotel and up the stairs until we're back in our room.

I spend the entire twenty minutes I'm in the shower thinking about what Francesca said. Ash has a heart? He can feel things? I mean, *obviously.* Just because he's surly and closed off doesn't mean he's not capable of basic human emotions. Having been his girlfriend, I figured she knew that.

I sigh, pulling my hair into a bun as I walk out of the bathroom. Asher is already in the bed, blankets and sheets haphazardly thrown over his legs, the waistband of his boxer briefs peeking out. He's not wearing a shirt. How promiscuous. A girl might get the wrong idea...

"Goodnight," I say, turning towards the couch.

He's watching a rerun of *Friends* with an intense focus, but his eyes flash to me briefly.

"Do you mind if I borrow a pillow?" I ask. "I'll use a towel for a blanket."

"Aren't there pillows on the couch?" he asks. "I need to sleep with four."

I blink at him.

"I'm kidding," he says and his focus shifts back to the TV. "And don't be ridiculous. You can sleep in the bed."

He doesn't look at me when he says it, but that doesn't stop me from staring at him. He's the most indecisive person I've ever met.

"You told me to sleep on the couch."

He shrugs. "I figured you would put up more of a fight. I'm disappointed."

"I didn't put up a fight because you made a valid point," I say. "You paid for this. I really can't make demands."

"You're not making demands. I'm telling you to sleep in the bed."

"Why?"

"We've established that I'm capable of being a decent human being," he says. "Now please stop arguing with me. I'm exhausted and you're giving me a headache."

I don't know why I'm arguing with him. It's not like I want to sleep on a couch. He's just confusing and annoying and I kinda, sorta want to strangle him.

But I don't.

Because that would be rude.

Instead, I slip out of my pajama bottoms and pretend that Asher doesn't look like the emoji with its eyes bugging out of its head.

I also pretend that he isn't staring at the Christmas trees on my underwear.

"I don't trust people who wear pants to bed," I tell him

as I climb in next to him. "And you must agree on some level because you're not wearing any either."

"You're deranged."

"You just invited this deranged person into your bed."

"I regret it immensely."

"I don't believe you."

"Go back to the couch."

"I think you just want to look at my butt again."

I can practically hear him blushing.

I'M in a Christmas-themed spin class and I'm never going to be able to listen to Wham! again without thinking about dying. Joey is a terrible roommate. Forcing me to get my daily recommended exercise at five in the morning. Before the sun is even up. It's cruel and unusual punishment.

I need pancakes.

And a shower.

I'm sweating in regions I didn't know could sweat.

"Natasha is on location in Tulum, so you'll have to come to pilates with me tomorrow. It's at six."

"I'm amazed you think I'm going to be able to walk tomorrow."

"Just make sure you're not sitting still too long today," she tells me. "You'll be fine."

Fine? There is nothing fine about the way my lady parts feel.

"It's supposed to snow tomorrow," I tell her as we walk through the locker room. "Like a foot and a half! I can't go to a pilates class in a foot and a half of snow! I can't go anywhere in a foot and a half of snow."

"You're from Buffalo," she says. "You basically lived in a foot and a half of snow."

"The city has made me weak," I say. "I can't handle snow and I break out in hives when I can't order a falafel at two in the morning."

"Have you ever needed to order a falafel at two in the morning?"

"No, but I like having the option."

I'm a big fan of options. Like the option to sleep-in an extra hour instead of being strapped to a machine that's designed to work the core muscles I don't have. Well... the core muscles I *could* have if I ate less chicken nuggets and exercised more.

Maybe I'll make that my New Year's resolution.

To exercise more.

I'm definitely not going to give up chicken nuggets.

"Olivia!"

Of all the places I could possibly run into my fake boyfriend's ex-girlfriend at six in the morning, it's in a women's locker room and all she's wearing is underwear. I'm pretty confident in my skin, but she has to be wondering how Asher went from long and lean to short and squishy.

Or maybe she's not thinking about that at all and I'm a *teensy* bit insecure.

"You look wrecked," she laughs.

"I promise you I feel worse."

"Was this your first class?"

"First and last!"

"We're going to try pilates tomorrow," Joey says.

"Oh, Ash loves pilates," Francesca says. "He can teach you a thing or two."

I ignore the look Joey is shooting me.

"He probably doesn't have the patience." I realize after

I say it that I shouldn't have. I'm writing him off the way most people do. Brash. Irritable. Self-centered. And while he puts up that front, I've seen the man beneath it all.

"Do you guys have plans for tonight?"

"I mean, it's supposed to snow."

"At least now he has an excuse for a low-key birthday, right?"

Birthday?

"You know him," I laugh. "Probably made a deal with Mother Nature."

How is it that I know his social security number but not his birthday?

"So." Joey turns to me after Francesca leaves for her class. Her eyes are closed and her lips are pursed. I can see equations forming over her head. "You're sleeping with your boss?"

"*No*," I say in a way that's not convincing at all. "Define sleeping."

"I knew something was up when he brought you home when you were drunk and then you went to the Ragnar Estate for *work*," she says as she wraps a scarf around her neck. "Honestly, Olivia, that's a disaster waiting to happen. He's a McGowan. They're all notorious for treating women like shit."

"That's not true."

"Levi has them on his payroll."

"Asher hates Levi," I say. "And we're not sleeping together. At least, we're not having sex. It's… it's all fake. We're trying to make his ex-girlfriend jealous."

"The one who just hugged you with her tits out?"

"Yeah."

"I don't think it's working."

"*I know*," I say. "It's like she's happy for us, or something."

"Imagine that." Joey whistles out a breath as we walk out of the studio.

It's still dark and the air is frigid, the light wind reddening my already splotchy cheeks. But the time and weather do nothing to hinder New York City's perpetual rush hour. Traffic is backed up for blocks. Drivers are half asleep and impatient. Headlights are blinding. I want to go back to sleep.

But I don't.

Because I'm a (mostly) functional adult with responsibilities and a job, so I whine all the way back to our apartment and take a cold shower (because the hot water isn't working) and I take the subway to work. By the time I get the bagels, I'm only thirteen minutes late.

I'm barely in my seat when Bree walks in, adjusting her skirt and top button of her shirt. Most days she's still getting dressed in the elevator. She's another one of those early morning spin class riders. I'm still trying to figure out the allure of sweating like a pig before the streetlights go off.

"You okay?" I ask. She's looking particularly green and queasy.

"I'm fine," she says. "Were you at the Ragnar Estate this weekend?"

There's no beating around the bush with her. "Why?"

"Because someone said they saw you there," she says as she falls into her chair. "And I for sure thought you would have told me that you were going up there. How'd you get invited? My parents own half of East Hampton and I've never been there."

"Joey," I say, signing onto my computer.

"I thought she hated you."

"I thought so too." I shrug. "But we went to spin class today and yesterday she got the cereal I like when she was at the store, which I really think was just an excuse because she doesn't want to admit that she also likes Lucky Charms."

"They are magically delicious," she says, and then grimaces. "I heard Asher was there."

"I heard Beyoncé's makeup artist was there too, but I didn't see him."

Bree isn't impressed, which I think is grounds for treason.

"He was being a dick on Friday," she says. "I mean, he's always a dick, but he was being exceptionally awful at the bar."

"No, he wasn't."

"Liv, he was acting like a possessive boyfriend. *She's not going anywhere with them.* Like? Who the fuck are you?"

"I was really drunk."

"We all were."

"Did you get home okay?"

"Yeah, I took an Uber. I wasn't about to have a three-some with Thing One and Two," she huffs. "Asher ruined everything."

"I'm glad he did," I say. "He shouldn't be painted as the bad guy because he took me home when I was too drunk to take care of myself."

"You're getting very defensive," she says curtly. "I didn't realize you thought so highly of Asher McGowan. Is that why you were kissing him at the Ragnar Estate this weekend?"

"I didn't see Asher this weekend."

"That's not what I heard."

"You hear a lot of things, Bree." I push back my chair and stand up, pretending my sore muscles aren't screaming in agony. "I suggest getting your hearing checked."

I brush past Emanuel so quickly that I barely hear him whistle, "damn, Elsa's got her gloves off today."

I'm panicking.

Because apparently word gets around fast in the gossiping capital of the world and I'm sure, by now, it's gotten back to Asher.

I'm not ready for him to end this.

You can't just kiss someone under the mistletoe and wake up with their hand on your boob and not catch feelings.

Or maybe you can.

Because boob groping requires consent and unwanted touching can be very distressing.

But I woke up warm and fuzzy and very okay with the proximity of hand to boob. And face to neck. And the fact that we were very much spooning. With the way Asher almost jumped out of the window when he woke up, you would have thought I had the bubonic plague.

I think he caught *The Feelings* too.

They're very contagious.

Sort of like the plague, but with less death and more boob touching.

But with a whole party of people talking about all the kissing we did, I highly doubt there will be anymore boob touching.

Which is a shame because I have really great boobs and Asher has very nice hands. I think about them on the short walk to his office.

When I get there, he's banging his head against his desk as the Menopausal Momager from the Seventh Circle of Hell screeches through the speaker phone. Her voice is enough to turn a birthday sour.

Still, I find it hard not to smile. There's something about Asher McGowan that makes every last atom inside of me burst into tiny pieces of confetti. He's surly and dramatic and *weird*, but there's something about his quiet breathy laugh and the way he smiles when he rolls his eyes at me. It's the little things. Like the way he holds the steering wheel or how he fusses with his hair when he's uncomfortable. It's how he's powerful and sexy but not domineering. When he touches me, it's always soft and hesitant and careful. He doesn't always show that side of himself, but I know it's there.

"Are you having a stroke?"

Asher leans back in his chair and tucks a pen behind his ear. He's dressed down today, wearing a gray pullover and a pair of fitted jeans, which suggests he doesn't plan to be at the office much longer. If I had the option, I wouldn't want to work on my birthday either.

"I feel like if you're going to ask someone that, it needs to be said with much more urgency," I say. "Like you'd actually try to get said person help if they were, in fact, having a stroke, which I am not."

"Well, now that we've settled that you're not having a stroke. Is there something else I can help you with, Ms. Langley?"

"That's a very professional way to address a woman whose right breast you're personally acquainted with."

"*Olivia.*"

"Yes, Mr. McGowan?"

"Are you done playing games?"

"Never."

"Right," he says as he pushes his chair back and stands up. "I'll be taking the rest of the day off, so I've emailed you a list of releases I need written. I would like them forwarded back to me when they're completed."

I watch him tuck his phone into his back pocket, his keys jingling in his hand. He's doing a great job at avoiding the giant elephant in the room. Our weekend together may as well have never happened.

"Is this for me?" He takes the paper bag before I get a chance to answer.

"As a matter of fact…" I grab the bag back from him. "It's not."

"Is that so?"

"*Yep.*"

He probably doesn't need to be standing as close to me as he is, but our bodies are practically flush and we're having a glare-off in the middle of his office. There's a flicker in his eyes that suggests I'm wrong. Maybe he hasn't forgotten about this weekend. Perhaps he hasn't stopped thinking about it. About me. About my right boob. We've definitely kept him up all night.

"Tell me, Ms. Langley, who else are you buying bagels for?"

"That's really none of your business, Mr. McGowan."

"I'd say it is."

"I wasn't under the impression that my bagels were exclusively yours."

His eyes narrow and mine narrow back. He's not going to win. He knows it, which is why he snatches the bag away from me.

"I need those releases by three o'clock."

"Right, four o'clock."

After he leaves, I wait until I hear the elevator ding before I collapse into his chair. I don't make a habit of going through Asher's drawers for fun. It's an activity I save solely for when I need something. Like his credit card. Or gum. Or the expensive chocolate he gets at the European import shop in Union Square.

Today I'm looking for none of that, but I steal the chocolate anyway. I finish the whole bar before I find what

I need. A phone number. I dial out on Asher's office phone and lean back in his chair like I run this place.

"*Hello?*"

"Morgan! Hi, it's Olivia."

∗ ∗ ∗

Ana calls me to her office just in time for lunch, which consists of garlic noodles and hot dogs with questionable amounts of mustard. I don't complain about free food, so I scrape the mustard off with a napkin and enjoy the fine cuisine of the 52nd Street hot dog stand. We eat an assortment of honey-roasted nuts for dessert.

"I let Billie know that you'll be working on the final arrangements for the gala with her," Ana says, wiping her mouth with a paper napkin. "I also told Asher that he would be without an intern for a week and he reacted exactly how you would imagine he would."

"Like a petulant child?"

Ana smiles. "He's… unique."

"I prefer difficult," I laugh. "Demanding. Hard to please. But I don't necessarily think those are bad things. He's good at what he does and he expects the people that work for him to have those same standards. I can respect that."

"He's certainly nothing like his father."

"Which is a miracle in and of itself."

Ana leans forward and smiles at me from across her desk. And in that moment, she's not my boss or my colleague or a publicist. She's a mother. And suddenly, I feel like I've just been caught sneaking in at two in the morning reeking of booze and teenage regret. It's a look I don't take for granted.

"Are you seeing him?"

"I… would never do anything to jeopardize my place in this company. I take my work and my future career very seriously."

"Olivia, I see the work you do. You don't need to defend yourself to me," she says. "I know workplace *things* happen. And I see the way he looks at you, so I don't know why I'm saying this, but I'm a mother first and foremost and I just want it to be known that I don't tolerate abuse of power. And if you ever feel like you're in a situation like that, I trust that you would come to me. I do a very good job of destroying men who think they're untouchable. It's probably my favorite pastime."

I read the papers after Willa's personal pictures surfaced. Ana Loveridge-Herrera is not a woman anyone wants to cross. Not as a publicist. Definitely not as a mother. She murdered an entire family's reputation with a few choice words. She deserves a statue. And a nice, long vacation.

"Thank you for looking out for me," I tell her.

"It's what I'm here for."

Ana goes over some of the finer details of the Winter Wonderland Gala before she has to get on a conference call with a hockey player who had a little too much fun in Mexico. I walk out of her office at the same time River walks out of his.

"Good afternoon, Mr. McGowan," I say as we wait for the elevator.

"Olivia." He doesn't look up from his phone.

The McGowans are men of many words.

I hate silence.

"Any big plans for tonight?" I ask.

"A Monday night with two feet of snow in the forecast? No, Ms. Langley, I don't have big plans."

I frown. "I meant for Asher's birthday."

River looks at me for the first time since we stepped into the elevator. "Today's Asher's birthday?"

"Yes?"

He chuckles. "For some reason I thought that he was born in April."

The doors part on my floor. I'm so stunned that I barely remember how to walk. What kind of father doesn't remember his son's birthday? I want to tell him that he should be ashamed of himself, but when I turn around, the doors are shut and River is gone.

* * *

Asher answers the door on the seventh knock. I'm standing in his hallway covered in snow and shivering, attempting to balance a six pack of Stella on a cake box while struggling to hold onto my purse and his birthday present. He doesn't offer to help. All he can manage is a frown.

"I'm busy."

"You're never too busy for me." I shove the cake and beer at him and invite myself into his apartment, which is welcomed warmth that practically leaves me melting onto his floor.

I kick off my boots before I get too far because I'm considerate and don't want to track snow into his house. And after I drop my bags onto the counter, I turn back to Asher and give him my come-hither-eyes as I rip off my jacket, revealing my very sexy snowman sweater and fleece-lined leggings.

"Happy Birthday, Mr. McGowan."

He frowns. "Who told you?"

"I'm very resourceful."

"Did you go down to city hall and get a copy of my birth certificate?"

"Of course not," I say. "Francesca told me at spin class this morning."

He blinks. "You went to a spin class?"

"That's what you're most surprised about?"

He snorts. "The amount of money I would have paid to see that."

"Me bent over a bike?" My lips curve into a smirk as a blush creeps over his cheeks. "Sounds much hotter than it actually was. My legs feel like Jell-O and my vagina—"

"*Olivia.*"

"Right, sorry, you don't care about my ailing lady parts."

His pained expression suggests that *maybe* he does.

"Should we start with your present or your cake?"

He sets the cake box and the six pack of Stella down. "This better not be some grocery store chocolate cake with gross sugary frosting. I have a very refined palate."

"Give me a little credit, Ash."

He briefly narrows his eyes to mine before running a fingernail under the slip of tape. It's the sticker on the top of the box that makes his face fall.

"I believe that's a vanilla sponge with layers of peanut butter mousse, strawberry jam, and marshmallow cream. Or as the woman at *Flower + Flour* called it: the *Oh God It's That Time of Year Again.*"

"You got my favorite cake?"

"I took three trains and an Uber to *get* your favorite cake."

"Why?"

"Because it's your birthday, Asher."

His face softens. He doesn't look upset. He doesn't look happy. He looks indifferent. Stunned. Shocked that someone would go out of their way for him.

"Do you want your present?" I hold up the bag to him.

It's purple with teal tissue paper. I figured he would appreciate the fact that I didn't use one of my many Christmas bags. After all, his birthday shouldn't be overshadowed by the biggest holiday of the year.

"Did I buy it for myself?" he asks when he takes it.

I glare at him. "I do have my own credit card."

"I'm surprised you remember how to use it."

"There's no card," I say. "I hope you're not offended. I couldn't find one I liked."

"Was there no fake boyfriend section?"

"Ex-husband. Second grade teacher. Gynecologist. But no fake boyfriend."

"How unfortunate."

"I considered drawing you one, but I didn't want Chloe to think I was trying to come for her spot on your fridge."

I catch a rare dimpled smile. As much as I love Asher in a well-tailored suit, I might love him relaxed in the kitchen light more. Leaning against his counter. In a pair of fitted sweatpants and the same gray hoodie from earlier. With messy couch-hair. And sleepy eyes.

"Robin Roberts' memoir?"

"You said you watch *Good Morning America*."

"I do." He's smiling, but he looks confused. Adorably perplexed. "Thank you."

"Happy Birthday, Asher."

I spring up onto the tips of my toes with every intention of kissing his cheek, but he turns his head just enough for me to catch the corner of his lips. There's a certain shyness that lingers over us that's never there when we're putting on a show. It's an unintentional realization. We don't have to pretend in the privacy of his home.

"We should cut the cake." I don't mean to whisper, but it comes out so softly that I barely hear myself speak.

"What kind of civilized person do you think I am?" he whispers back.

"Then may I suggest getting us some forks?"

"You think I'm going to share my cake with you?"

"I think you're going to feed me cake while I lay on your couch."

"What sort of fantasy land are you living in, Ms. Langley?"

"One where you also give me a foot massage, Mr. McGowan."

I hold his stare for a second longer before I spin around dramatically. I'm very good at making myself feel at home, so I flop onto the couch I've had fantasies about. It's so soft. Like a cloud. I'm moving in.

"It's so *warm*." I bury myself under the blanket I ordered last week.

"Listen," Asher shouts from the kitchen. "You can't steal my blanket and my cake."

"Of course I can. Do you know who I am?"

"Literally the most annoying person on the planet."

"Please shower me with more compliments. Preferably about my boobs. I know how you feel about the right one, but the left one feels very underappreciated."

He ignores that comment. "Do you want a beer?"

"No, I don't like Stella."

"*Excuse me?*"

"Sorry we can't all be as sophisticated as you."

I pretend I don't hear him mocking me under his breath and I grab the remote off the coffee table. He's watching *Live! With Kelly and Ryan*. I've decided to stop being surprised by the things he likes.

"Hey! They were just about to do the trivia question."

"I didn't realize how seriously you take your morning talk shows."

He glares at me as he hands me a glass of wine.

"Look at you trying to wine and dine me. Who knew you could be romantic?"

"You have some very low standards for romance if you think this is it."

"C'mon, Ash." I sit up as he sits down, the box of cake nestled on his lap. "Cozied up on the couch. Snuggled under blankets. Snow falling outside. Christmas movies. *Cake*. We're living a *Lifetime* special."

He takes a bite of cake. "When do I get accused of murdering you? Because I won't even try to deny it. I'll walk into the courtroom and say *you're welcome*."

"You would be very lonely without me."

"I would definitely have to buy less Tylenol."

I roll my eyes and open my mouth.

"Don't beg, Olivia, it's unbecoming."

My lips barely fall into a pout before he shoves his fork into my mouth.

"*Oh my God.*" I might start crying. "That's so good."

"It was one of my finer creations."

I take a sip of wine. I'm definitely going to cry.

"I don't suppose this is a four dollar *Trader Joe's* special?"

"I think it was a two hundred dollar limited edition."

I'm trying very hard not to spit red wine all over his couch. "Why did you open a two hundred dollar bottle of wine?"

"Because you said you didn't like beer?"

"But the beer cost, like, twelve dollars. I can't replace this."

"I don't want you to replace it? You're just…supposed to enjoy it."

I shrink back into one of his many throw pillows and

take another long sip. "You're doing a very bad job at not making this romantic."

"Let's see how romantic you think I am when I finish this entire cake."

I watch him shovel two forkfuls into his mouth before I sit up and scoot closer. He glares at me and shifts away, a protective arm around the box.

"You're not being very nice right now," I tell him.

"I don't think I've ever been nicer," he says and takes another bite. "I've given you expensive wine and haven't kicked you back out into the snow."

"Fake Boyfriend of the Year."

I'm on my knees and inching closer, like a lioness on the prowl, ready and waiting to pounce. If you look up the word *seduction* in the dictionary, it's a picture of me. Asher won't be able to resist me for much longer.

"You look terrifying."

"Terrifying or the star of your next wet dream?"

"Terrifying, you fucking weirdo. Go away."

"Give me the cake, Asher. This is not proper birthday etiquette."

"And what exactly is proper birthday etiquette?"

"Sharing your cake with—"

He shoves his fork right into my mouth and laughs when I choke.

"Sorry, was that not what you meant?"

Scowling at him and trying to chew is proving to be difficult. There's too much in my mouth. I resemble a chipmunk.

"You're a mess," he laughs and swipes his thumb over my lower lip, collecting a glob of strawberry jam that never made it into my mouth. He licks his finger clean.

Which may have turned me on more than it should.

"This is, like, the best peanut butter and jelly sandwich I've ever had."

"Eight-year-old Asher was a gourmet genius."

"How did you even come up with this? Are you some sort of peanut butter and jelly connoisseur?"

He laughs shyly under his breath. "It's stupid."

"I bet it's not."

He takes a bite of cake and then offers me one. No begging, crying, or whining needed. I hold his stare as he pulls the fork from my mouth, which may have been a little more erotic than I intended. I probably could have done without moaning, but I can't help what good food does to me. This cake is better than sex.

Well, better than any sex I've had.

I have a sneaking suspicion that sex with Asher might take the figurative cake.

"My parents were always working when I was a kid, so I spent a lot of time with nannies," he says as he hands the whole cake over to me, which is probably the sexiest thing he's ever done. "This isn't some sob story about how I was neglected. My mom made sure she was home every night to put me to bed and my dad… made sure my tuition was paid. And I don't know… maybe this is selfish because I know people had it worse off than I did. Sad little rich boy whose parents buy him expensive things to keep him happy. I sound like a spoiled prick."

"I mean, money's nice, but there are some things it can't buy."

"All I wanted was for one of them to remember that my favorite color was orange. Isn't that sad? My parents didn't know what my favorite color was. Or that I didn't like bananas. Or that I had nightmares about Ronald McDonald for an entire summer."

My mom remembered everything. Even the things I didn't want her to remember. Like how I broke her favorite candy dish. Or how I brought her bra in for kindergarten show-and-tell. Even that snide comment I made under my breath in the car at 12:38 p.m. on the third Tuesday in June of 2009. My side of the pizza always had pepperoni. My eggs were always scrambled. No sandwich ever had crusts. To this day, I still don't know how she managed to do it all by herself.

I don't think I ever thanked her.

"I started coming up with these really outlandish requests just to see if they paid attention. A train set with green and purple train cars. A snowboard with yellow and orange stripes. A cake with peanut butter, *strawberry* jam, and marshmallow frosting. A tropical fish tank with eleven blue fish—"

"A double-toasted cinnamon raisin bagel with extra cream cheese? A venti half-caf quad-shot half whole milk half almond latte with three sugars and five dashes of cinnamon?"

"And it's still never right."

I don't realize my legs are in his lap or that my fingers are twirling a strand of his hair until he turns to me and smiles.

"He didn't even wish me a happy birthday today," Asher says. "I rode the fucking elevator up to the office with him and do you know what he said to me? *Your broth-er's not coming in today. I need you on a conference call in ten minutes.*"

"Ash—"

"I don't think he's ever told me he loves me," he says. "And you know what? It's fine. I don't love him either. He's a bastard."

When I decided to come here tonight, I anticipated us arguing over the cake. I figured he would appreciate the thought I put into his gift. I thought we'd argue over what we'd watch on TV and *maybe* we'd make out a little. Or a lot. With some friendly over-the-clothes touching. And maybe a little under-the-clothes touching too.

Instead, he puts his heart on a silver platter. The most honest he's ever been with me. Maybe even himself. I want to hug him. Mostly, I want to find River McGowan and tell him what an awful father I think he is.

"I really know how to bring down the mood," Asher laughs and steals the bite of cake that's been sitting on the fork before he takes my empty glass off the table. "I'll get you more wine."

"You know how I get when I'm drunk."

"Sloppy and horny?"

"You're a lucky man."

He walks over to the kitchen. I'm half tempted to change the channel, but I resist. Instead, I stand up and walk over to the window.

"Ash? Do you have any of that expensive chocolate you keep in your desk?"

"How do you know I keep expensive chocolate in my desk?"

"Urban legend."

Outside, the snow is falling in thick, fat flakes, masking the sidewalks in a crisp layer of white. The lamps glow against the frosted windows of empty stores, illuminating the abandoned street. The traffic lights change from green to yellow to red in an endless loop. There are no cars or people or signs of life. Moments like these are rare. I stop and drink it in.

"It's so quiet." I can feel Asher behind me, his chest flush with my back. I relax against him.

"I think that's my favorite part about the snow," he says, handing me my wine.

"That the city just stops?"

"You can think for a minute."

"All I can think about is how fun it's gonna be to get home," I laugh into the glass. "I might have to shovel my way down to the subway—if it's even running."

God.

I'm going to have to walk home in a foot of snow.

"Stay." He says it quietly and without hesitation. "The roads look terrible."

"Are you concerned about my safety?" When I turn around, he pops a piece of the expensive chocolate into my mouth.

"Of course not," he says. "I'm not about to let you disturb the peace."

"You'd much rather I wreak havoc in your apartment?" I take a step closer despite already being pressed against him. "What sort of trouble can I get into here?"

He shoves another piece of chocolate into my mouth. "Sit on the couch and be quiet."

"I only like to be bossed around in the bedroom."

"*Olivia.*"

I grin up at him and saunter over to the couch, where I place my wine on the coffee table before falling back dramatically against the cushions. "Fine, bring me more pillows and blankets. I'll be a good girl and go to sleep."

"This is where you're going to sleep?"

"Where else would I sleep?"

He shrugs, which only makes me grin.

"I didn't realize the invitation extended to your bedroom."

He looks everywhere but at me. "You could sleep on my terrace for all I care."

"Sounds like you really want me in your bed."

"I don't."

"Well, if you insist."

I finish off my glass of wine, turn off the TV, and make my way towards the stairs that lead into Asher's loft.

The small upstairs is just an extension of the downstairs. Modern and industrial and simple. A black bed frame sits against an exposed brick wall that's lined with a floating shelf that houses two lamps and two potted bonsai trees. Beneath a thick, white duvet, I see a familiar pattern on his sheets. But it's not the snowmen that take me by surprise—it's what's in the corner.

"You have a bathtub in your bedroom," I say, "A bathtub that's filled with shoes."

"I told my realtor that a tub in the bedroom was impractical," he says as he walks over to his dresser, pulling open the top drawer. "She insisted it sets a mood."

"I imagine coming home to me up to my neck in bubbles would set a mood."

I watch his hand tense around a t-shirt. "I think it's much more suited for storage."

He says that now, but when he does come home and finds me up to my neck in bubbles, he'll definitely have a change of heart.

"Here." He hands me a long-sleeved shirt that's cerulean blue and orange.

"You're a Mets fan?"

"Kills my father a little every day."

"We should get married at Citi Field," I tell him. "Really put the nail in the coffin."

He rolls his eyes at me and pushes me towards the bathroom door.

"You didn't give me pants," I tell him.

"I believe you told me you don't trust people who wear pants to bed."

"I know, but it's still polite to offer. You might give a girl the wrong idea."

"Would you like pants, Olivia?"

"Of course not," I say. "Who wears pants to bed?"

It doesn't take me long to change, but I take a few extra seconds to snoop. Asher has a weird amount of floss and quite the selection of condoms. If my calculations are correct, he should be much happier if he's having this much sex. I want to bring a handful back into the room with me, but I fear he might have an actual aneurysm.

He's already in bed when I open the door, laying back against his pillows with his eyes focused on his phone, which is very rude when there's a girl in his bedroom only wearing his shirt and a *really* cute pair of underwear. I sigh loudly and when I know I have his attention, I pull an elastic from my wrist and reach up to fasten my hair into a bun, the shirt rising just enough for him to catch a glimpse of my *Grinchy* panties.

"It's rude to stare, Asher."

"Then maybe you shouldn't try to put on a show in my bedroom."

"Trust me, if I was putting on a show, you would know," I say as I pull down the blanket. "And you would be begging me for more."

Asher lifts a brow. "I don't beg, Olivia."

"Perhaps you haven't had the right reason to." I'm crawling over the blankets and sheets to get closer to him. "I'm feeling *very* generous. How would you like to spend the last few hours of your birthday?"

Our lips are practically touching and I want to kiss him more than I've ever wanted to do anything in my life. I know it's killing him. I can see it in his eyes. It's killing him not to touch me. He's white-knuckling his snowman sheets, his sad attempt at resisting the urge to put his hands all over me. I'm not sure why he's so intent on making the both of us miserable.

"Go to sleep, Olivia."

I let out this annoyed gurgling sound that I didn't know I was capable of making as I flop back against my pillow.

"You're such a buzzkill."

"So I've been told."

"We're both adults."

"I'm aware."

"And we're both attracted to each other."

His silence is deafening.

I have visions of wrapping my hands around his neck.

Not in a kinky way.

"Don't give me that look," he says. "You know I'm attracted to you."

"So we're two adults who are attracted to each other and yet…"

"And yet…"

Asher kills the lights and the room drowns in darkness. I'm too exhausted to puzzle all of his mixed signals back together. I'll save it for the subway ride to work tomorrow and I'll probably still be trying to sort it out on the ride back home. Men suck. We should send them to another planet.

"Olivia?"

"You had your chance, buddy. Give yourself a birthday present."

"Goodnight."

I don't say it back.

Mostly because I'm in shock when his arm snakes around my waist and he pulls me against him.

He does a fantastic job of confusing me.

10

I HAVE twelve alarm clocks that go off three minutes apart starting from 4:55 a.m. and lasting all the way to 5:31 a.m. Asher loses it after the fourth, which is how I find myself pinned underneath him as he rips my phone off the nightstand, powering it off in a bleary-eyed rage. I'm half awake, but still manage to moan sleepily as his body presses mine into the mattress. Good morning to me.

"You have *this* many alarms that go off *this* early and you're *still* late for work?"

He flops back over to his side and I'm annoyed that he takes all the warmth with him. He can't just bury me in his body heat and then roll away, leaving me shivering and cold. It's rude.

"A lot of time and effort goes into making me look hot." I shuffle through the sheets to get close to him, slipping my hand over his stomach and entwining my legs with his. I use his chest as a pillow.

"C'mon, no cuddling."

"Says the man who hasn't stopped touching me since we got into bed."

"You're so clingy," he says. "When's the last time you shaved your legs?"

"When's the last time you shaved yours?" I giggle and brush my calf against his. "Stop pretending you don't love this."

"I don't."

The circles he's tracing over my back say otherwise.

"You know… I don't understand the point of being in a fake relationship if I'm not getting any benefits."

"And what sort of benefits are you looking for, Ms. Langley? Medical? Dental? 401k? Pension?"

"Cuddling, for one. And it wouldn't kill you to tell me I'm pretty. And maybe kiss me once in a while. And, y'know, other stuff."

"What kind of other stuff?"

"You're a smart man. I shouldn't have to tell you," I say. "But sadly, this little tryst must end. I have to trudge through two feet of snow to get a double-toasted cinnamon raisin bagel with extra cream cheese for my tyrant of a boss."

"He sounds awful."

"He's terrible," I say. "Devilishly handsome but terrible."

Asher's fingers toy with the waistband of my underwear, drawing out a pleasant hum from me. He has exceptionally bad timing if he wants an early morning romp.

Thankfully my boss will be *very* understanding when I show up an hour late looking completely ravished.

"They're not opening the office," he finally says. "We're working from home today."

That might be the hottest thing he's ever said to me.

"Does that mean I can go back to sleep?"

"Yes."

"Does it also mean you'll make me pancakes?"

"Only if you do the dishes."

I curl into him. "I don't make deals with the devil."

"And I don't make pancakes for girls with sandpaper legs."

"Mm, yes, you do." I grin. "Because this girl with sandpaper legs is allowing you to keep your hand on her butt."

"Go back to sleep, Olivia."

"So bossy."

"I believe you told me you like to be bossed around in the bedroom."

"Only under naked circumstances."

"You have a lot of stipulations."

"It's part of my charm."

"You're charming alright." He not-so-subtly squeezes my ass. "Go back to sleep, O."

I don't typically give a man what he wants so easily, but I'm sleepy and warm. I drift back to sleep to the sound of Asher's breathing and a car backfiring.

* * *

To: *Loveridge & McGowan Employee Network*
Cc: *Ana Loveridge-Herrera, River McGowan*
From: *Olivia Langley*
Subject: *Light That Menorah & Ugly Sweater Day!*

Gone away is the work day!
Here to stay are the PJs!
Ana and River called a snow day!
So we get to play!
There will be no walking in this winter wonderland!

I know what you're thinking! *Olivia, we really wanted to hear you sing your new hit Christmas single that's destined to top all the charts and become a holiday classic!* And I'm here to tell you that there's an audio attachment for your listening pleasure. I know, I know. I'm far too kind. Please shower me with compliments and Sephora gift cards.

And while I'm sure you were all ecstatic when you found out about this very snowy snow day, I know you were devastated when you realized it fell on the first day of Hanukkah and Ugly Sweater Day! But have no fear! Olivia is also here to tell you that we'll be celebrating tomorrow! Wear your ugliest sweater to work and stay for our Menorah lighting extravaganza! Prizes will be awarded to the most hideous! (Sweaters not Menorahs).

Yours truly,
O. Langley
Social Media Intern & Santa's Executive Helper
Loveridge & McGowan International
98 W 52nd St, New York, NY 10019
olivialangley@lmi.com

P. S.: Asher, I do not sound like a rabid koala bear.

I wake up to a plow scraping the pavement. The quiet of a New York snowstorm is replaced by a noisy clean-up. I can hear Asher's neighbors cursing as they chisel ice off their cars. Not everyone has the luxury of a snow day.

The realization that I'm alone spawns an annoying sense of disappointment. Doesn't Asher know I have a long list of plans that don't include getting out of bed? He has no idea how much fun he ruined. I consider making a point by reciting the *very* long list *very* loudly until he storms up here in a fit of broody rage and does number five to me for *hours*, but I smell coffee and hear pans clank, so I get out of bed because I need to be caffeinated and fed if I want to get through that list.

I don't scream in sheer agony when my feet hit the floor like I do in my apartment when I'm greeted with cold wooden planks. Asher has heated flooring, a ridiculous luxury that I didn't realize I needed. He's making it very hard for me to ever leave.

He's in the kitchen, hunched over his back counter, cursing at an espresso machine that's not listening. Let's just say ogling Asher in his boxer briefs doesn't make for a bad morning.

"It's rude to stare." He glares at me over his shoulder.

"Sorry," I say and slide up onto the stool in front of his computer. "I was just admiring all the hard work you do. The pilates is really paying off."

"I don't do pilates," he says a little too quickly.

"Okay." I don't try to conceal my smile, which only makes the wrinkles on his forehead grow. I type in his password. "You should probably use something stronger than your home address. Anyone could guess this."

"Anyone? Really?"

"Yes, you wouldn't want this to get into the wrong hands."

He sets a cup of coffee in front of me and leans forward. His eyes are smoldering. Why won't he kiss me?

"Who knows what someone could do with access to all of your personal accounts."

"Perhaps they'd buy me an essential oil diffuser?"

"Jasmine is supposed to be very relaxing," I tell him. "And ylang-ylang is a known aphrodisiac."

"I'll keep a note of that."

"I'm sure you will."

Asher holds my stare a second longer. I'm ready to grab his neck and kiss the hell out of him. He doesn't give me the chance.

"Get to work, Olivia."

I focus on his computer screen and the background—a stock picture of Yosemite at sunrise. Everything is crisp and clean and perfectly organized. Everything has a place, except for the file in the upper right hand corner of his desktop.

LB Testimonials.

Huh.

Curiosity, as it seems, also kills the Olivia.

"What exactly am I dealing with today?" I ask.

"A pregnant mistress and a Housewife meltdown."

"Scandalous," I say. "Are we denying the pregnant mistress?"

Asher looks back at me as he dumps pancake mix into a bowl. "Of course we're denying the pregnant mistress."

"And the Minnie Talcott situation?"

He scratches the back of his neck and sighs. While he's hard on most of his clients, I've found that Asher has a soft spot for Minnie Talcott, a model turned designer turned reality show star, who has seven Pomeranians and notoriously only washes her hair with water flown in from Switzerland.

"Minnie is deeply saddened by the events that took place at Monday's Fashion Institute award ceremony. She struggles daily with anxiety but is seeking treatment and counseling. She hopes that this will shine a light on mental health awareness."

I'm typing what he says verbatim because it's better than anything I could have put together. This is why they pay him the big bucks.

"She's my godmother."

"Minerva Talcott?"

"Yeah, she's my mom's best friend."

"You come from such a strange world."

"It definitely makes for interesting holidays. And by interesting I mean totally ridiculous and I usually sneak away from whatever black tie affair we're at to watch Disney movies with Chloe."

"Cool Uncle Asher knows all the words to *Love Is an Open Door,* doesn't he?"

"Bet your ass he does."

I'm smiling and he's smiling and we're smiling in his kitchen. It's easy and normal. Of all the ways I thought today would go, this is not any of them. But I'm happy and Asher looks happy too, so I channel all of this positive energy into denying that Ryker Hammond, a married race car driver, got his twenty-year-old mistress pregnant.

The griddle sizzles as pancake batter splatters against it. Asher is humming. Today, I find it oddly endearing. He seems so relaxed, a rare sight for the perpetually uptight man. I want to slide up behind him and wrap my arms around his waist. Maybe nuzzle my face into his well-sculpted back. Kiss his shoulder blade. Make him laugh.

I don't.

Mostly because my phone rings and ruins the moment.

It's Bree.

"Hello?"

"Why are you answering Asher's phone?"

I pull it away from my ear and realize it's not my phone. Mine is still upstairs. *Fuck.*

"Can you believe he made me come all the way here in a foot and a half of snow to write press releases?"

Asher looks insulted when he looks back at me with his eyebrows pinched. I smile and shrug.

"Seriously?" Bree asks.

"Yes," I huff dramatically for emphasis. "He's such an asshole."

I smile sheepishly at him when he sets a plate of pancakes in front of me. He's still glaring.

"I feel like it's illegal for someone to force you into work when the office is closed. He can get into a lot of trouble."

"It's not that big of a deal," I say. "He got me a car."

"I don't understand why he needed you there."

"He didn't trust my WiFi."

"I'm sure," she says, unconvinced. "Are you sure you're not on a snow day booty call?"

"Seriously, Bree? We have a professional relationship."

"Please define professional for me."

"I don't need to justify anything," I say. "I assume you're calling for a reason."

"Tell Asher I can't get in contact with Melodie Tran's manager, and *Celebrity!Now!* is demanding the statement by noon."

"Okay, he'll deal with it." I hang up the phone and resist the very strong urge to throw it across the kitchen. I don't know what her problem is.

"This asshole is taking these back." Asher picks up my plate and carries it over to the table.

"Hey!"

"If you're going to slander me over the phone, you don't deserve my pancakes."

I don't like that logic even if it seems perfectly fair.

"Asher," I follow him across the kitchen. I'm a puppy begging for scraps. "Don't be mean."

"Says the girl who just called me an asshole."

"I was trying to sound convincing."

"Did it work?"

"Of course not."

I'm all pouty lips and fluttering eyelashes. He won't be

able to resist me. Looking adorable as hell. Standing in his kitchen. In only his t-shirt and my underwear.

"You're a menace."

He puts my plate down on the table opposite of his. I grin and bounce up onto the tips of my toes to kiss his cheek.

Asher uses real maple syrup and not the chemically enhanced kind I buy at the grocery store. It's organic and purely Canadian. I wouldn't expect anything less from the man who once made me walk seven blocks back to a Greek restaurant because they put feta on his salad.

"What did Bree want?"

"Other than to accuse me of having a less-than-professional relationship with you?"

"Well, you are sitting in my kitchen in only your underwear and my t-shirt. That's not exactly business casual."

"Whose side are you on?"

"There aren't any sides. I'm merely stating that our relationship isn't exactly as professional as it should be. You've slept in my bed. You've kissed me. You've made countless sexual advances."

I glare at him. "My sincerest apologies, Mr. McGowan. It will never happen again. Will you excuse me while I put on pants?"

"No, I will not, Ms. Langley," he says. "Eat your pancakes."

"But this is very unprofessional," I say. "My boss should not be making me pancakes in questionably sized boxer briefs."

"As my employee, you should not be questioning my authority."

"Oh, I'll question your authority."

We both choke out a laugh and we're red-faced and out of breath. Laughing with Asher over pancakes on a snow day from work. I didn't realize this was on my Christmas list.

"What did Bree really want?"

"She can't get in contact with Melodie Tran's manager and *Celebrity!Now!* wants the statement on her engagement by noon."

"Of course they do."

"Tabloids don't stop for snow." I pull the fork from my mouth and smile.

We finish breakfast in silence. I'm okay with it. Sometimes saying nothing says enough. It's comfortable. Normal. Like we do this every day.

"Alright," Asher finally says. "You start writing the release. I'll do the dishes."

"No."

He frowns. "Excuse me?"

"I'll do the dishes," I say. "You write the release."

"Who's the boss here, Ms. Langley?"

I lean over the table to grab his plate. "*Me.*"

In a perfect world he'd grab me by the collar and pull me in for a kiss. We'd forget about work and the dishes and we'd go back to bed. Definitely not to sleep.

But this isn't a perfect world and he doesn't kiss me. I walk over to the sink and turn on the tap. We work to the beat of Asher's fingers against the keyboard. I rinse the plates and place them in the dishwasher. I catch Asher's eyes when I bend down.

"It's rude to stare, Mr. McGowan."

"I'm just making sure you're loading that the right way, Ms. Langley."

"I can assure you I'm more than capable of loading a dishwasher."

"Says the woman who's not capable of ordering my coffee right."

"You know," I start and put my hands on my hips, "You're gonna miss me when I'm gone."

"And where exactly are you going?"

"My internship is up in January," I say. "You'll have to find someone else to boss around. I'll be sure to leave detailed notes. Credit card number not included."

Asher licks his bottom lip and moves his eyes back to the computer screen. "You're not going anywhere, Olivia."

"That sounds vaguely threatening," I say. "Are you going to chain me to your desk?"

"Fortunately for you, I'm not into keeping captives."

"Fortunately for you, I am."

My attempt at sounding extra sexy leaves Asher in a fit of hysterics.

"Don't laugh at me."

"But you make it so easy."

"See if you have a bagel on your desk tomorrow."

"Empty threats, Ms. Langley."

I don't dignify him with a response, and I finish loading the dishwasher. My sights are set on the couch and that heated blanket. I'm going to take full advantage of this snow day. We're going to watch *so* many Christmas movies. Asher is going to lose his mind.

"What should we watch first?" I swan dive onto the couch, and burrow myself into the pillows and blankets. I'm never leaving this spot. *Ever.* Asher just got himself a very hot roommate. We're everyone's favorite trope. "*Elf? Home Alone?* My personal favorite: *To Grandmother's House We Go?* Or we can go in the more *romantic* direction. *Love Actually? The Holiday?* Jude Law is so hot."

He rips the remote out of my hand. "I'm offended you didn't suggest *The Santa Clause.*"

"I'm offended you haven't offered to make me hot chocolate."

"You're more than capable of walking into the kitchen to make it yourself, Ms. Langley."

"I think you just want to stare at my ass again, Mr. McGowan."

The dimples in his cheeks suggest I'm not wrong.

"Don't give me that look," I tell him.

"What look am I giving you?"

"Your cocky douchebag eyes."

"Is that what gets you going?" he laughs.

"You have no idea."

"And what exactly are these cocky douchebag eyes saying, Olivia?"

"Really dirty things," I say and he looks down at me with a sly smile and for a moment, I think he's going to crawl on top of me and show me what his cocky douchebag lips can do.

I'll never be able to watch *The Santa Clause* without getting turned on again.

But there's a knock on the door that's so fierce that it causes Asher to jump back.

"*Uncle Asher! Let me in! It's a snow day!*"

The doorknob jiggles as Chloe grows frustrated.

"Shit," Asher curses. "Hold on, Chlo."

He's already upstairs and putting on pants before I can dive further under the blankets. Spending the day with Asher's very cute niece was not in my plans.

"*Uncle! Asher!*"

"Chloe, we've talked about patience."

I lift an eyebrow at him as he runs down the stairs and shoves his arms through the sleeves of a shirt. They've talked about patience? What was that conversation like? Asher has none.

"*Why's the door locked? I can't get in. I can always get in.*"

Asher ignores her question and throws a pair of sweat-pants at me.

"This is very unfortunate," I say as I put them on.

He watches as I jump and wiggle my way into them. He swallows.

"Yes, I'm aware."

I'm back under the covers when Asher walks over to the door, ruffling his messy hair with each step. When he finally opens the door, Chloe barges through with Morgan following closely behind.

"You get to watch me while Mommy tells someone off in court," Chloe announces before she sees me. "Why is Olivia here? Why is she in your clothes?"

A blush that matches Asher's warms my cheeks.

"Why *is* Olivia in your clothes, Ash?" Morgan asks.

"Did you have a sleepover?" Chloe asks as she jumps on the couch next to me. "Was it fun? Did you watch movies? Eat candy? Yesterday was Uncle Asher's birthday. Did you know that? Did you get him a present? What was it? Do you guys kiss?"

"*Chloe*," Morgan says.

"Sorry."

Morgan turns to Asher. "Do you mind? It's just for a couple hours. But if you're *busy,* I can—"

"It's fine."

She kisses his cheek. "Thank you *so* much. Bye, Chloe! Mommy loves you!"

When she leaves, Chloe smiles at both of us.

"Uncle Asher?"

"Yes?"

"Can we build a snowman?"

* * *

Asher drips melted snow onto the table we sit down at. We're crammed into a corner of *À La Boulangerie* with everyone else who lives in a two block radius of Green Street. It's not the only place open, but it is the best place that's open. They serve their hot chocolates with an extra shot of melted bittersweet chocolate on the side, which I strongly believe is the only way to serve hot chocolate.

"Uncle Asher, you're making a mess." Chloe is in a chair by the window. Outside, the snow is slushy and gray, a mirror image of Asher, who has not smiled since I lobbed a snowball at his head.

"That's what happens when you're attacked with frozen matter."

"You mean snow?" she asks.

"Yes."

"Then why didn't you say that?"

"Because Uncle Asher has to be difficult." I grin madly at him when he glares at me.

"Uncle Asher isn't buying anyone hot chocolate if they continue to attack him."

"Don't be a weenie."

I laugh. I know I shouldn't, but I do. Chloe looks so pleased with herself. Asher wavers from being totally offended to biting back his own laughter.

"You become more like your mothers everyday."

"Thank you," she says.

Their dynamic is something out of this world. If I could freeze this moment and replay it forever, I would. Even when Chloe gets under his skin, Asher looks at her like she's the only thing he's ever loved.

"Hot chocolates all around?"

"And pistachio macarons!" Chloe says.

"Hot chocolates and pistachio macarons," Asher says

as he looks at me. For a fake boyfriend, he knows the way to my very real heart.

"And a chocolate croissant?"

"And a chocolate croissant."

My eyes linger on Asher as he zigs and zags through the crowd of people and the occasional stray chair. He mouths quiet apologies and runs his fingers through his soaking wet hair. His teeth chatter lightly, his skin red from the wind and snow. I want to warm him up in very dirty ways.

"Olivia, you're drooling."

"I was thinking about that chocolate croissant."

"You're looking at Uncle Asher the way Mommy looks at Jennifer Lopez."

Damn. Even a six-year-old can see through me.

"Are you in love?"

My eyes nearly fall out of my head.

"No, I'm not in love."

At least I don't think so. I feel something. Definitely stronger than like. Lust? No. That makes it seem like what I feel is only physical when it's not.

"Well, you should be," Chloe says. "Uncle Asher makes the best ice cream sundaes. You're missing out."

"Well, when you bring ice cream sundaes into the equation…"

"He can be very grumpy, but Mommy told me a secret to make him laugh and it works every time."

I lean in closer. "I'm a very good secret keeper."

Chloe leans in. "Tickle his neck."

That… is *very* useful information.

"I was thinking," Chloe starts.

"You? Thinking?"

Asher sets a tray down on the table. Three porcelain mugs are toppling over with mounds of whipped cream that are dusted with peppermint crumbs, a chocolate filled pirouette cookie speared through the side. Along with my chocolate croissant and Chloe's pistachio macarons, Asher also ordered a raspberry tart.

"I'm always thinking!" Chloe says. "Mama says my brain's gonna explode if I keep thinking too much!"

"And what has you thinking so much today?"

"Can Olivia come to my Christmas recital?"

It's the wrong moment to take a sip of my piping hot drink. I almost spit it all over her.

"Olivia is very busy, Chlo," he says.

"You're very busy and you're coming."

Asher glances across the table at me, his lips parted as if he's ready to speak. He doesn't.

"I'll try my hardest to get there," I tell her. "I'll have to sweet talk my boss into giving me the morning off."

"Isn't Uncle Asher your boss?" Chloe giggles.

I nod. "He's a very hard man to persuade."

"I think you can do it," she says. "Especially if you do the *thing*."

The *thing*.

The secret to make him laugh.

"What thing?" Asher asks.

"I'm sworn to secrecy," I tell him.

His eyes shift between the both of us. "You two are trouble."

To prove his point, Chloe reaches over and grabs the pirouette out of his mug of hot chocolate.

We spend the afternoon playing hangman on paper napkins, shivering each time the door opens and sends a frigid breeze through the café. Chloe wins every round, which Asher deems unfair, but when she smiles at him, he turns to mush.

I'm realizing I might have the same effect on him.

Because when I eye the last bite of his raspberry tart and bat my lashes, he's all heavy sighs when he pushes it over.

Outside, New York is back to its usual hustle and bustle, just with more snow and ice. I'm holding Chloe's hand and she's pointing out all the buildings she's going to own when she's the most powerful person in Manhattan. I don't crush her dreams when she tells me she's going to be the king. Maybe she will be. The world is changing. Perhaps New York will secede from the United States and form a monarchy. Perhaps Chloe would be at the helm of it. Given the current state of our government, I can only hope.

We're halfway down the cobbled street that leads to Asher's apartment when I feel the sting of cold, wet snow against my neck. My shriek is in sync with Asher's laugh. I don't get to glare at him. My boot glides over a sheet of ice and I unintentionally give another bid to the USA's ice skating team. My gold medal performance is accompanied by Chloe's silver. A snowbank breaks our fall.

Asher laughs until he realizes Chloe is crying. Her purple leggings are gashed at the knee, blood trickling out of the scrape. He scoops her up, kisses her forehead, and when we get back to his apartment, I embarrass myself by doing the *Bandaid Dance* that my mother did on the daily during my childhood. It's worth it when Chloe laughs.

And it's double worth it when Asher cracks one of his elusive smiles.

* * *

I consider moving into Asher's shower. It has double shower heads and a rain effect with just the right amount of water pressure. I'm a prune by the time I drag myself out.

Asher leaves a shirt and a pair of boxer briefs on his bed for me. I don't realize how small they actually are until I have to squeeze my butt into them. I put on my bra— because I'm not one of the lucky ones that can meander around without one—and then the shirt before going downstairs.

Asher is draped lazily over the couch, one leg twisted into a throw blanket and the other planted on the floor, his head resting in one hand as he flicks through the channels.

Morgan picked Chloe up shortly after we returned to the apartment, which means we are very alone. Perfect conditions for snow day antics.

I decide to be forward. No one gets anywhere by not making a move. And if Asher won't, I will. There's nothing wrong with a woman taking charge of what she wants.

I'm in his lap before I realize, dripping confidence and seduction. He's going to be putty in my hands.

"Can I help you?" He snarls at me when I slide my hands over his chest.

"You look very annoyed for a man with a hot girl on his lap."

"You're blocking my view."

"As if there's a better view than me."

The corners of his lips flicker. For someone who's so bothered by me being on top of him, he doesn't hesitate putting his hands on my hips.

"You have a very nice shower," I tell him.

"I'm aware."

"It's very spacious."

"What are you suggesting, Ms. Langley?"

"Just making an observation."

"I can also make a few observations."

"Care to elaborate?"

Asher's fingers brush against the exposed skin of my back. "You're a menace."

"You're trying very hard to resist me." I shift in his lap, which makes him suck in a sharp breath. "Which is funny because you can't keep your hands off of me."

"Says the girl on top of me."

"I'm very willing to switch positions."

His grip on my hips tightens, suggesting that he's very okay with the position we're in now. So I slip my hands over his shoulders and behind his neck and grin at him with a menacing smile. His eyes turn electric, a shock zipping through me as he holds my stare.

It's now or never, Olivia.

"I'm going to kiss you," I tell him.

"I know you are."

"Are you suggesting I'm predictable, Mr. McGowan?"

"One could assume what your intentions were when you climbed on top of me."

I almost want to crawl off of him and play hard to get, but his hands trail from my hips to my back to my bum and our lips are so close that I can practically taste his. Now is not the time to tease the hell out of him.

My lips barely brush his. It's a soft kiss. Subtle and shy and quick. I press my lips to his jaw, sharp and defined and so tempting, and I trail my way down to his neck, where I blow a soft breath against his nape until I hear a quiet laugh escape his mouth.

"You're not supposed to know about that."

"Mm, but I do."

I kiss my way up his neck and over his jaw and when I reach his lips, it's lightning. Fireworks on the Fourth of July. The first stroke of midnight on New Year's Eve. We're magic.

He tastes sweet. They're raspberry and chocolate kisses, rich and deep and almost sinful. His hands are everywhere. All over me. He doesn't know where he wants to touch first. I smile into him before I roll my hips in calculated motions. He moans into my mouth.

When he toys with the hem of my shirt, I realize there's too many layers between us. I nip his bottom lip before I pull away to allow him to take off my shirt. He throws it somewhere near the coffee table and then puts his hands back on me, trailing tiny bumps over my entire body.

I've never wanted someone as much as I want him.

I don't have to ask if the feeling is mutual. I can feel it. He wants me just as much as I want him.

He runs his thumb over the underwire of my bra, his fingers disappearing around my back. He undoes the clasp with skilled ease. He barely has it off before he's sitting up and forcing my back onto the couch. The shift in weight is delicious.

As much as I love control, I might love Asher in control more. His lips touch my neck and I make a sound I didn't know I could make. He alternates between soft bites and eager kisses, which leaves me arching into him in desperation. I want more of him. I slide my hands under his shirt and then push him away to pull it off.

His body is gorgeous. Lean and lanky but softly sculpted. I want to lick him all over.

But he's still in charge and his lips move from my neck to my chest and he's mapping my body like I'm a destination he's trying to discover. When his tongue swirls over the swell of my breast, I moan so loudly that I almost drown out the sound of my phone.

It's my alarm.

"Fuck," I say and it's not in a fit of pleasure.

It's panic.

It's Tuesday.

I'm going to be late for work.

"Fuck fuck fuck." I wiggle out from underneath Asher, who looks terrified and confused as to why we're not kissing anymore.

"O," he says, sitting back on his heels as I scramble to put on my bra and shirt. "What's wrong?"

"I'm so sorry," I tell him, fastening the clip of my bra. "Please don't be mad."

"I'm not mad, Olivia," he says, watching as I pull on my shirt. "I'm confused."

"You look really frustrated." I try not to laugh. He looks like he's in pain.

"Yeah, well…" he laughs.

"I'm really sorry. I have to go," I say.

Pants.

I need pants.

I grab my leggings that are hanging over a chair, still damp from the snow.

"I promise I'll make it up to you."

His eyes shift and they're electric again. "I might hold you to that, Ms. Langley."

I kiss him again and I don't want to stop. It takes every ounce of willpower I have to drag myself out the door.

When I arrive at the restaurant thirty-seven minutes late, Ivan whispers into my ear that this is my final warning.

11

THERE'S ONLY one remedy for a quiet office:

Mariah Carey and her Grammy Award-winning background singer, Olivia Langley.

I get to the office early—not to prove a point to Asher that I'm not *always* late—but because it was stupid to go to sleep when I didn't get in from the restaurant until after four. Ivan had me scrubbing dishes with the overnight bakers as my penance for being late. I went home, took a shower, changed, and downed two cups of coffee before grabbing bagels and a four-shot latte to get me through the day.

I caught my second wind by the time I got to W 53rd Street and 6th Ave, so when I got to the office, I was raring and ready for an early morning solo dance party while I hung up Hanukkah decorations.

I haven't stopped thinking about Asher. He was the reason I sent the wrong order to the wrong table—the reason I shattered a bottle of white wine, why I had to apologize to a woman for spilling salad dressing on her lap.

He is most definitely the reason why I'm living in a permanent hot flash.

I can still feel his lips.

God.

Get a grip, Olivia.

You can't have an orgasm in front of a menorah.

Focus.

I channel all my energy into dancing the taste of Asher's lips off of me while I hang garland made of the Star of David and dreidel. The security guard downstairs must be loving the show. I bet he'll suggest I audition for that new reality show *America's Best Dancer.* I should call Francesca. Maybe the Rockettes are looking for a five-foot-one blonde with jiggly thighs and great boobs.

"Are you having a manic episode?"

Asher's voice hits me like a bus. He's leaning against his doorframe with his arms crossed. He's wearing a black crewneck sweater and fitted gray jeans with artfully messy hair and sleepy eyes. I want to jump him.

"What are you doing here?" I ask.

He furrows his brow. "I… work here?"

"It's early."

"Which is why I'm surprised to find you doing a terrible Mariah Carey impersonation down the halls. I figured I had at least another hour before you strolled in thirteen minutes late."

All I can think about is him on his couch with his mouth all over me. I feel lightheaded.

"I couldn't sleep," I say. It's not a total lie. I didn't have time to sleep.

"Yeah, me neither."

Asher up all night. Losing his mind at the thought of me on top of him. Kissing him. Grinding into him.

Olivia.

"Your bagel's on my desk," I tell him. "I didn't get your coffee yet. I was waiting till it was closer to the time that you come in."

"And how would you know what time I come in when I'm always here before you?"

A smile flickers over my lips. Asher's trying to conceal his dimples, but he's failing miserably. We can never go back to whatever we were before. His mouth was on my boobs.

I finish hanging the Hanukkah garland with Asher's help. I don't ask for it, but he's there holding the end of the string as if he suddenly became some holiday-decorating guru. This is the man who wouldn't have had a Christmas tree if I didn't fraudulently purchase him one.

"You're quite the little helper," I say.

"Not quite Santa's Executive Helper."

"But close."

We're standing so close that I can smell the lime basil of his body wash—the same scent that lingered on me all night, a quiet reminder of where I'd been and who I'd been with. It was torture.

Like it is right now.

I need to touch him.

"We're standing underneath the mistletoe," Asher whispers.

I glance up. "How trite."

He steps closer and I feel his hand slip around my back as his fingers tangle into my hair, his thumb brushing my bottom lip as his head tilts and his mouth forms a smile. I don't remember how to breathe.

"I'm going to kiss you," he says.

"I know you are."

It starts out soft. He traces our mouths together with careful certainty. It's slow. He's teasing me. He knows I'm always in a rush. He's taking his time, like we're not on the clock. Making out with my boss was not on the list of responsibilities when I applied for this internship. It's a welcomed surprise.

He loses his patience shortly after he licks his tongue into my mouth. It's a whirlwind of missed steps and staggering feet as we bump into walls and desks until we stumble into his office, where he kicks the door shut before lifting me onto his desk.

It's frenzied.

My hands are in his hair and his lips are on my neck. The fact that I'm sitting on a stapler doesn't faze me.

"You look hideous in this sweater," he says into my mouth.

My brain translates that into, "you would look better without it on."

"I haven't stopped thinking about you since you ran out of my apartment."

"Sorry." It comes out as a moan when he nips my bottom lip.

"Come over tonight."

I'm stunned and not because he found the spot on my neck that makes my toes tingle.

"I have a date," I tease.

"With who?" He doesn't sound vaguely jealous.

"Betsy," I say. "I've been neglecting her."

He groans. "She can come too."

"I don't think you're ready to be formally introduced."

He traps me in a deep, slow, head-spinning kiss. I'm dizzy and breathless. When his hands sneak under my sweater, I'm electric.

"How appropriate is this?" I ask him, my legs wrapped tightly around his waist.

"About as appropriate as you prancing around my

apartment in my t-shirt and your underwear," he laughs. "Speaking of which… you ran out so fast you left them there."

"Keep them," I say. "I'm sure they'll look good on you."

He smiles into me and I might explode. I want to start every morning this way. Heavy make out sesh and bagels. Who needs fairytales when Asher's lips and funfetti cream cheese exist?

"Asher—"

We hear the knock, but the door opens before we can pull ourselves off of each other. Bree looks like she won the lottery.

"Most people lock the door," she says and looks at Asher, whose hands are still tucked into my shirt. "Melanie Tran's manager needs to change the conference call to ten."

She leaves as quickly as she came, leaving nothing but a rush of panic in her wake. This was the moment she's been waiting for. A slip up. A lie I can no longer deny.

"Shit."

I push Asher away from me despite the fact that nothing feels better than his hands all over me. I spend the entire sprint to Bree's desk adjusting my sweater and wrestling my boobs back into my bra.

The security guard must really love that.

When I get to her desk, Bree is opening a sleeve of crackers and sipping ginger ale. She looks calm and cool and collected, like a serial killer or a sociopath. She's going to murder me with a letter opener in a fit of vengeful rage.

"Bree—"

"It's not what it looked like?" she laughs. "I tripped and Asher's lips broke my fall?"

"It's not that serious?," I say, despite knowing that we

might be a *little* serious. "Honestly, we're just having fun. What's a little mouth on boob action? I mean, I've gone further with guys I barely know!"

She doesn't look convinced.

I sigh. "It's complicated."

"No, it's not," she says, opening her laptop. "You're sleeping with your boss, just like half of the other people in this city. You're not special, Liv."

"I didn't say I was."

"I just hope you're not looking for your happily ever after," she says. "Because you're not going to get one. This is what they do. You're not his first intern. You're not going to be his last."

"It's not—"

"Like that? He's different? He's not. He's going to fuck you and he's going to make you promises and then he's going to move on to the next girl. It's a cycle, Olivia."

"One you seem to be very familiar with," I say. "You do spend an awful lot of time in River's office."

She doesn't say anything.

Neither do I.

I walk back to Asher's office, but he's gone.

* * *

Billie glances over the rims of her wine-colored glasses before she pulls them off and turns to me, an act she's been repeating for the entire hour and a half we've been at *the Met*. If memory serves me right, she wants me to take another picture.

"Olivia," she starts, "what's your opinion on roses?"

"In general?"

"As centerpieces."

This feels like a trick. She just spent twenty minutes on

the phone with a florist who was supposed to be bringing samples over to the office tomorrow. She wants me to tell her roses are a good idea. Reassurance. I didn't realize someone as experienced as she is needed it from me. An intern. Who didn't realize she was wearing two different boots until she was walking over here.

Lying gets me nowhere.

"I think they're predictable," I say. "When we have this type of venue, I think a more minimalist approach is better."

Billie laughs. "I didn't expect the word *minimalist* to come out of the mouth of the woman responsible for the three different types of string lights hanging around the office."

"Trust me, it leaves a sour taste," I say.

Billie smiles as she slides her glasses back on. "I agree about the roses."

"How do you feel about fake snow?"

"Let's not go overboard, Olivia."

She dials the florist's number while I snap picture after picture. Different shots. Different angles. If this whole publicity thing doesn't work out, I can always try my hand at photography.

"You two look like you're up to no good."

I turn around when I hear Ana's voice. She's dressed for a spring day. The two feet of snow outside are no match for her hot flashes. Willa, however, is bundled so tightly that I have to wonder if she can breathe.

"Always." Billie grins. "Olivia and I make a great team."

"I'm slightly terrified," Ana says, pushing and pulling the stroller that Lily, her seven-month-old, is in. "But mostly intrigued."

"As you should be," I say.

"Can I treat you two event planners to lunch?" Ana asks.

"I have a date with Saks," Billie says.

"That's my kind of date," Ana laughs, shifting her eyes to me. "Olivia?"

"I should really be getting back to the office," I say. "I probably have a million emails."

"If Asher can take the rest of the day off, so can you."

His name makes my heart beat out of rhythm. I haven't seen him since this morning, and the way we left things was not ideal. I plan to stop by his apartment tonight. If not to finish what we started, then to at least have a conversation about where we go from here, especially when Bree has been unusually quiet.

For lunch, Ana brings us to a tavern by Central Park that makes soft pretzels with a five cheese dipping sauce, which just happen to be two of my favorite food groups. I also order a salad because, well, I need to balance things out.

"Willa, when do you go back to London?" I ask.

"Not until the end of January," she says. "I'm leaving the day after Christmas to meet Ollie and Daphne in Seoul for our friend Tosh's movie premier, and then we're all flying to Thailand for New Year's."

"You must be so excited."

"I am."

"Well, I'm not." Ana frowns and bites off a piece of pretzel. "It's bad enough you go to school in London. You're not even here on your breaks."

Willa smiles. "You're just mad your live-in babysitter won't be at your disposal."

"That's not true," Ana says. "I like you for your snarky attitude and those granola balls you make."

I lose my appetite the same way I do whenever I catch

a rerun of *Gilmore Girls*. I don't begrudge Willa and Ana for their relationship, but I can't ignore the pang I feel in my chest when I see Ana brush a strand of hair away from Willa's face. It's pure adoration. The kind of love only a mother can give.

I shove another pretzel in my mouth to stop myself from crying.

* * *

Asher ignores all my text messages. I convince myself he's catching up on sleep, so to kill some time I stop by a boutique near his apartment to pick up a gift for my Secret Santa. I find a cute hat and mitten set for Eleanor to go along with a necklace I found at a little shop in Brooklyn.

Another text to Asher goes unanswered, but that doesn't stop me from walking into his building. Obviously, Bree catching us in the act freaked him out. It freaked me out too, but it's not like we've been hiding it. We went to a very exclusive event together where plenty of people saw us kiss. Compared to them, Bree is relatively low on the totem pole. I have more to lose than he does.

I knock on his door not once, not twice, but twenty-seven times. The doorman told me he was home. He's a light sleeper. There's no way he can't hear me.

"Ash," I call. "Asher, open the door."

Nothing.

"It's Liv," I say. "C'mon, Ash, open the door."

Still nothing.

I knock again and again and again until—

"What?"

For someone who was catching up on sleep, he sure looks exhausted. His clothes are wrinkled, his hair is a mess, and the cold glare suggests he's grumpier than usual.

"Hi?" I smile and hope it softens his mood. I'd offer sexual favors, but now might not be the time.

"What are you doing here?" he asks.

"I believe you invited me over," I say. "I brought Betsy."

I say it to make him laugh, but he doesn't.

"Okay, do you want to talk about what happened this morning?"

"Not really," he says and moves to shut the door.

I put myself between it. "Well, I do."

Much to his dismay, I force myself into the apartment. Even before all the kissing and boob touching, he never looked *this* unhappy to see me. Is this the same man who was taking off my clothes last night?

"You're upset." I lean against his counter while he walks over to his toaster and pulls out a bagel that seems to be triple-toasted.

"Of course I'm upset," he says. "You're in my apartment and I don't want you to be."

"About ten hours ago you invited me over to have sex."

His body stiffens. "People can change their minds, Olivia."

"I know," I swallow. "But we had a really good couple of days and I don't understand why you're pushing me away. Is this because of Bree? Because it's really not a big deal. If anything, it's a good thing."

"It's a good thing?"

"Yeah, I mean, less pretending, right?"

"Less pretending," he says slowly, running his fingers through his hair.

"Most of the office already suspects, which is a testament to how convincing we've been."

"Convincing," he laughs and scratches the back of his neck as he walks around me and turns towards the door.

"Because this whole thing is a fucking joke, isn't it, Olivia? Like everything is a fucking joke to you."

The blood drains from my face and my arms and legs. I'm bleeding out on his kitchen floor.

"What?"

"I'm done with this."

"Done with what? Me?"

"Whatever this is." He pulls open the door. "If anyone asks, we broke up. I'm sure they won't be surprised."

"Ash—"

"I'd say it was fun while it lasted, but it wasn't," he says. "Leave before I call security."

It's fight or flight. I can't cry. I can't show him all the ways my heart is breaking. He doesn't get to see me hurt. He doesn't deserve it.

"Bree was right," I whisper. "I'm just another one of your *interns*."

"If that's what you need to think."

"It's what I know."

"You can't act like a victim when this charade was your idea."

After he slams the door in my face, I eat an entire pint of mint chocolate chip ice cream on the subway ride home. When I walk into my apartment and find Joey and Paloma sitting on the couch, I burst into tears.

12

PALOMA HAS a cure for sad boy problems that doesn't include eating another pint of ice cream and crying myself to sleep but does include lots of free alcohol and dancing, which is how I find myself at an exclusive club opening in the Meatpacking District the following night.

Boudoir is dark and broody, a perfect visual representation of my current mood. Sections of curtained off rooms line the back wall, black velvet hiding secrets only the leather couches can tell. The clusters of half-moon couches, that have floral cushions straight from a backyard in the 70s, are littered with pretty girls and wandering eyes. Antique chairs and potted trees fill the empty space. It's oddly smokey.

This sounded like a good idea when I was all snotty and in tears last night, but being here feels like actual agony.

I called out of work today. I'm a coward with splotchy eyes and I couldn't let Asher see how broken up I am about our break-up—*our fake-up.* It may have started as a way to show Francesca how happy Asher was, but it transpired into something more. I liked being around him. I liked the side of him he didn't show others. I liked how easy it was for me to wear him down. I liked that soft smile. That quiet laugh. The way he always found a way to touch me. I've had sex with men who didn't make me feel a fraction of what Asher made me feel when he pulled me closer.

I didn't want to catch feelings, but I did. And to be so easily disposed by him hurt me in ways I never imagined. Deep down, I know he feels the same way. Because he opened up to me. He showed me that other side—that vulnerable side, the one that needed me closer. You can't just turn that off. He can't have me on his desk one minute and want nothing to do with me the next.

It doesn't make sense.

"Olivia!" Anouk towers over me but still manages to throw her arms around me. "Look alive!"

"I am alive." That much I'm aware of. I'm very much alive.

"Get it together, girl," Natasha says. "You look sexy as hell and you can have any guy in this room. Asher who?"

She's right about one thing: I do look sexy as hell. I'm wearing a black long-sleeved mini dress with a deep v-neckline and a choker collar. If this was a month ago, I would have walked right up to the bar and worked my charm, but the only person I want to flirt with is Asher.

I'm going to be *tons* of fun tonight.

We sit on a couch in the VIP section and a bottle service girl brings us over a bottle of champagne that probably costs half of my yearly salary. Natasha practically spills the whole thing on the floor. She's not even drunk yet.

"Tonight," she starts, waving what's left of the bottle, "is about getting Olivia laid."

"Olivia will settle for getting a little buzzed," I say as she fills my flute with champagne.

"You need to get under someone else to get over him," Anouk says.

"I don't think it works that way," Joey says. "Especially when she doesn't want to be over him."

Joey and I seldom agree on things. She likes documentaries. I like reality TV. She buys organic soy yogurt. I eat cereal for dinner. She doesn't believe in aliens. And, well, I do. But as far as Asher goes, we're on the same page.

I don't want to be over him.

I barely got to be under him.

"Okay, *fine*," Anouk says. "Let's just see where the night takes us."

The night mostly takes me to the women's room where I help Natasha pull down her skin-tight leather skirt. We talk about her upcoming shoot with a French lingerie brand and she gives me the phone number of her aesthetician that does all her waxing.

Is she trying to tell me something?

Probably.

I missed half of my right ankle when I was shaving this morning.

We stop seven times on the way back to our table because Natasha has to hug and kiss everyone she knows. She introduces me as her pocket-sized publicist, which I am now considering changing my Twitter handle to.

When we finally get back, Joey looks like she's ready to murder someone. It's her usual look. I don't think much of it until I see her typing furiously on her phone.

"What's wrong?" Natasha asks. "Where'd Paloma go?"

"Levi's here."

Natasha, who was a drink away from being one with the floor, is now sober. "I have mace in my bra."

I can't decide if that's convenient or dangerous.

"Well, you better get ready to use it because if he even looks in my direction I'm going to castrate him with a bobby pin."

I'm well aware of Joey's opinion of Levi, but I never thought to ask why she and all her friends thought so low of him. This went further than him being a little too charming.

"What did he do?" I ask.

Joey's eyes snap open, like that was the worst possible question I could ask. I regret it instantly.

"How do you work for the McGowans and not know what Levi does? They make a business out of covering it up."

"I only work with Asher," I tell them. "And he's not Levi's biggest fan."

"Yeah, well, his father and brothers don't share those sentiments."

Natasha clears her throat. "Just don't let him buy you a drink."

"What?"

"Loves an unconscious girl." Joey downs the rest of her drink and slams the empty glass so hard on the table that it almost breaks. She gets up and walks over to the bar.

"We'd only heard rumors until our friend Alice met him in London," Anouk says. "If Joey hadn't found them…"

Joey went to London in September for Fashion Week. I vividly remember her leaving on a Saturday night. She left me strict instructions to not overwater the cactus she keeps in her room. I took the job seriously. I sent her pictures every day just so she knew we were getting on fine without her. She never responded. I thought it was Joey being Joey, but now I realize there was more going on than just hair and makeup and haute couture.

Natasha goes into more detail.

They were at an afterparty at a club in Shoreditch. Levi had been buying drinks for Alice all night, and despite Joey's warnings, Alice left with him. When Joey got back to the hotel room they were sharing, she found Levi on top of Alice, who wasn't moving or responding to Joey's screams.

Levi left, but not before his handler forced Joey to sign a nondisclosure agreement.

Hollywood's best kept secret was built on threats and denial.

"Is Alice okay?" I ask.

"She wants to speak out, but they paid her a lot of money not to."

Maybe it's the champagne, but I can't wrap my head around this. The firm I work for supports this? Bullying women into silence? Protecting a predator for financial gains? Ana would *never*. Not after her own daughter was exploited. She would be the first to throw Levi in jail.

"Does Asher know?"

"How can he not?'

The whole walk to the bar, I tell myself he doesn't know. I down a cosmo in one gulp and tell myself again.

Asher doesn't know.

Asher doesn't know.

Asher doesn't know.

"Livi."

It's a whisper. A quiet echo in my ear that I don't want to hear. I pretend I don't. It was said in passing. Meant for someone else. It's a popular name. I would bet the thirty-seven dollars in my checking account that there's at least three other Olivias here tonight. Maybe I'll take an exit poll.

"*Livi*." I feel his breath hot against my ear and then I feel his hand—inappropriately low on my back. "You've been driving me crazy all night in this little dress. I can't believe Asher let you out of his sight. I wouldn't have let you out of the house."

"Asher's not my keeper."

"Thank God for that."

That doesn't stop me from wishing he was here. Because he always made me feel safe and protected. Even when he was grumpy and annoyed and complaining about the coffee that the barista made wrong for the seventh time, he was never threatening. Agitated. Unreasonable. Irritable. But not threatening.

And when he touched me—when he touched me my entire body sang. I melted into him. I wanted to drown in the feeling of his body pressed against mine. In his bed. Between the sheets. Every sleepy sigh and *pull me closer*.

God, I could never be close enough.

I wanted that with Levi once. I wanted our *Hallmark* Christmas special. I wanted to fall in love the way it happens in the movies. Starry eyes and happily ever afters. But the man in front of me is not the man from the screen.

He never belonged on the pedestal I put him on. He was a figment of my imagination. Someone I dreamed him to be. He's the reality check I never asked for.

"Will you join me for a drink?"

"I'm with friends," I say.

"Just one drink." He moves his hand lower. "I can never get you alone."

"And why exactly do you need me alone?" I ask. "Because you're certainly not concerned about privacy when you're touching my ass."

"My apologies," he says and removes his hand. "I don't know where I left my manners. Do you need me to get on my knees and beg for forgiveness? Because I will. And I promise I'm very sincere."

"Sincere," I scoff.

"*Very* sincere," he says. "I promise no one has ever apologized to you the way I will."

"That won't be necessary."

"At least let me buy you a drink," he says.

"Really, it's okay. I reached my limit a glass of champagne ago."

"Please, I won't be able to live with myself if I know you think I'm anything less than a gentleman."

I glance around the club. I don't see Natasha or Joey. Anouk is consumed in a conversation.

I know how to take care of myself. I've been doing it for as long as I can remember, but that doesn't mean I'm opposed to being rescued. I know when to ask for help. This is one of those times.

But tonight, I have to handle Levi on my own.

"One drink," I tell him.

"One drink here and then another drink at my penthouse? In my hot tub? Overlooking the Manhattan skyline?"

"One drink."

"Then I choose the drink at my apartment. It's clothing optional." He smiles and it's so convincing. If I didn't know any better, I would have gone with him. I probably would have fallen out of my clothes long before we got out of the car and into the hot tub.

I probably would be unconscious too.

"One drink," I repeat. "Here."

"I guess I have to take what I can get, Ms. Langley."

I don't like the way that sounds coming out of his mouth.

"I'll have a scotch neat," Levi says to the bartender. "And whatever this gorgeous woman is drinking."

"Club soda with lime, please."

"*Livi.*"

"*Levi.*"

"You're a handful," he says. "I like that in a woman."

When the bartender comes back with our drinks, I make sure it's a smooth transfer into my hand.

Levi walks us back to one of the curtained off rooms his handler is guarding. I recognize him from the office. He's big and bulky and terrifying. When Anouk said Joey was forced into an NDA, I almost didn't believe it. Joey doesn't get forced into anything, but this man—he seems persuasive. Even when he winks at me.

We sit on a slate gray, tufted leather couch that's placed in front of a wall splattered with shades of red and yellow and electric blue. The chandelier above is covered in a red velvet shade. It's mood lighting. Under different circumstances, I could see myself having a few drinks and getting a little handsy.

Tonight, I'm trying to keep a respectable distance, which Levi thinks is an invitation to slide closer.

"I feel like I don't know you, Livi."

"Because you don't."

"And I think that's unfair because I'm sure you know plenty about me."

"Rumor has it you're part warlock."

"Wikipedia?"

"And you eat thirteen slugs a day."

"Did Asher tell you that?"

"I read it in a magazine," I say.

"It's all true," he says. "I eat slugs and I cast love spells on beautiful women."

"Love spells?" I almost laugh.

"I'm going to charm you right out of that dress, Livi."
He slides closer, his arm resting on the back of the couch.
He's grinning at me. "But first, I'd like you to tell me about
yourself."

"There's really not much to know." I shrug. "I'm
twenty-two. I'm from Buffalo. Graduated last spring. I like
reality TV and eating dry cereal straight from the box."

"How'd you get mixed up with Asher McGowan?"

"I applied for an internship and hoped for the best," I
say. "You two grew up together?"

"We went to the same schools, but Asher was that
pretentious kid who thought he was too cool for everything," Levi says. "But I'd rather not talk about him when
there are much more interesting topics we could be
covering."

"Like what?" I ask. "Christmas? Wrapping paper
patterns? Global warming? UFOs?"

"You're so cute, Livi."

And then he kisses me.

Our mouths fit together all wrong.

There's no anticipation. It's straight to the point. He's
rough and hard and demanding. He's in control and he
makes sure I know it.

When I feel his hand slip under the hem of my skirt, I
hear Asher's voice in my head.

"If you ever find yourself alone with Levi, please call me."
"I just need you to trust me."

I push Levi away and giggle enough to sound convincing. "I think we need to slow down a little."

"Of course," he says and takes my glass from me. "Let
me get you another drink."

"That would be great. Thanks."

He's not stupid. I'm not either. I know his handler is

still at the door. I can't leave, so I pull my phone out of my bag and find Asher's number.

I call him four times before Levi gets back. They all go to voicemail.

"I hope this is club soda," I say when Levi hands me the drink.

"Why don't you take a sip and find out?"

His eyes are burning holes into mine. I'm on fire. Not in a good way. I don't know how to talk my way out of this one.

"I'll take it back if it's wrong."

I take a sip and pray there's no lasting effect.

"Well?" he asks, but his lips are on my neck before I can answer. When I try to move away, he moves closer. I'm crammed into a corner, half-sitting, half-lying, and Levi doesn't take the hint.

"Levi," I say. "Can we slow down?"

"Livi," he groans into my neck. "I've been waiting so long to have you like this."

"We only met a few weeks ago."

"And that's a very long time to have you just in my head."

"I'm just… I'd rather we just stay friends."

"Friends," he laughs and it's sinister. I see a shift in his eyes. This isn't the man that romances women on the big screen. This isn't a man who romances women anywhere. "Like you're friends with Asher?"

"I'm not—"

"Olivia, you need to know whose bed to sleep in if you want to make it in this industry. And let me tell you: it's not Asher McGowan's. It's mine," he says into my ear. "And I can end your career before it even starts."

I can't move or speak or breathe. He looks straight

through me, pinning me further into the couch. I want to scream, but when I open my mouth, no sound comes out.

"Don't fucking touch me."

The black velvet curtain flies open. I see Joey against the dim club lights. She's six feet of pure rage and she's shaking. I never want someone to look at me the way she's looking at Levi.

"Get your hands off of her." She doesn't give him another option. She drags me off the couch, leaving Levi raw-lipped and furious.

"We keep meeting like this, Josephine."

"Yeah, it's kind of funny how you continue to be a fucking vile piece of shit," she says, tucking me against her side. "You're gonna rot in hell."

"Is that a threat?"

"It's a promise."

Outside, Natasha is waiting with a car. The cold shocks the life back into me and when Joey looks down at me, I burst into tears.

I think about my mom and how I need her to hold me and whisper into my ear that everything is going to be okay. But that's a luxury I don't have, so I try to put on a brave face. I tell myself everything is going to be okay. Tomorrow will be better.

It doesn't have the same effect.

But then Joey wraps her arms around me and squeezes me tightly. She doesn't say anything about the tear stains I leave on her borrowed designer dress.

When we get home, I use our five minutes of hot water to scrub my skin clean of Levi. I brush the taste of him out of my mouth. And I make myself a promise before I go to sleep.

Levi is never going to touch another girl the way he touched me tonight.

I'm going to make sure of it.

Emanuel is on the verge of tears when he calls me from the deli two blocks away from the office. In the background, I hear Maja yelling in Polish. Something is wrong with the order. This is what happens when people don't follow my rules.

"Did you read my email?"

"Yes."

"Did you take the lunch order directly to the deli in person?"

"No."

"Did you call in the order?"

"Yes."

"Did the email specifically say not to do that?"

"Yes."

I'm on my way back from the museum, so I swing by the deli to rescue Emanuel from Maja, who I find to be the sweetest woman ever. I don't understand a word she says to me, but she always sends me away with two loaves of chocolate babka. I have a sneaking suspicion that Emanuel won't be getting *any* chocolate babka.

"Oh, thank God," he says when I walk through the door.

I'm pretty sure Maja says the same thing in Polish.

"I'm trying to sort through everything to make sure it's all here like you *very specifically* said in the email—"

"So what you're telling me is that you're picking and choosing what information you took from it?"

"There were thirty-four bullet points, Liv!" he says. "But whatever! I'm missing a sandwich and a salad and I don't know which ones!"

"There are six salads and six sandwiches," I count.

"And there should be seven."

"No, there should be six because you were supposed to order Asher's from the vegan place across the street. It was bullet point number eleven."

"Asher's not vegan."

"I know, but that's the only place that could assure me that they use Bolero carrots in their carrot and ginger soup."

"Are you serious?"

"I wish I weren't."

After assuring Maja that everything was okay, she gives me a chocolate babka as we leave. Emanuel thinks we're going to share it, but I'm actually going to eat it under my desk while I avoid an inbox full of emails.

"I didn't get a chance to tell you this morning," Emanuel starts as we exit the elevator and walk towards the conference room, "but you look wrecked."

"Thanks, Manny. I feel wrecked."

"Late night?"

"I went out with Joey and her friends. Too much free champagne."

"That'll do it."

It didn't help that I got no sleep. I tossed and turned until I heard Joey get up for her morning spin class. I almost invited myself along.

Almost.

I couldn't get the taste of Levi out of my mouth. Mostly, I couldn't get Asher off my mind. He never returned my calls. I didn't expect him to, but a small part of me hoped, which just led to disappointment and anger.

We were never real.

That's what I keep telling myself.

I cut Emanuel loose before we get to the conference

room. It doesn't take two people to unpack a few paper bags. And I'm a nice person, and I'm grateful that he's been helping out with my workload while I've been helping Billie organize the gala.

But as soon as I turn into the room, I realize that being nice got me nowhere.

Asher has his back to the door, but Levi's eyes catch mine immediately. His lips curve devilishly. I almost vomit on my babka.

"*Livi.*"

Asher's neck cranes enough for our eyes to meet for a moment. He looks exhausted. Like he tossed and turned all night.

Good.

I hope he has puffy eyes for days.

Because I will not be there to buy him a stupidly expensive jade facial roller.

"I can't stop thinking about that little black dress you wore last night," Levi says. "I had high hopes I'd see it again today. I had higher hopes that I'd see it on my bedroom floor."

It's easy to ignore him when I see Asher's face fall out of the corner of my eyes. For someone who looked like he wanted to watch me fall down an elevator shaft mere seconds ago, he suddenly looks awfully concerned that I'd spent the night in the same vicinity as Levi Booker.

"What's with the look, Ash?" Levi says. "There's plenty of her to go around."

When he grabs my ass, my entire body goes cold. I don't say anything. I can't speak. I can't think. I can't move. I'm just there. Existing as an object for Levi to touch and grope at his pleasure.

"Get your hands off of her." Asher's voice fills the room.

"She likes it," Levi says. "Don't you, Livi? Tell Asher about all the fun we had last night."

"Levi, I'm not going to tell you again." Asher is out of his seat. I have visions of him jumping over the table and pouncing on Levi. Funny how he wants to rescue me now. When it's convenient for him.

"Ms. Langley, I'm glad you're already here. We have a few matters to tend to."

Levi drops his hand when River walks into the room and commands our attention.

"Do you need me to make some phone calls?" I don't know what else he would want me to do, but I'd walk all the way to Honolulu if it meant I got to leave this room.

"No, that won't be necessary," he says and opens a navy blue folder and pushes it towards me. A single sheet of paper rests inside:

NONDISCLOSURE AGREEMENT

"I trust that you understand why we need you to sign this."

Because everyone else does? Because I'm not a person? Because I'm just another piece of this web of women Levi Booker chews up and spits out?

"Why does she need to sign an NDA?" Asher's white-knuckling the table.

"It's nothing against you, Livi," Levi says and he almost sounds sweet. "It's just a precaution."

"A precaution?"

"Yes—"

"Olivia, please go down to my office," Asher says, grabbing the folder from me.

When I look at him, I see the man I was snowed in

with. The one who held me all night. Who made me pancakes. And fed me expensive chocolates.

Not the man who threw me out of his apartment.

The one who told me we were done.

"Asher, she needs to sign—"

"She's not signing anything," he snaps. "Olivia, go to my office."

"This is a legal matter, Asher."

"Then call my lawyer."

"Don't be ridiculous."

"I've never been more serious."

I leave the room because I feel like I'm suffocating. I need fresh air. Space to breathe. None of the **20 REASONS WHY YOU SHOULD MOVE TO NYC** blog posts I read mentioned this sort of thing. They prepared me with the best Chinese takeout and how to get cheap theater tickets. They didn't warn me about serial assaulters and nondisclosure agreements.

"Olivia."

The elevator parts and I enter, ignoring Asher's calls.

"Olivia."

I press the button for the ground floor and when the doors begin to shut, Asher slams his hand between them.

We don't say anything. It's like we're searching each other for answers we already know.

"I called you," I say, my voice a distant tremor.

"What happened? Did he touch—"

"Do you know?"

"What?"

"Do you know?" I ask again, this time louder. "Do you know that Levi roofies girls and then takes them to hotel rooms and waits for them to be unconscious before he *assaults* them? Do you know that he also pays them off and makes them sign NDAs? Do you know that your father covers it up?"

He doesn't have to say anything.

The way his eyes drop to the floor tells me everything.

"You knew."

When the elevator doors close, I start to cry.

13

"Hey, Olivia! It's Francesca! I wanted to see if you were free tomorrow to go thrifting. I'm running into a rehearsal now, but shoot me a message so we can set up a time and place! Bye!"

I LISTEN to her message between hefty bites of mushroom risotto and gulps of Red Bull. I only have a five minute break. I don't have time to chew. Or even comprehend that my ex-fake-boyfriend's ex-girlfriend wants to go shopping with me. A week ago, I would have jumped at the opportunity. Today, I'd rather jump in front of a train.

Not a moving one.

One that's idling.

Something to traumatize me—and probably a platform full of people—into realizing that these are outrageous and irrational thoughts to be having over the actions of a man.

Men have been disappointing women for centuries.

And if I'm going to throw myself in front of a train, it's not going to be because of a man.

It'll be because the government found my blog about the extraterrestrials.

"Liv, Ivan's looking for you." Celeste takes my risotto and places it in the sink behind me before Ivan sees that I've taken an extra seven seconds to swallow.

I'm exhausted and have been since before I got here. I've already waited on two tables of twelve. Christmas parties are fun when you're at them, but when I'm not the one drinking on my boss's dime, I don't find them merry and bright, especially when they send four plates back that they insisted were wrong.

They weren't.

I want to crawl into a cabinet and sleep for seventeen years.

"Olivia." Ivan's voice brings the kitchen to silence, which isn't easy when, at any given moment, someone is cursing at an inanimate object. But Ivan's voice is enough to wake the dead and make them want to die all over again. It also makes my skin crawl.

And makes me vomit a little in my mouth.

"I just sat you another party," he tells me.

"I already have two."

"And now you have three," he says tightly. "And you'll cover tables thirty-two and thirty-three while Oscar takes his lunch."

He's still punishing me for being late and will continue into the new year. I'm used to it. I shouldn't be, but I am.

"The party is a group of hotel investors. I expect you to treat them with the utmost respect."

"As opposed to spitting in their food?" It slips out, but I don't regret saying it. I'm tired of people speaking to me like I'm not a person.

"You're on thin ice, Olivia," he says through his teeth. "We'll be speaking in my office after your shift."

Ivan storms off and leaves me with a bad taste in my mouth. My usual response is to lie down and play dead, nodding quietly at his lewd requests to undo a few more buttons or to be a little more *friendly*. I always bend and break, crumbling to his feet because I can't afford to not have this job. He knows that, which is why I'm his easiest target.

"I'm surprised he didn't ask you to give each of them a lap dance." Celeste is frowning next to me.

"He'll probably suggest I blow him when we're speaking in his office later."

Celeste grimaces. "Just quit, Liv. There are thousands of restaurants in New York."

"He knows a lot of people. He'll slander me around town."

She shakes her head. "I'll take thirty-two and thirty-three for you."

"No, it's fine," I say. "They're small tables."

"You're too good, Livi. You deserve better."

I don't have time to stand there and agree with her, so I give her my best brave face and walk back into the dining room.

The lights are dim and the tables are crowded, busy chatter illuminating the restaurant. I straighten the skirt of my black, button-down dress. It fits tightly against the curve of my hips and lands an inch above my knee. Ivan would have me in heels if it wasn't such a hazard.

I arrive at table thirty-two and I'm reciting my lines before I look up.

"Good evening, I'm Olivia. I'll be your—"

I don't expect Asher to be staring back at me, awestruck and lips parted, eyes like a deer in headlights. I also don't expect him to be with a woman, whose beauty is encased in coiled curls and smooth dark skin.

A date.

He's on a date.

I straighten up.

"—server tonight. Can I start you with a drink?"

Asher forgets how to speak, which is a far cry from the man who has left me twenty-seven voicemails since yesterday.

"Olivia, please call me."

"Olivia, I need to speak with you."

"Olivia, this is important."

"O. Please just call me."

It was easy to avoid him at work. The gala is in four days, so I spend most of my working hours (and sometimes more) at the museum with Billie. But my absence at the office doesn't mean River has forgotten about me. I had another NDA delivered to my apartment. Joey was home when his assistant dropped it off. She put it through the shredder and sent the scraps back to the office.

Maybe I'll put my heart through the shredder and mail it to Asher.

Better yet, I'll serve it to him roasted on a silver platter with a steak knife through it.

"Your wine listing," his date says, scanning the menu. "Which Cabernet would you recommend?"

"The Beringer private reserve."

"We'll take a bottle," she says.

"Of course," I say and glance at Asher. "Is there anything else I can get you?"

"Do you have Stella on—"

"No," I say too quickly. "But we have a craft that's similar."

He swallows. "Grey Goose and—"

"Soda with lime. Perfect, I'll be right back."

I should have let Celeste take the tables and dealt with the repercussions from Ivan. If I had time, I would have gone into the kitchen to cry, but I don't, so I walk over to the table of twelve with my head held high and greet them with the biggest smile I can muster up.

"Good evening, I'm Olivia. I'll be your server tonight," I say. "Can I start you off with some drinks?"

They spew off their orders with wild eyes and cheeky grins. I do my best to ignore the fact that they're all sizing me up, nudging each other when I have to lean down to hear them over the noise. They're all middle-aged and wearing fancy suits. Half of them have rings on their fingers.

Their poor wives.

I take the orders over to the bar, where Maritza is backed up and looking flustered.

"Breathe," I tell her. "You're doing fine."

She smiles quickly at me and I coach her through some of the drinks. She knows what she's doing, but I'll take any excuse I can to prolong my journey back to Christmas party hell.

"Olivia." Asher's voice hits me like a car, knocking the air out of my lungs.

I ignore him and tell Maritza to hand me the bottle opener.

"Olivia, we need to talk."

"I'm working."

"I can see that," he says. "Why didn't you tell me you have another job?"

"I checked with HR before I started my internship. They said it wasn't an issue."

"That's not—why didn't you tell *me*?"

"Does it matter?"

"I mean, no, it doesn't—"

"So why would I tell you? You're my boss, Asher. What I do outside of Loveridge & McGowan really isn't any of your business."

"Right."

"Now, if you'll excuse me, I have a job to do," I say, taking the tray Maritza slides to me. "And you have a date. I'll be over shortly to take your order."

I leave Asher in the dust and walk back to my table of ten. I give them their drinks and excuse myself before I walk over to the other table I was sat. Once I get their order, I turn to Asher and his date.

"Are you ready to order?"

"Yes, we are," she says and I can't ignore the smirk that lingers on her lips.

I wonder what her name is and what she does for work and what it is about her—other than her striking beauty— that Asher likes.

"Would you recommend the duck or the filet?"

"The duck is excellent," I tell her.

"I'll have that," she says, closing the menu.

"And for you, sir?"

"I'll have the filet. Medium-well."

"And instead of the mushroom risotto?" I already know he won't want that.

"Does the macaroni and cheese have—"

"No, it doesn't have fontina," I say. "It's a cheddar-gruyere blend. From New Zealand."

His eyes don't move from mine. "I'll have the roasted root vegetables."

"Of course. Is there—"

"You're *Olivia.*"

I look at his date, my brow lifting at her suggestion that I'm a special breed of *Olivia.* "Yes?"

"Vivian." Asher's tone is warning.

"You're Olivia," she says again, smiling at me. "What a small world."

I don't know what she means, but Asher eyes his fork

like he's ready to maim himself.

Please, let me do the honors.

"It's great to finally put a face to the name."

Why does she know who I am? What did he tell her about me? How I can never get his coffee right? That I'm the most annoying human to exist? That I write in purple ink? I bet they laugh at me.

"She's oblivious."

"It's like talking to a wall."

"She's a complete and utter idiot."

Why is she wearing a wedding ring?

What's that saying?

Like father, like son.

"Is there anything else I can get you?"

"No," Asher says. "That'll be all."

I nod curtly and power-walk to the kitchen to get their order in. The faster they get their food, the faster they leave, and the faster I can get some semblance of peace.

"Are you okay?" Celeste asks as I fumble with the touch screen.

"Yeah," I lie. "I'm just ready for this night to be over."

"I'm ready for this year to be over."

I can't remember a time when I ever wanted December to end. I would relive Christmas every day if I could—never take my decorations down or watch a movie other than *Love Actually.* But this season took a turn and I don't feel that same cheer I felt a few weeks ago.

I'm ready for this year to be over too.

I take a few deep breaths, count to three, and walk back into the dining room. My table of hotel investors are waiting *patiently* for me.

"Are there any questions?"

"I have a few." He has salt and pepper hair and dark

brown eyes that he hasn't taken off my chest. "What perfume are you wearing? You smell delicious."

"I don't think I'm on the menu." I laugh because that's what I do when I'm uncomfortable.

And then he laughs too and so does the entire table.

"Benny and I have been trying to guess how old you are. I say twenty-five. He seems to think you're younger."

"I am," I say.

"How young?"

I cough. "Do you have any questions about the menu?"

"No," he says. "Just about you."

I freeze when his hand slides over my back, jerking me forward.

"Ivan said you were his best waitress."

"That was nice of him," I say. "But I don't think this is appropriate."

"Oh, c'mon," he laughs and he smacks my ass lightly before grabbing a handful of it. "We're just having a little fun."

I try to pull away, but he holds me there. "I'd like to take your order if you're ready."

"Yes, I'll take you on this table with your legs spread."

I feel it bubbling deep inside of me, brewing long before I was old enough to realize what it was. Always passive. Always polite. An uncomfortable giggle and a quick glance around the room. It was an unwanted kiss on the playground at eight years old. It was a bra snap in seventh grade. A boob graze in eighth. It was a tongue shoved down my throat during a dare. A cat call at fourteen. An uncomfortable hand job at fifteen. A frat house of guys calling me a slut. A boss who asks me to show a little more skin. It's Levi Booker pushing me into a couch. It's fifteen years of silence.

I'm done being passive and polite.

I'm tired of being quiet.

"Who the hell do you think you are?" I snap. "I'm not some rag doll you can do with what you please. I'm a person. I deserve to be respected. Get your fucking hands off of me."

"You're feisty." He pulls me closer and the table laughs.

"Let me go, you vile piece of shit." I manage to grab his glass of Merlot and throw it in his face.

"Who do you think—"

I'm forced out of his grasp. Partly from my spastic wiggling and partly from the help of someone else. I look back and it's Asher, eyes blazing with rage. He drops my arm and tries to step in front of me. I don't let him.

"You're a disgusting person," I say. "I hope you know that. I hope you go to sleep at night and know you're the equivalent of a pile of dog—"

"I couldn't help but overhear you sexually harassing this woman." It's Vivian. She wraps her hand around the back of his chair one finger at a time and speaks calmly. "In fact, I think this whole restaurant heard you sexually harassing this woman."

"I think you misunderstood."

"I don't think I did," she says, turning to me. "Olivia, did I misunderstand?"

"No."

"Like I was saying, sexual harassment is a criminal offense and I happen to be a very expensive lawyer that you will have to pay for when Ms. Langley takes you to court and a jury finds you guilty."

"It was all in good fun."

"I don't think it—"

"What's going on here?" Ivan snaps in my direction. "William, are they giving you a hard time?"

"Yes, they're making some nasty accusations," he says. "Olivia was getting a little friendly and—"

"A hundred people will tell you that's a lie," Vivian says. "Are you the manager?"

"Yes, I am."

"Olivia will be filing a police report," Vivian says. "I expect you'll be complying with state and federal regulations. I also expect that you're up to date on your state-mandated sexual harassment training."

"Now, just wait a minute," William tries.

"No," Vivian says.

"Olivia, I need to speak with you in my office."

Ivan is glaring at me, the whole restaurant watching. I can say no. I don't have to go with him.

But I do.

Because he deserves a piece of my mind.

"I'll come with you," Asher whispers, a concerned look in his eyes.

"No, that won't be necessary."

"Then let Vivian."

"No."

I follow Ivan's heels through the dining room and into the kitchen. Celeste is waiting, but I don't get a chance to speak. The look I give her says enough.

This is it.

Ivan's office smells like cigarettes and too much air-freshener. Papers are strewn across his desk, a sea of uncapped pens on the floor. How does anyone work like this? He's an unorganized, messy slob. And that's putting it nicely.

"You've been testing my patience, Olivia," he says.

"He grabbed my ass."

"I told you to be nice. William invests a lot of money into this hotel."

"So I was supposed to *let* him touch me?"

"Yes," he snaps. "And you will not be filing a police report."

I'm stunned. I knew Ivan was an unreasonable perv, but I didn't realize he was this far gone.

"Yes, I am."

"Olivia, you're treading on thin ice. You will not make a mockery of our customers."

"I'm filing a police report."

Ivan looks up at me slowly, lips twitching and eyes glowing. And then he laughs.

"You're fired."

My heart plummets into my stomach.

No, no, no.

This can't happen.

"That's not fair."

"Life's not fair, babe."

"I don't even think it's legal."

"Of course it's legal," he laughs and falls into his chair. "You're insubordinate and continuously late. I can't have a waitress who doesn't know how to show up when her shift starts."

I feel the mushroom risotto in the back of my throat. I'm going to be sick.

No, no, no.

This can't happen.

This *shouldn't* happen.

This is why people don't speak up.

Because when they do, their life that's already ruined is completely destroyed with no repercussions to the person who pulled the trigger. They move on. They live. While victims suffer.

"You can leave now."

I don't realize I'm walking until I see Celeste, who throws her concerned self at me.

"Liv," she says.

"It's over."

"What?"

"He fired me."

"He can't."

"He did."

I grab my hat, my jacket, and scarf and I don't look back as I slip out of the service entrance.

The wind is cold and brittle and harsh against my skin, a few stray tears chapping my cheeks. I'm not going to cry. I refuse to be that girl sobbing on the subway. I was already that girl once this week. Twice might give everyone the impression that I'm mentally unstable.

I'm not.

I'm very stable.

Maybe not at this exact moment.

But generally speaking, I can keep it together.

In public.

When I get home, well, that's a different story.

When I get home, I'm going to cry until I make myself sick.

I've never been fired from anything. Not even from the pizza place I worked at in high school that I accidentally set on fire. I'm a model employee. Sure, I've had some slip ups over the last few weeks, but only because I've been busy.

I didn't particularly like Ivan. He made me uncomfortable and asked me to do things that were ethically questionable, but waitressing at an upscale restaurant was fast and easy money—money that I *desperately* need to make ends meet. My internship will be over in a few weeks.

What happens then? I won't be able to pay rent or buy food or afford transportation.

I'll be homeless for Christmas.

"Olivia."

I'm at the crosswalk and reaching for the push-to-walk button when I hear Asher shout. He's half out of breath and wheezing when he gets to me, but I ignore him and jam on the button again. I'm pretty sure these things don't even work.

I'm not going to speak to him or look at him or acknowledge him in any sense. I'm going to stand here and wait patiently because I can't afford to be reckless and get hit by a taxi or a rabid cyclist. I occupy myself by making a list of all my recent purchases and how I now have to return them.

"Olivia, please—"

When his hand grazes my arm, I snap.

"Don't touch me." I jerk away from him, my eyes narrowed into a glare. "I'm sick of people who touch me without asking. There's no reason for you to put your hands on me. I knew you were there. I chose to ignore you."

"I'm sorry, I shouldn't—"

"You're right—you shouldn't have," I say, glancing back at the light that still hasn't changed. "Now that we've established that, you can go back to your date."

There's a brief pause.

A cab driver rolls down his window and flips off an Uber that cut him off.

"I'm not on a date," he says. "Vivian is my lawyer. And she's married to my sister."

My heart doesn't jump. There's no rush of hope or relief. I don't feel anything except the bitter cold against my bare legs.

"Olivia, are you okay?"

I laugh. Hysterically. Manically. I'm a freak show on the corner of E 77th Street and Madison Ave. People are staring at me. Maybe I'm not stable. Maybe I'm very, *very* unstable.

I'm losing it.

And I start crying.

"Am I okay?" I ask and the light finally changes and I walk across the street like I'm some new off-Broadway production called *The Girl's Gone Mad.* "I was just sexually harassed and got fired. No, I'm not *fucking* okay, Asher."

He starts to follow me when there's two seconds left on the timer. How brave. Wouldn't want that pedicab to hit him.

"He can't fire you for this."

"Of course he can."

"Legally—"

"Legally, he can," I snap, carefully avoiding a slick spot of black ice as I maneuver onto the sidewalk. "I've been on warning for being late multiple times, which you're very familiar with. I'm always late, right?"

"Olivia—"

We're in front of a bridal shop with a window display that's filled with snow-frosted trees and glitter that sparkles against the twinkling lights, illuminating a long-sleeved gown that's adorned with lace and pearls. I walk a few feet further, because I refuse to have this argument in front of something so breathtakingly gorgeous. I'd much rather do it in front of the rat that's frozen to the bottom of the mailbox.

"Remember when we were in bed together and you asked me how I still manage to be late when I have twelve alarms set?" I ask. "It's because I usually don't get home until two in the morning and I'm exhausted. And sometimes trains breakdown and busses are late and I get that you don't understand any of that because you have a car service that's *always* on time. And then I have to wait in line to get your breakfast at what seems to be the most popular bagel shop in Manhattan. And your coffee! Your *fucking* coffee! They *hate* me. Those baristas run away when I walk through the door because they know it's never going to be right the first or the second or even the third time. *That's* why I'm always late, Asher."

"Olivia—"

"And I try so hard." I'm crying. *God*, I really didn't want to cry in front of him. "And I know it's my own fault. I know I do too much. I try to please too many people. But that's me. I don't want to disappoint anyone. So I take on the extra work. I go to that event I told you I couldn't moderate. And I stay an extra forty-five minute to finish those emails, and then I miss my train and the bus and then I'm late for my other job—the one I *desperately* need because I have no one. It's just me. I don't have the luxury of calling my parents for some extra cash. I don't have a trust fund or a rich relative waiting to bail me out. I have to support myself. And that means dealing with a handsy boss and gross customers because the tips are good. And that's sad, isn't it? That I have to suffer the gross side effects of misogyny to make a living."

"Olivia." Asher looks as defeated as I feel.

"But I don't have to worry about that anymore," I laugh. "I'll be unemployed and homeless by the end of the month. What a way to ring in the new year."

He shoves his hands into his pockets. His face, normally rigid and stiff from his long list of frustrations, goes soft. "You're not going to be unemployed."

"Oh, are you going to keep me on payroll as your play-thing? Just like your father does with Bree?"

His switch flips in an instant. What was once gentle and tender turns sharp. Anger flares in his eyes, his sudden fury warming the whole block. Maybe even the whole city. And state. Possibly the whole country. The world just might explode.

Asher is livid.

"Fuck you, Olivia."

And I'm stunned.

"You don't get to put me in a box," he snaps. "Not when you came onto me. Not when you made me the punchline of your joke."

"Excuse me?" I snap right back at him, ignoring the looks we get from the people walking by. "I made you the punchline of *my* joke? Exactly what joke did I make you the punchline of? Because if you haven't noticed, I'm not laughing."

"Us, Olivia," he says. "You and me. We were the joke."

"Is that what you think?'

"It's certainly what you thought."

"Excuse me?"

He licks his lips, his eyes glancing to the night sky before returning to mine. "What's a little mouth on boob action? It's not that serious? I've gone further with guys I barely know? Less pretending? We were so convincing?"

His snide anger is a mask for how hurt he actually is. He overheard what I'd said to Bree. Now he's trying to hide the fact that he felt more than he was willing to admit, accusing me of not feeling anything at all when I felt everything all at once.

"You think this meant nothing to me? You think *you* meant nothing to me?"

He shrugs. "It was an act."

"An act. Of course." I force down the lump in my throat. "You were my fake boyfriend, right? Because my real boyfriend wouldn't have ignored my calls when I was alone in a room with a known predator. Do you remember that conversation, Asher? The one when you told me to call you if I was ever alone with Levi? Remember when you told me to trust you? And I did and I called and you didn't answer?"

"I didn't know that was why you were calling."

He won't look at me. A few more tears escape my eyes and I push them away with the heel of my palm. My mascara is most definitely running down my face. I probably look wrecked, but I don't care. Because nothing is as bad as how I feel.

"And you know what the worst part is?" I say when his eyes finally catching mine. "It's not even that you ignored my calls. It's that you knew—that you've *known* and you continue to let him and *your father* get away with it."

He holds my stare and it's the first time I see him—the man I was definitely falling in love with—and it feels real and honest, but I know better. Nothing about what Asher felt about me was real.

We were fake.

"There's a lot you don't know, Olivia," he says, his voice eerily still.

"I'm starting to realize that," I say. "But soon—soon everyone is going to know because I'm going to scream it from the rooftops. And I'm not going to stop until the whole world knows who the real Levi Booker is and the lengths you people went through to make sure no one ever found out."

"Olivia."

"I'm telling Ana."

I give him one last look and it's a long one. I hope he feels what I feel. I hope his skin is crawling. I hope he's afraid to fall asleep tonight.

And when I'm satisfied—when he knows that all the cards are in my hands—I turn around and start walking towards the subway station.

But Asher's not done. He leaves me with three final words.

"Ana already knows."

14

FRANCESCA IS FANNING through a rack of t-shirts while I try not to fall asleep against a floor-length mirror. We're at *Odds & Ends*, my favorite thrift store in Queens, where I'm on a first name basis with the manager. She usually ushers me into the back so I can check out new items before they go on sale. But she's not working today; the assistant manager is. We are not on a first name basis and he never looks up from his issue of *National Geographic* to acknowledge me, which I usually find rude, but today I'm too tired to care.

Long story short: Francesca and I are slumming it with the other bargain shoppers.

"What's your stance on faux-fur?" Francesca asks.

"Love a faux-fur vest," I yawn. "I've been eyeing this purple faux-fur coat at the *Skeleton's Closet* in SoHo. It's children's sized. My boobs are too big for it, but the rest fits fine, so I just won't be able to zip it up. I'm waiting for it to go on sale."

At least I was waiting.

I won't be buying much of anything until I find a new job.

"I, like, never get to wear fun clothes," she laughs. "I have a wardrobe of yoga pants and leotards."

"It must be rewarding, though."

"It is," she says. "It's grueling, but it's the only thing I've ever felt passionate about."

"That's great," I tell her. "You should love what you do, and you're amazing. Honestly, I could watch you for hours. I wish I could move like that."

"You should come to a class!"

"I'm not very graceful. I do my best dancing alone in the kitchen," I laugh. "Or after drinking heavily. Vodka gives me rhythm."

"I'm not opposed to boozy ballet."

"Then sign me up!"

We laugh, but in the back of my head I know there will be no boozy ballet. We no longer have a common denominator. Once Francesca realizes Asher and I broke up, we won't be going on anymore thrifting dates, which is fine, I guess. The ex-girlfriend and the current girlfriend was never a likely friendship.

"We need to find me something to wear tonight," Francesca says, flicking another hanger down the rack.

"Where are you going?"

She looks at me with quizzical eyes and laughs. "The ugly sweater party? At the *Demerci*? Asher said you two were going."

"When?"

"This morning," she says. "I ran into him when I was leaving pilates. He looked a mess, but when I asked, he said you guys would be there."

"Oh."

I try not to get hung up on him looking a mess.

Because him being a mess means he got as much sleep as I did. Up all night. Staring at the ceiling. Wondering how a week could change everything.

It's a strange feeling to be simultaneously angry and heartbroken. Half the time, I don't know if I'm crying because he disappointed me or because I miss him. Sometimes I cry because I'm upset that I'm crying over him.

Most of the time, I cry because I hate that I've been silenced for so long—that I've let men walk all over me. Allowed them to make me uncomfortable. Granted them permission to treat me as less than the person I am. I'm not an object to be used for their gains.

I'm a woman.

And I'm done being bullied.

"Is everything okay?"

"Yeah," I say even though that's an absolute lie. "No, not really."

"Is it Asher?"

I can't tell if she's fishing for information, or if she's generally concerned. I give her the benefit of the doubt. Whatever her intentions were when befriending me don't matter now.

"I don't think we're going to work out."

"What?" she gasps, her eyes widening into tiny oceans of gray. "Why?"

"We're very different."

"I know," she laughs. "That's what makes you guys so great together."

"No, I think we're too different."

Francesca drapes an old Rolling Stones tour t-shirt over her forearm, and gives me a sympathetic smile, like she knows what I'm feeling, like she's been here before.

"Look, I don't want to sound like the ex who thinks she

knows Asher better, but he's been this way for so long that I don't think he knows how to be any other way."

"What way is that?"

"He's closed off and stubborn and crotchety. He has control issues galore. Everything is done on his terms. I know it's exhausting."

She's not wrong. Asher is all those things. But I'm a glass-half-full kind of person, so I never got frustrated with his long list of otherwise negative quirks. I use them to my advantage. I push his buttons. Force him out of his comfort zone. Make him see things a little differently. Sure, he does most things reluctantly with a snarl or a frown, but he does them. He's not incapable of change. And frankly, it's not my job to change him. It has to come from him. He has to want it. I can buy him all the Christmas trees in the world —fill his whole apartment with mistletoe and garland and animatronic reindeers—but ultimately, it's up to him if he decides to keep them up.

"Me and Asher…" Francesca sighs. "We weren't serious at the start. I don't even think we were serious at the end. And I was okay with that at first, but at some point I wanted more than just a physical relationship. And Asher couldn't give that to me, so I had to find it somewhere else—"

"Did you—"

"Cheat on him? Yeah, I did. Because I was frustrated and unhappy. And I know that's not an excuse, but Asher made it so hard to open up. I felt like I couldn't be honest with him."

Asher failed to mention all of this. He'd been so open about his feelings for his father. Why wouldn't he be honest about this? Why couldn't he tell me the truth?

"You're good for him," she says. "And I know that it's a two way street and you have to be happy with the relationship as well, but if your hesitance is stemming from his inability to open up then tell him that. Be honest with him. Because I don't think he wants to lose you."

"How do you know?"

"Because I've never seen him smile the way he does when he looks at you."

* * *

Asher texts me just before noon. Instinctively, I ignore it. I know what he's asking, and I haven't decided if going to this party is a good idea. What's the point of keeping up the charade? He made it clear that we were over. Francesca knows we're having *problems*. I'm still upset about the events that transpired from my night at *Boudoir*. I'm pretty sure the only way tonight will end is with me in tears.

I'm so tired of crying.

Also, I don't have anymore of my expensive eye masks and I can't afford to buy more.

For my skin's sake, I should just stay home and polish off a tube of cookie dough.

But a small part of me feels guilty. Okay, a *big* part of me feels guilty. My need to please everyone is not something that I can fix overnight. It's going to take time to learn how to put my feelings first. And even though I'm angry with Asher, I still miss him. My heart and my head have been battling over this for days. Both are far too stubborn to surrender.

So I find my ugliest sweater and pair it with a skirt and my favorite booties and I finally open Asher's three text messages when I'm on the train to the *Demerci*.

I know I'm the last person you want to hear from, but there's a party tonight at a gallery on the Lower East Side.

I don't know why I told Francesca we'd be there, but you
don't have to show up. I'll understand if you don't.

It starts at 8:00 at the Demerci.

It's ugly sweater casual.

A cloud of smoke greets me in front of the gallery. I
smile tightly at the cluster of cigarette smokers and try not
to breathe as I walk inside.

I've never been afraid of a room full of people. Usually,
I can strike up a conversation with anyone. I love talking.
Aside from ordering take-out, it's my biggest talent. But
tonight I find no comfort in the crowd of strangers. I don't
feel like talking, which probably means I should seek
medical attention immediately.

I don't want to be here.

And that's a shame because I look really cute in my
ugly sweater.

Asher isn't here. Neither is Francesca. I check the text
again. I'm at the right place at the right time. I sigh and
walk over to the open bar. I order a ginger ale with lime.
Tomorrow's the Afternoon of Giving at the children's
hospital. It's not appropriate to be hungover around a
bunch of sick children.

I sip my drink and make my rounds, admiring the
photos taken by Nawaar Qadir. The exhibit, *A Night of
Celebration*, chronicles holiday traditions from around the
world. Quiet glimpses into the lives of people from
Pakistan and Peru and Tanzania and all the places in
between. They're all unique in their own way yet encom-
pass the same message: family. Not every photo is one with
a smile. There are tears and heartbreak and pain. A
woman from Laos is draped over a hospital bed and

clutches her chest in pain. The title is simply *New Year's Day*. Behind her, a man stands with a newborn in his arms. The end of one life and the beginning of a new one. Hope and future. It's beautiful in a tragic way.

Still, the picture leaves me shaken. A lump forms in my throat that I try to force down. I can't cry here, so I put on my brave face, which, recently, has become my only face.

Fake it till you make it, Liv.

Thirty minutes pass quickly. I've walked the whole first floor alone. It's starting to feel like a joke. Francesca doesn't show. Asher stands me up. They're probably laughing over expensive wine as she tells him everything we talked about at the thrift store.

I'm looking at a photo of children in Moscow and deciding what flavor of ice cream to get on my way home when Asher walks in. He's wearing a black sweater with the *Coca-Cola* Santa on it. I'm shocked he attempted to get into the holiday spirit.

I'm more shocked when he holds the door open for Francesca.

They came together? This really is a joke. I can't believe I fell for it.

"Olivia!" Francesca hurries over to me. She has on a red sweater dress with a reindeer pattern, her long legs on display. She's so hot. I want to date her.

"Hey." I force a smile when my eyes catch Asher, who looks exhausted. His hair is tousled, a wayward strand curling down his forehead. A week ago, I would have smiled, kissed his cheek, and brushed his hair from his eyes.

But today we idle in place, neither of us flinching.

"Sorry I'm late," he says quietly. "An accident had 1st Ave backed up."

"It was awful," Francesca adds. "I got out of my cab and walked the rest of the way here."

"You must have been freezing," I say.

"I was," she says. "I need to find something to warm me up."

I'm sure Asher will volunteer.

"Ash, do you want a drink?"

"Yeah."

"Grey Goose and soda?"

He nods and once she walks over to the bar, we're alone.

"I wasn't sure if you'd come," he says.

"Neither was I."

The uncomfortable silence is new. We're all tension. We avoid each other's stare. Asher shoves his hands into his pockets. Rocks on his heels. I eye the door. We're so broken.

"Have you talked to Ana?"

"No," I say, biting the corner of my lip. "We have a meeting tomorrow."

"On a Sunday?"

I shrug. "The gala's on Tuesday. We won't have a chance to talk before then."

Asher nods and takes a slow breath. He looks like he wants to say something, but he doesn't. He swallows and scratches the back of his neck. His eyes land on the floor, avoiding mine.

"This open bar thing is going to be dangerous." Francesca's voice breaks our silence. She hands Asher his drink and smiles. "This is my second drink. I drank the first while he made yours."

"Don't you have a show tomorrow?" Asher asks.

"Not until seven," she says. "Plenty of time to recover."

"I'd be hungover until Christmas if I took advantage of the open bar," I say.

"That sounds like a challenge."

"One I'm usually up for," I laugh, taking a sip of my ginger ale. "Where's Brent?"

Francesca doesn't try to conceal her eye roll as the rim of her glass grazes her lips. "He had better things to do, and by better I mean his cousin invited him to Vegas for the weekend."

Her tone leaves Asher wincing. I can see the war flashbacks in his eyes. He seems very familiar with her current state of aggravation, an annoyance he's clearly bestowed upon her once or twice or seventy million times.

Though, some of it had to have been warranted. She did cheat on him. And cheating is still cheating no matter how emotionally unavailable the other partner is.

"I need a refill," Francesca says. "Anyone else?"

"I'm good," I say.

"I'll take a double," Asher says.

"My kind of man."

It stings.

Her kind of man.

Why would she have cheated on *her kind of man*?

Her kind of man should have been someone she was willing to work with, not someone she would drop for the next *best man.*

Her kind of man should have been enough.

Why am I getting defensive?

I like Francesca. I listened to her reasoning this morning and didn't judge her. Why am I now?

Get a grip, Liv.

I catch Asher staring when I turn back to the pictures. My body goes warm, heat rising up my neck. I hate that he does this to me.

This picture, I decide, is my favorite, and one I would gladly purchase if I had the funds of a billionaire heiress. It's titled *Midnight in Roma.* It's a photo of a little girl, who is looking to the sky in absolute wonder. Snowflakes fall around her, a rare sight in Italy. She's holding her mother's hand. If I could see her mother's face, I imagine she would be smiling too.

"What do you like about it?" Asher's voice startles me.

"She's looking at the snow like it's magic," I say. "It's like this is the most enchanting moment of her life. You can see the grip she has on her mother's hand. She's so happy. Look at her smile."

"It's pretty spectacular."

We stand in silence, both staring at the same picture, sharing the same feelings. It's intimate.

"Olivia—"

"I am already feeling this." Francesca stumbles over to us and hands Asher his drink while she downs her own.

It's a constant loop. Francesca gets a drink. She giggles and laughs with her friends. Even Asher is contributing to the conversation. I melt into the background, which is unusual. I've never melted into the background a day in my life. I thrive on attention.

But tonight I make myself scarce. I slip away from the group unnoticed and make my way to the upstairs gallery. I haven't seen many people up there. I'm hoping to be alone.

The walls are lined with photos of New York City on New Year's Eve. The ball dropping. Couples kissing. Confetti. The aftermath of trash on the ground. An eerily quiet Brooklyn Bridge. A sad woman in an empty subway car. A different story for the same night.

I walk over to a wide arched window that gives a full view of the cobblestone street. A woman walks by pushing a stroller. A couple gets into an argument. A man struggles to parallel park his car.

Like really struggles.

Like really *really* struggles.

"Olivia?"

For the second time tonight, Asher's voice startles me. When I turn around, he holds out a glass to me.

"It's eggnog," he says.

I take it. "Thank you."

I turn back to the window and take a sip. It's spiked heavily with brandy.

"How long has he been trying to park?" Asher asks.

"About ten minutes," I say. "I almost want to go down and help him."

"That would be a blow to his ego."

"Kind of makes me want to do it more."

We shrink back into silence. It's not uncomfortable, but the underlying tension is still there. It's strange to feel this way with him. Our tension has always been sexual.

"I should have answered my phone," Asher says. "I'm so sorry, Olivia. It should have never gone as far as it did—"

"Asher—"

"He'll never touch you again."

"I know that," I say. "It's not me I'm worried about."

"Olivia." He pushes his fingers through his hair. "It's complicated."

"It doesn't seem very complicated to me."

Asher licks his lips. "I promise it's being dealt with, but—"

"There shouldn't be any buts, Asher," I tell him. "There's no gray area. It's black and white. Right and wrong."

"I know—"

"Do you? Because when I decided to go into publicity, I didn't realize this was the kind of industry I was getting myself into. And it's definitely not one I want to

be a part of. I cannot sit back and watch him get away
with this."

"He's not going to."

"And why should I believe you?"

Asher pauses. His lips part as if he's about to give me a
hundred and one different reasons why I should believe
him. Pleading his case with every last breath.

But he doesn't.

His eyes fall to the floor.

"You have absolutely no reason to."

He leaves me alone and I'm stunned into silence. His
honesty hits me like a punch in the gut and another to the
heart. His words were soft and vulnerable. I can still feel
his pain, the most honest he's been with me in days.

He's full of regret.

I'm just not sure about which part.

* * *

It takes me forty-five minutes before I have the courage to
walk downstairs and tell Francesca (and probably Asher
too) that I'm leaving. I pray to God that she doesn't insist
that he leaves with me.

The crowd of people has thinned and as I walk over to
where Francesca is standing with a few girls, I notice that
the photo of the child in the snow has a tag on it. Someone
bought it. I hope it gets a good home. It deserves to be
admired every day in a room with good lighting and high
ceilings.

Francesca's contagious laughter greets me. A smile
appears on my lips at the sound. She's talking with every
part of her body, fluidly moving her hands and her hips,
telling a story through motion. I'm mesmerized. Like I
always am when I'm around her.

"Liv! I thought you left." She throws her arms around me and I can smell the liquor on her.

"I was hiding upstairs," I confess. "But I am heading out now."

She frowns. "Did you have a good time?"

"I did," I say. "The photographs are beautiful. If you speak to Nawaar, tell her the stories she tells are so moving."

Francesca hugs me once more. "I'm so glad you came. I know things are rough right now, but give it time. You're good for each other."

I force my smile despite my quivering lips.

Outside, it's bitterly cold, but the lack of wind makes the temperature bearable. The subway is three blocks away. If there aren't any delays, I should be home in twenty-five minutes, which will give me six hours of sleep before I have to get up for my morning meeting at Ana's house in Brooklyn.

I shove my hands into my coat and tuck my chin into my chest for warmth. And, well, to mask the cigarette smoke clouding the sidewalk. I pass a bar and a high-end shoe store and steps that lead into a designer's showroom.

That's when I stop.

Not because of the dress made of Swarovski crystals in the window, but because of the person sitting on the stoop.

It's Asher. His head lolls on his neck. I can see his brow furrowed, his forehead wrinkling as he stares at his phone. He's plastered.

My head tells me to keep walking.

But my heart…

My heart can't keep her damn mouth shut.

"Asher?"

He looks bewildered when he sees me.

"Hi," he says.

"What are you doing?"

"Sitting."

"I can see that. Why?"

"Because standing is… a lot."

"Are you waiting for a car?"

"I think so?"

"Did you order one?"

"I think so?"

I sigh and take his phone from him. The app should show me where the car is and the estimated wait time.

"Asher, you didn't order a car."

"I didn't?"

"You ordered twelve lemon loaves from a *Starbucks* in Utah."

"We'll never make it there before they close."

I sit down next to him on the cold stone steps and find the Uber app. I order a car for him and give him his phone.

"It'll be here in five minutes."

"The lemon loaves?"

"No, the car."

"Oh," he says. "But what about the lemon loaves?"

"They're in Utah."

He frowns. "That's a shame."

I brace my feet on the step, ready to stand, but I don't move. Leaving him drunk on a stoop feels wrong.

Leaving you alone with Levi was also wrong, my head says.

In his defense, my heart says, *he didn't know she was with Levi.*

He still ignored her call.

He obviously regrets it.

I want to see the receipts.

Look at him!

I'm looking.

"I still have your panties."

My cheeks are already red from the cold, but a heat rises up my neck at Asher's words.

"I washed them," he says. "I'm not some pervert who likes dirty panties."

"I... didn't think you were."

"I haven't washed my sheets, though," he continues. "They still smell like you. Sometimes I wake up and think you're there."

"Asher—"

"I should have been there," he whispers. "He shouldn't have touched you. I would have never let him touch you."

His voice shakes. I think he's going to start crying and I know I'm going to start crying. This isn't how I want the night to end. Crying on a stoop with Asher, because everything that was supposed to be fake is very, *very* real.

When the car pulls up, I help Asher stand. He towers over me, and my heels make it almost impossible to maneuver us both down the few short steps to the curb. I somehow manage to get the door open and shove Asher into the backseat. I'm ready to send him off, but I see him slumped over helplessly. How is he going to get up to his apartment? How is he going to get into bed?

Olivia, my head warns.

Shut up, my heart replies.

I slide in next to him. I don't even have the door shut before I feel his head on my shoulder.

It takes us fifteen minutes to get to his apartment. I get out of the car and pull Asher with me, thanking the driver before we stumble into his building. I've never been more thankful for the security guard in the lobby. He rides the elevator and holds Asher up while I pat him down in an attempt to find his key.

He giggles.

I roll my eyes and find his keys in his coat pocket.

"No, keep doing that," he says.

I shake my head and unlock the door.

"Thank you, Elliot," I say to the security guard. "I can take it from here."

I guide Asher to the stairs of his loft. His couch is preoccupied with half-wrapped Christmas presents, so it's not an option. We take each step slowly.

"C'mon, Ash, just a few more."

"Here's fine."

"I don't think it'll be very comfortable."

He groans, but we make it to the bed. I manage to get his coat off before he tumbles face-first onto the mattress. I pull his boots off next and round the bed to put them back in their rightful place—the bathtub in his bedroom that doubles as a shoe bin.

But, to my surprise, it's empty.

I glance over at Asher, who hasn't moved.

Why did he clean it out? He said a bathtub in the bedroom was impractical. It made better storage. What changed his mind?

I place his shoes on the floor of his closet and force my mind not to wander. It has nothing to do with me and the vivid picture I painted for him of what I would use that tub for.

He did it for himself.

We both know you're lying, my heart says.

"Olivia?" Asher's voice is muffled by his pillows and sheets.

"Yeah?"

"I think I'm in love with you."

15

WILLA LOVERIDGE MAKES spectacular granola balls.

I've eaten five in the past ten minutes in an effort to keep my mouth occupied. God knows the kind of trouble it would get me into if I didn't keep it busy. So I chew and I chew and I chew and I try to grasp that I'm at the Loveridge-Herrera townhouse on a Sunday morning.

Ana is still in her bathrobe.

Willa isn't wearing a bra.

I wish I knew this meeting was pajama-casual.

I wouldn't have put on pants.

"I think I'm in love with you."

I eat another granola ball.

Those are some very big words from a very confusing and very drunk man who ordered twelve lemon loaves from a *Starbucks* in Utah thirty minutes prior to making such a confession. I mean, what kind of man orders twelve lemon loaves when he could order twelve banana-nut loaves? And what kind of man tells me he loves me when he's drunk when he could, I don't know, tell me when he's sober?

I shove another granola ball into my mouth.

I almost ignored Ana's phone call this morning. After getting seventeen minutes of sleep, taking three trains to Brooklyn was the last thing I wanted to do.

But despite Asher's vodka-tonic confession and my whirlwind feelings, we have bigger issues to deal with.

Ana knows about Levi.

She's *known*.

She destroyed Mason Stueck, Willa's slimy ex-boyfriend who plastered her naked pictures all over the internet, so why is she protecting this monster? Why is he so special? Because he's worth millions? Because he's powerful? Because the world's collective heart would break if America's sweetheart turned out to be a special kind of demon?

It doesn't make sense.

There are too many missing pieces.

"There's a lot you don't know, Olivia."

Well maybe someone should start informing me.

"Are you ignoring me?"

My ears perk at the sound of an unmistakably Scottish voice coming from the phone Willa abandoned in favor of ladling waffle batter into an iron.

"I'm trying to," Willa says. "But you didn't get the memo when I left the country."

"Did I also not get the memo last night when you were telling me all the vulgar things—"

Willa drops the ladle into the bowl, batter splashing onto the countertop as she dives to hang up the call with Ollie. Her cheeks burn red when Ana looks over at her from the kitchen table, a spoonful of mashed banana teasing Lily's lips.

"He got dropped on his head a couple times when he was a child," Willa says.

"Mhm," Ana says. "Let's hope those vulgar things include condoms and—"

"*Mom.*"

"It's my job to make things uncomfortable."

"Well, it's not your job to make things uncomfortable for Olivia."

"It's my job to instill professional wisdom in Olivia," Ana says. "That being said: safe sex is great sex and don't keep your read receipts on."

"How profound," Willa says as the waffle iron beeps.

"I'm full of wisdom," Ana says. "Now, please take Lily and your waffle into the other room because Olivia and I have business to tend to."

Willa grumbles under her breath, spooning strawberry compote onto her waffle before rescuing Lily from mashed-banana hell. They disappear into the living room, leaving Ana and me alone.

Ana walks over to where I'm sitting at the breakfast bar, taking control of the waffle iron. There's a plop and a fizzle and she closes the top. She looks calm and cool and collected, which I find bizarre for a woman who is four months pregnant and the mother of a seven-month-old. Not to mention she's protecting a sleazy actor who takes advantage of women. That must be exhausting.

"We have some things to discuss," Ana says. "I'm sorry that we're doing this so informally. I hoped to not be in my pajamas, but you weren't in the office on Friday and I won't be in tomorrow. I figured conversations are always better over waffles."

Normally, I would agree.

But maple syrup and globs of melted butter do little to sugarcoat the acts of a sexual predator.

"I would like to make you a job offer."

"Ana—"

"Social Media Specialist."

"I—"

"It's not going to be with Loveridge & McGowan."

Wait.

What?

"You look very confused."

"That's… an understatement."

The iron chirps and Ana pauses to remove a waffle, plating it before sliding it over to me. I'm not hungry. It feels like there's a pile of bricks sitting in my stomach.

"There are things that are about to happen that will change the company."

"Do these things involve Levi Booker?"

If Ana is surprised by my question, she hides it well. She doesn't flinch. Nor does she look up from the batter she's ladling into the waffle iron.

"Asher told you."

"No," I say. "He won't tell me anything, just that there's a lot I don't know."

"It's complicated."

"Yeah, he said that too."

"Please don't be upset with him," Ana says. "We made a decision not to get anyone involved."

"But I am involved," I say. "I was involved the moment Levi put his hands on me. Just like all those other girls. We're all involved."

"I know," she says, her eyes falling to the counter. "And I will never be able to do enough to make this better."

"You could stop protecting him."

"We're not protecting him." Her voice is sharp. "Believe me, as soon as I found out what was going on, I got someone on Levi's security team to make sure it didn't happen again. Like I said, it's complicated. There are NDAs involved and contracts and a lot of overpaid attorneys who bend all sorts of laws. There's a reason Asher wouldn't let you sign that NDA. It would legally bind you to Levi's team. He's trying to protect you."

I look down at my waffle. It's cold and sad, begging to be soaked in butter and syrup. I feel sick and confused. I'm sad and angry. I feel everything at once. It makes me dizzy.

I don't need to be protected.

I need honesty.

Ana's hand slips over mine, forcing my eyes to meet hers. "I would never protect someone like Levi Booker or River McGowan."

Deep down, I knew that. There had to be something more—something bigger. I shouldn't have doubted her.

And I shouldn't have doubted Asher.

* * *

To: *Loveridge & McGowan Employee Network*
Cc: *Ana Loveridge-Herrera, River McGowan*
From: *Olivia Langley*
Subject: *An Afternoon of Giving*

Don't forget that this Sunday we'll be volunteering at New York Children's hospital's Christmas Extravaganza! The event starts at noon and will run until 4:00 p.m. We'll be decorating gingerbread cookies, making snow globes, and other holiday crafts. There will also be a donation box for toys!

I hope to see everyone there!

Yours truly,
O. Langley
Social Media Intern & Santa's Executive Helper

Loveridge & McGowan International
98 W 52nd St, New York, NY 10019
olivialangley@lmi.com

* * *

"Do you *really* know Santa?"

"Of course I do." It's the easiest lie I've ever told. I sound very convincing. Well, as convincing as a woman with finger puppets on her hand can sound.

"Tell us a secret only Santa would know," a little boy decked out in snowman pajamas says.

I gasp and clutch my chest. Rudolph and Mrs. Claus fall off my fingers. I hope it doesn't traumatize the group of children sitting on the floor around me.

"I can't tell you Santa's secrets," I say before lowering my voice into a whisper. "I'll end up on the Naughty List."

He purses his lips at me as if he's giving my statement some good thought. Maybe I'm not convincing at all.

But then the girl next him nudges his side. "If she tells us, we might end up on the Naughty List too."

Children have the best logic.

The little boy taps his index finger to his lips, clearly pondering his friend's statement. Eventually he shrugs.

"Yeah, you're right. Can I have your finger puppets?"

I laugh and pluck an elf and a penguin from my ring finger and pinky while he scoops up the two that fell on the floor. I leave the kids to create their own show.

The playroom of the New York Children's hospital is glittering with green, red, and gold tinsel. Candy cane and snowman decals cling to the walls, gaggles of blindfolded children play pin the ornament on the tree and pin the candle to the menorah. I smile when they fumble over each other. Their laughter is exactly the medicine the doctor ordered. I know what it's like being stuck in a hospital room throughout the holidays. If I can make it a little better for them, then that's a Chrismukkah miracle in itself.

"Look at that angel!" I glance over the shoulder of a little girl with a pink crayon in her hand.

"She's a rebel," Emanuel says as he colors in his picture of a sleigh. "Dominique and I decided that angels should be able to color their hair pink too."

"And she's got purple streaks!" Dominique says.

"She certainly does," I laugh. "She really pulls them off too."

"Manny says he's gonna hang this up in his office."

I squeeze Emanuel's shoulders. "Maybe we can get a few more."

"Of course," Dominique says. "I'm an artist. This reindeer is going to be green."

"That's very progressive," I say. "Keep up the good work."

I skirt through the room and watch Alba and her son decorate cookies with two little boys. Not every child was cleared to attend the party, so the hospital made sure to send cookies to the rooms of the kids who couldn't come. But for the kids that could make it, they have piles of sugar cookies to decorate with globs of royal icing and plenty of sprinkles.

Along with a craft table, there's also a holiday card station and an area where the kids can watch an endless stream of holiday movies with bowls upon bowls of popcorn and cups of hot chocolate with gooey marshmallows and whipped cream.

And as happy as the children look, their parents look even happier. They're all on a physically and emotionally draining journey. A few hours away from the machines and routine checks? It's priceless to them. Anything to get away from those same four walls and a ticking clock. A breath of fresh air. A new kind of hope. For a moment, they can forget why they're here.

I would give them a million of these moments if I could.

Because I know what it feels like when you can't forget —when you can't escape the room and the machines and the revolving door of doctors and nurses and the clock that's a constant reminder that time is slowly running out.

I spot a little girl sitting by herself at the greeting card table and take it upon myself to plop down on the tiny stool next to her. I don't know why everyone else is complaining about them. I fit on them just fine.

"Hi," I say.

"Hi!" She looks up and smiles. "I'm Valentina. What's your name?"

"Olivia"

"Did you get your appendix taken out too?"

"I got my tonsils out when I was seven," I tell her. "Did you get your appendix taken out?"

"Yeah," she sighs. "Then I got infected."

"Are you feeling better?"

"A little bit," she says. "My nurse, Maya, says I might be able to go home tomorrow."

"That's exciting!"

"My mom says I should make her a card to say thank you," Valentina says. "She sneaks me extra popsicles and Jell-O cups."

"I think she would love a card."

"Will you help me? Sometimes I don't spell words right."

"Of course."

Her piece of red construction paper reads *Marry Kris-mas*. I smile.

"Is that right?"

"Almost," I say. "But let's start over."

She frowns for a moment, but then shrugs and grabs a piece of green paper. I spell Merry Christmas for her, but I don't correct her when she writes her *R*s and *S*s backwards. They give the card character, and Valentina looks too proud for me to burst her bubble.

"*Olivia!*"

I turn around at the sound of a familiar voice and I'm unable to fight the smile stretching my lips.

Chloe is standing in the doorway wearing a metallic pink bubble jacket and matching snow boots, her curly hair tangled into two puffs on the top of her head. Behind her, Asher idles hesitantly, like he's not sure if coming was a good idea.

But Chloe bounds in fearlessly, making up his mind for him. They're staying whether he wants to or not.

"Chloe." When she throws herself into my arms, the wind is knocked out of me in the form of a laugh.

"I thought you'd be at Uncle Asher's this morning, but I got there and it was just him." She frowns. "Where were you? How come you didn't get breakfast with us? Uncle Asher let me have *two* chocolate chip banana muffins *and* hot chocolate with *extra* marshmallows and caramel."

"No wonder you have so much energy," I say. "I want you to meet my friend, Valentina."

Chloe looks at the girl next to me. "Hi! What's your favorite color? Do you like Shopkins? What about Ninja Turtles? I met Spiderman once. He smelled like bologna and charged Mommy ten dollars to take a picture with me."

Valentina looks overwhelmed for about two seconds. "I met Mickey Mouse once!"

"Me too!" Chloe sits down on the stool next to her. "Can I use your orange crayon?"

Childhood friendships are so simple and innocent. Good thing we're in a hospital because my heart is about to swell and burst, which I'm pretty sure isn't good for my cardiovascular system.

Out of the corner of my eye, I see Asher's shadow. He pulls out his own stool. He's too tall. His knee knocks the table, sending a green and yellow crayon onto the floor. Chloe scowls at him.

I, however, can barely look him in the eyes. We give each other fleeting glances. How much of last night does he remember? I'm not sure I want him to remember as much as I do. How do we come back from that? Seven words. Twenty-one letters. They changed everything.

"Thank you," he finally says. "For bringing me home."

Okay, so he remembers last night.

"It was the least I could do," I say. "Couldn't just leave you on that stoop. Who knows how many more lemon loaves you would have ordered."

"What?"

Okay, so he remembers *some* of last night.

"There's a *Starbucks* in Utah that you should probably avoid."

"I'll try to remember that on the off chance I ever go to Utah."

"I hear the skiing is good. Lots of trails to hike. Tons of national parks. It's very outdoorsy."

"Olivia," he says, forcing my eyes to meet his. "I shouldn't have said it."

"Right." I swallow and look away. "You were drunk. You didn't know what you were saying. You don't have to apologize."

"I shouldn't have said it when I was drunk."

When I look back at him, his gaze is unwavering. It hasn't left me.

"When should you have said it?"

"I don't know," he says. "It just shouldn't have been last night and I shouldn't have been drunk."

I don't know how to respond to that. Does that mean he meant it? Is he in love with me? If so, he has a very strange way of showing it.

"Did you talk to Ana?" he asks.

"Yeah."

"Did she tell you?"

"Not everything," I say. "Just that it's complicated, but you're not protecting him and you two made a decision not to get anyone else involved."

"The last thing I wanted was to bring you into this," he says. "If I answered my phone—"

"If you answered your phone, I would still be involved," I tell him. "I was involved as soon as I went into that room with him."

"But if I didn't act like a dickhead when you came to my apartment—"

"You were upset," I tell him. "We can play the what-if game for the rest of our lives, but it doesn't change anything. What's done is done. We just have to move forward. It doesn't do anyone any good rehashing the past."

He nods. "Where does that leave us?"

"I have no idea."

I don't exactly know how to move forward. There's still a huge puzzle piece that's missing. Do I just trust that he and Ana are taking care of it? Does he want a real relationship? Because I can't do that if he plans to keep more secrets from me. I need honesty.

And someone to kiss me on demand.

"Olivia, do you think Maya will like a Santa sticker?"

"I think she'll love one," I tell her.

"Who's Maya?" Chloe asks.

"My nurse. I'm making her a Christmas card."

"Olivia's mom is a nurse! She made up the Bandaid Dance," Chloe says before looking at me. "Can I make her a card?"

My heart slips into the pit of my stomach and the smile on my lips falters just enough for Asher to notice.

"Of course you can," I say. "She would love that."

"What's her name?"

"Charlotte." It comes out as a whisper.

"Does she like glitter?"

"Who doesn't love glitter?"

"One time Uncle Asher let me put glitter eyeshadow on him. It was pink."

"And I had to scrub my face for three days," he mumbles.

Chloe and Valentina giggle.

"I'm going to grab you guys some hot chocolate. I think they have peppermint."

"Extra whipped cream!" Chloe says.

"And marshmallows!"

I slide off my stool and catch Asher's eyes once more before I walk over to where Emanuel is standing near the refreshment table, two chocolate chip cookies in his hand and a few feathers glued to his fingers.

"Was that as painful for you as it was for me to watch?"

"What?"

"You and Asher and your torrid love affair."

I glance back and watch as Asher helps Valentina spell a word.

"It's complicated."

I almost choke on that statement. It's such a cop out. I'm ashamed of myself.

"Aren't most things complicated? Easy isn't really fulfilling."

"That's not totally true," I say. "Refrigerated cookie dough is easy and very fulfilling. Autocorrect. Listening to your favorite song. Taking a walk. Eating an entire pizza. Very easy. Very fulfilling."

"You're nuts"

"Probably."

"Speaking of nuts…"

I place three gingerbread men and sugar cookie on a plate when Emanuel's voice trails off. I look in the direction he is and turn away quickly when I see Bree.

"Who invited the Grinch?" he asks.

"Everyone was invited."

"Surely, she should have realized that didn't include her," he says. "She's going to frighten the children. Haven't they been through enough?"

I stifle a laugh as the familiar florals of Bree's perfume hit me.

"Bree," Emanuel says tightly. "You realize this is an event to help children, not eat them, right?"

"Kids love me."

"Because you lure them to a gingerbread house in the forest built of candy canes and gumdrops?"

"I'm offended that you think I'd step foot in a forest."

"God forbid you ruin those knock-off Gucci loafers."

"First of all, they're not knock-offs, they're vintage. Chrissy Teigen wore the same pair to the Thanksgiving parade," she says. "Second of all, I would *never* wear them outside."

"Because you're afraid one of your fashion friends will call you out for wearing knock-off Gucci loafers?"

"You're an awful person."

Emanuel bites the head off a gingerbread man. "Sometimes, but mostly I'm just tired of your bullshit. It was funny at first, but honestly, you're not as untouchable as you think. I don't care who you're fucking."

Bree's eyes bug out. Emanuel? He just shrugs. Me? I choke on air. This is not the time nor the place to have this kind of conversation. There are children writing letters to Santa. Today is about yuletide cheer. Not checking off Bree's trysts on her workplace Naughty List.

"Is everything okay over here?" Asher's voice trickles into my ear. I can feel the heat of his body against my back, but he's not touching me.

"Everything's wonderful," Bree says. "We were just talking about relationships in the office. Asher, what's your stance on sleeping with interns? What about interns sleeping with clients?"

"Don't bring them into this," Emanuel says.

"So it's just okay for me to get slandered?"

"What exactly has Olivia done to you? Except pick up your slack?"

"Right." Bree laughs. "Precious Olivia can do no wrong. The office sweetheart. Asher's plaything. A notch in Levi Booker's bedpost. Tell me, Liv, have you signed that NDA yet?"

I don't know where any of this is coming from, but I suspect there's more going on with Bree than she lets on.

"Bree, you should go," Asher says. "You're upset with the wrong people."

"Is that what you think?"

Tears brim her eyes. I've never seen Bree cry before. It's not something that was on my list of sights to see. What kind of person wants to see someone cry? Not me. I'd rather comfort someone.

But I don't think Bree wants a hug right now.

I'm pretty sure if I put my arms anywhere near her, she'd strangle me.

"Bree—"

"Fuck you, Olivia," she whispers.

She leaves as quickly as she came. We stand in stunned silence, the chorus of *Frosty the Snowman* playing in the background. This must be how the tiny people in snow globes feel when they get shaken up.

"Well, I certainly enjoyed watching the Grinch trying to steal Christmas," Emanuel says. "I'm gonna go find something stronger to put in this hot chocolate."

Asher watches as he walks away before turning back to look at me.

"You okay?"

"Never better," I laugh. "I don't know why she suddenly hates me so much."

"Jealousy will do that to a person."

"Why would she be jealous of me?" I ask. "She lives in an apartment in Greenwich Village. Her parents are television producers. She met Oprah. I sleep in a bedroom with no heat, have seventy-five thousand dollars in student loans, and eat cereal for dinner."

"I don't think her jealousy stems from material things," he says. "You're a good person, Olivia. Money can't buy that."

A warm and fuzzy feeling sends tingles through my body. It's familiar—the same feeling I got when I spent the night with him.

"I thought I was a pain in the ass?"

"You are," he says. "But that doesn't make you any less of a good person."

"I appreciate that." I smile. I forgot how nice it feels to smile with him. "I don't think Bree is bad—"

"Uncle Asher!" Chloe slides between us.

"Indoor voice, darling."

"Valentina's nurse says she has to go rest, but we can go read her a story," she says. "Can you help me sound out the big words?"

Asher laughs. "Yeah, I'll be right there."

"Olivia, you can come too!"

I smile. "I have to go supervise the craft table."

"Okay," she says and thrusts a piece of red paper at me. "This is for your mom."

I see the sticker of an angel and try to keep my composure. "She's going to love it."

Chloe smiles so big that her entire face lights up and then she tugs on Asher's hand. "Let's go! I already decided we're reading *The Polar Express*."

As Chloe drags him out of the playroom, I open the card.

Merry Christmas, Charlotte! Thank you for teaching Olivia the Bandaid Dance. I hope Santa brings you a new bike.

Love,
Chloe Elise Fisher-Walton and Uncle Asher

I don't get a chance to cry.

Someone starts screaming about feathers that somehow got glued to their face.

* * *

After scrubbing purple finger paint off my hands, I head for the nurses station to see if they need help passing out the special goody bags to the children who couldn't make it to the party. I get halfway there before something in room 513 catches my eye.

Chloe is sitting on Asher's lap, *The Polar Express* open in front of them. She drags her pointer finger across the page, repeating each and every word before announcing a very proud, "the end!"

Valentina is already asleep, but that doesn't stop Chloe from smiling.

"I did such a good job," she says. "I should be a professional reader."

"I thought you wanted to drive fire engines?"

"I can do both," she says. "Will you give the nurse my phone number so I can talk to Valentina again?"

"Of course."

"She has a baby brother," Chloe says. "I'm gonna tell Mommy and Mama that I want one too."

Asher laughs and helps her into her jacket. When Chloe races out of the door, they catch me eavesdropping.

"Olivia, were you spying on us?" Chloe asks.

"Not very well," I say. "I got caught."

"It's okay," she says. "Now you get to walk us to the elevator. Uncle Asher is taking me to see the swans in Central Park. Sometimes they attack each other. Do you want to come? Uncle Asher will buy you a hot dog."

"Can I take a raincheck?"

"It's not raining, silly!"

Asher smiles. "It's a saying."

"Can I save the invitation for another day?" I clarify.

"Why can't you come today? Do you not like watching swans attack each other? Sometimes they chase people. That's funny too. I promise you'll have a good time. What if Uncle Asher buys you two hot dogs *and* honey-roasted nuts?"

"Chloe," Asher sighs. "Olivia might have other plans."

"With who?" She looks up at me. "I thought Uncle Asher was your boyfriend. Do you have two boyfriends? Or a girlfriend? A boyfriend *and* a girlfriend?"

"I have a big day tomorrow," I tell her. "We're setting up for a gala at the museum."

"Is that like a ball? The ones princesses go to?"

"Sort of," I laugh.

"Are you going to wear a pretty dress?"

"I plan to."

Chloe looks up at Asher. "Will you take a picture of her so I can see?"

His cheeks flush. "That's up to Olivia."

Chloe turns to me, grinning.

"I'll make sure you get a picture."

Chloe squeals and grabs my hand. "I'm so excited!"

Calling it a walk to the elevator is an understatement. She *drags* me there. While we wait in the doorway for Asher to give the nurses Chloe's information, she tells me about the swans at the park. There are three of them— Hercules, Angel Eyes, and George Stephanopoulos. Hercules was married to Angel Eyes, but Angel Eyes left him for George Stephanopoulos, so Hercules bit off a piece of George's wing. I don't know if she has a very wild imagination, or if I should call animal control.

"All set," Asher says when he comes over to us. "The nurse will give your phone number to Valentina's mom."

Chloe smiles slowly. Her eyes shift up and then back to us. Her smile grows.

"Are you going into sugar shock?" Asher asks.

"You're standing under a mistletoe," she sings. "We all know what *that* means."

Asher takes a breath but doesn't let it out. He's a good talker. He'll get himself out of this somehow. He'll tell Chloe it's not appropriate. That she can't expect us to kiss just because we're standing under a mistletoe. It's trite. Cliche. This isn't a *Hallmark Channel* movie.

This morning I wasn't sure if I ever wanted to kiss Asher again. His drunken confession left me confused and his sober admission just puzzled me more.

But I know one thing. I miss him and that has to mean something.

So I lift myself onto my tippy toes and catch Asher's eyes before I kiss his cheek.

And then, much to my surprise, he turns his head and his lips capture mine.

To: *Loveridge & McGowan Employee Network*
Cc: *Ana Loveridge-Herrera, River McGowan*
From: *Olivia Langley*
Subject: *Winter Wonderland Gala!*

At the Metropolitan Museum of Art we have an authentic Japanese sushi bar
And we can pretend we're super bougie celebrities
We'll have lots of fun with all the paintings
And if you knock one down, you'll probably get arrested

We'll dance and we'll sway, the influencer way
Walkin' to the Winter Wonderland Gala

That's right! Tonight is the night! Join your favorite clients and least favorite colleagues at our Winter Wonderland Gala at the *Metropolitan Museum of Art*! We're going to have a holly jolly good time!

Yours truly,

O. Langley
Social Media Intern & Santa's Executive Helper
Loveridge & McGowan International
98 W 52nd St, New York, NY 10019
olivialangley@lmi.com

* * *

JOEY'S FLIGHT leaves in three hours, but her sense of urgency doesn't exceed how fast she can spoon globs of peanut butter into her mouth. She's still in her bathrobe. Her carry-on is empty. She hasn't looked away from the episode of *90210 Prep* that's on the TV. I'm pretty sure she hasn't blinked in seventeen minutes.

"Don't you have a car coming in an hour?"

"Yes."

I glance up at her from where I'm sitting on the floor before returning my attention back to my reflection in the mirror I'm holding. My eyelids are glittery and so is our rug.

"Are you going to fly to Oslo without your bra and panties on?"

"Wouldn't be the first time."

I snort and pick up my mascara. The gala is also in three hours, but unlike Joey, I'm almost ready. Not because I feel like being exceptionally early for once in my life, but because Asher's picking me up and that thought alone has made me *exceptionally* nervous.

I got the text before any of my alarms went off, which meant he was getting as much sleep as I was.

Asher
Can I pick you up tonight?

Even though I knew my answer as soon as he asked, I couldn't muster a reply until my final alarm went off.

Olivia
As long as you bring me a latte.

Asher
I can't promise they'll make it right.

Olivia
I'm not as fussy as some people.

Asher
Are you insinuating that liking my coffee a certain way makes me fussy?

Olivia
Of course not.
I'm telling you that makes you fussy.

Asher
I'm rethinking offering to pick you up.

Olivia
I'll see you at 8:00.

A few text messages and I was wired, which meant I voluntarily went to a barre class with Joey before the sun came up. My energy lasted until my third *relevé plié*. I was not made to be a nimble ballerina. I feigned a pulled muscle and went to the bagel shop across the street.

Before I could stop myself, I ordered a double-toasted

cinnamon raisin bagel with extra cream cheese. It was my auto-response whenever I walked into such an establishment. If I walked across the street, I would have surely ordered the *right* coffee that the barista would make the *wrong* way. But I didn't. I sat at a table by the window, watching the snow flurrying against the sunrise, and ate the grossest bagel in existence.

Can I really love a guy who insists on eating his bagel that way? It seems unlawful. Unholy. He needs to go beg for forgiveness. Maybe get exorcised. The devil is clearly wreaking havoc on his soul.

Possibly mine too.

Because I still love the absolute weirdo.

And that absolute weirdo kissed me.

And I haven't stopped thinking about it.

"What are your plans when you get to Oslo?"

Joey looks at me and then at the mascara wand I totally didn't steal out of her makeup bag. "I have a photoshoot that will probably give me frostbite and hypothermia because apparently print-ads for snow boots require models in bikinis, and then I'm meeting my parents in Copenhagen for Christmas with my grandmother and her girlfriend."

"Sounds fun," I say. "Minus the potential frostbite and hypothermia."

Joey shrugs. "Honestly, I already have a headache. I have twenty cousins and none of them know what an indoor voice is. I'm already trying to come up with an emergency plan to get me out quick—oh, you could call me and tell me the apartment is on fire!"

"I feel like that's not something we should joke about," I say. "Our smoke alarm doesn't work."

"Even better!" she says. "Our apartment is on fire and you're in the hospital for smoke inhalation."

"Carbon monoxide poisoning is exactly what I wanted for Christmas."

"See, we both win," she says. "Call me on Christmas. The airport will be dead. I'll be able to get a flight out. I bet they'll upgrade me."

"You're a terrible person," I laugh. "Don't you want to see your family? That's what the holidays are about."

Joey scoffs. "I would much rather be on an island in the sand with a couple magazines and a lot of cocktails—oh, maybe I'll fly to Ibiza instead."

"Nothing says Merry Christmas quite like tan lines and the blistering sun."

"It sounds amazing." Joey throws her head against a pillow, a dreamy smile flickering over her lips. It's like she's already there, drunk off fruity drinks and soaking in the sun. "You can come if you want."

"To Ibiza?" I laugh, capping the tube of mascara.

"Yeah," she says. "Or you can come to Copenhagen too, if you want—if you don't already have plans for Christmas."

"I don't."

"You're not going to spend it with Asher?"

"Oh." I swallow. "No, I'll probably just spend it here. Or, I don't know, maybe I'll look into helping at a shelter."

"The offer still stands."

"I really appreciate it."

But I can't afford a trip to Copenhagen or Ibiza. I can barely afford an Uber to the Upper East Side. Also, I don't want to impose on anyone's holiday traditions.

"I really should get ready, but…" Joey sighs at the TV. "Maritza is about to confront Keegan about taking Paisley to winter formal."

"She slaps him."

"Olivia! Spoilers!"

"Sorry," I say, swiping bronzer over my cheeks.

"I'm not surprised," Joey says. "I worked with Maritza's sister, Margarita, on a shoot last year and she was a nightmare. Crazy must run in the family."

"Anything to get those views."

"Don't I know it," she says. "Speaking of disgusting celebrities, how are things on the Levi front?"

"Complicated," I sigh. "Ana and Asher are handling it. I'm not really sure what that means, but they don't want me involved."

"You're already involved."

"That's what I told Asher," I say. "But I'm learning to pick my battles."

"I shredded another NDA while you were in the shower," she says. "If it doesn't get handled soon, I'm sure you'll be getting a court summons for Christmas."

The only person getting summons to court should be Levi.

"I'll bring it up to Asher again," I say. "He's picking me up tonight."

Joey lifts a brow but quickly shakes her head and laughs. I don't need to ask. I know what she's thinking.

"*That lasted long.*"

In my defense—

Who am I kidding? I can't defend myself. I'm the girl who constantly loses the battles of heart versus head. At this point, Asher could smile at me and I'd melt into a puddle of Olivia goo.

He kissed me.

Underneath the mistletoe.

If I was on my bed, I'd be rolling around, screaming into my pillow, like I did all night.

Get a grip, Olivia.

You're twenty-two—a mature adult, not a love-sick teenager.

"Olivia?"

"Yeah?"

"You okay? Thought I lost you there for a minute."

I try to think of something to say, but my head is filled with visions of Asher in a suit.

I fall back against the rug and sigh.

* * *

"My car's here!"

I don't get to say goodbye before the door slams shut, so I turn my attention back to my reflection in the mirror —lacy strapless black bra and a pair of matching cheeky panties. I put on a silky light blue dress that gives off just enough cleavage and stops right above my knee. I twist and turn and frown.

Panty lines.

I take off the dress and look in the mirror again.

Not wearing underwear to a work event is totally appropriate, right?

A sharp knock cuts through the apartment.

I sigh.

Joey probably forgot something. Her keys, most likely. I'm not surprised. She spent five very frantic minutes running around the apartment. I can't believe she remembered herself.

It's a very brisk walk to the door. I shiver as my feet touch the cold floor. I should have turned on the space heater, but it's too late now. It takes forever to get this place warm and I'm leaving soon.

"Do you think I need to wear panties?" I'm asking the question before I get the door open.

It's not Joey.

Asher has his back to me, his hands shoved into his coat pockets. When he turns around, he's startled. Rightfully so. His eyes double as they skate—rather slowly—up my body.

I flush all over, suddenly shy in front of the man who has seen me in less. The man who has had his tongue in my mouth and his mouth on my breasts. We've already been up close and personal.

"Yes," he says stiffly. "You need to wear panties."

"Do you want to see the dress before you decide?"

"Nope," he says. "I just want you to keep your underwear on."

Well.

That ruins my entire outfit.

I sigh and step aside to let him in. He's hesitant but eventually follows me, closing the door behind him.

"You're early," I say, walking towards my room.

When I glance back, I catch him staring at my ass. He blushes.

"I thought there'd be more traffic."

I hum and convince myself it was because he couldn't wait to see me.

"Just give me a minute," I tell him. "I'm almost ready."

My door clicks behind me and I resist the urge to bang my head against it. This isn't how I envisioned the night beginning.

It's not even how I envisioned it ending.

A kiss goodnight, sure.

But I had no plans to show Asher what was or wasn't underneath my dress.

Deciding against the light blue dress, I fan through my rack of clothes. I find a navy midi dress with a v-neckline and short lace sleeves. The skirt has enough of a flare that no one would question whether or not I was wearing panties.

"Where was Joey going in such a rush?" Asher asks from the living room.

"Airport."

"Where's she going?" he asks.

"Norway for work," I say. "And then Copenhagen to spend Christmas with her family."

"And you're staying here for the holiday?"

"I am." I pull my dress over my head.

"Why aren't you going home?"

I catch my reflection in the mirror. My makeup looks fantastic. I'm not about to ruin it with the threat of tears, so I ignore his question and continue to twist and turn towards the mirror to get a better look at my back. If barre class taught me anything, it's that I'm not flexible enough to do up my own zipper. "Ash?"

Silence.

"Asher?"

"Yeah, sorry, do you know that your neighbor sells electronics out of the trunk of his car? I'm watching him right now. He's not very stealthy."

"Oh, yeah, that's Mark," I say. "He sells other things too. Last week he gave me a really good deal on a toaster."

"Was it stolen?"

"I'm not sure. I didn't want to ask," I laugh. "Can you come help me?"

"I'm no good with makeup," he says. "Chloe says I need to watch YouTube tutorials."

I stifle another laugh. "It's not makeup related."

My bedroom door opens slowly, Asher's head peeking through the frame. Our eyes meet in the reflection of the mirror.

"Can you zip me up?"

He holds my stare for a moment that's long enough for my body to erupt in tiny bumps. I hate that he has this effect on me—that all he has to do is look at me and I'm gone. I'm not a person. I'm a hormonal reaction.

Pull it together, Liv.

He's a step too close. I can feel the heat from his body radiating against my back, and I have to bite back the urge to shiver when I feel his thumb brush against my skin. Through the mirror, his eyes stay locked on mine. And for some reason, this feels more intimate than fooling around on his couch did.

"All set," he whispers but makes no move to put distance between us.

"Do I look okay?"

"You look beautiful."

I feel a heat creep up my neck again and I break our stare as the blush reaches my cheeks. "We promised Chloe a picture."

"I believe that request was only for you."

"I'm sure she wants to see how handsome her uncle looks in his suit."

"I highly doubt that," he says. "She's going to give me a *Queer Eye* critique before telling me to change."

"She has a lot of opinions for a six-year-old," I say. "But that's not a bad thing."

"She's definitely her mothers' daughter."

I grab my phone and aim the camera at the mirror. "Smile."

"I'd rather not."

I elbow him. "*Smile.*"

* * *

When we get to the museum, Asher helps me out of my coat.

"I'll make sure they don't call animal control on this," he says.

"That's mean," I say. "Do you hear me criticizing your shoes?"

"My shoes are Saint Laurent and cost fifteen hundred dollars. Your jacket looks like a poodle got the electric chair."

"But it only cost seven dollars at a thrift store."

"Which was seven dollars too much."

"Remember forty minutes ago when you said I looked beautiful?"

"You do look beautiful," he says. "You also look like an electrocuted poodle."

I scoff. "You really know how to make your fake ex-girlfriend feel special."

He pauses for a moment, his face falling in the slightest way. He recovers quickly but not fast enough for me not to notice.

Fake ex-girlfriend.

I don't know why I said it, but what other way was there to describe it? If the feelings weren't fake, what does that make us? Coworkers who casually kissed? And spooned? And put their mouth on the other's boobs? I'm not sure there's a proper way to classify that sort of relationship.

"I'll meet you inside," Asher says before walking over to the coat check.

I sigh.

Good going, Liv.

You ruined what little progress you made.

Inside, the lobby is sparkling. Tiny white lights are draped over bare branches, illuminating the room like the winter wonderland I envisioned. Soft piano notes of Christmas classics sing in the background. I've been staring at these walls for weeks straight, but being here at night with a crowd of people transports me to an entirely different world. It's magical. I take pictures from every angle, so I don't forget.

Behind me, I feel the presence of another person, and when their hand grazes my lower back, I turn warm all over it.

It's Asher.

Well, I assume it's Asher until their cologne wafts around me. It's all too familiar, but not the soft earthy scents of wood and vanilla and sage that he uses.

"Just the girl I was looking for."

My stomach turns when his lips lower to my ear. "Get your hands off of me, Levi."

"I want to talk," he says. "We have some unfinished business."

"We have nothing to talk about," I snap and pull away from him. "Get your hands off me before I make a scene."

"Don't be like this, Livi," he whispers, his lips pressed to the crown of my head. "Where's the girl who was ready to drop her panties for me the first day we met?"

"She realized how vile you are."

"Ouch," he laughs. "That hurt."

I jam my foot down on his.

"*Bitch*—"

"Yeah, and you better not forget it."

His eyes catch mine in a flare of rage. If the room wasn't crowded with people, he wouldn't have given up so easily.

"This isn't over."

"Yes, it is," Asher says tightly. He's standing behind Levi with a stone-cold expression on his face.

Levi rolls his eyes. "This doesn't involve you, Asher."

"You can contact Olivia's lawyer if you have something to say," he says. "Her name is Vivian Fisher-Walton."

I have a lawyer?

I'm pretty sure I can't even afford a free consultation.

"Sharing a lawyer?" he laughs. "I didn't realize you two had gotten so serious. Is it an open relationship? Because I'm pretty sure Olivia had her tongue in my—"

"You need to leave," Asher says. "Now."

"Is that any way to speak to a client, Asher?" he asks. "Your father personally invited me."

"Then go bother him."

A grin flickers over Levi's lips before his eyes catch mine. "I'll be seeing you, Livi."

"Yeah, in hell."

"Feisty," he says. "You must be fun in—"

"*Go*," Asher snaps.

Eventually, he does. Asher keeps his eyes on him until he disappears into the wings of the museum for only the artwork to judge him.

"Are you okay?" Asher asks.

No.

I'm not.

And I won't be until Levi is stopped.

"I don't want him to hurt someone else," I say.

"He's not going to."

I don't ask him to elaborate. I know he's not going to. I just have to trust that Asher and Ana know what they're doing.

Because God knows I don't.

* * *

I'm holding a mistletoe to *Perseus with the Head of Medusa* while Emanuel takes a rather suggestive selfie with Perseus' lower regions.

"Talk about a work of art," he says, scrolling through his camera roll. "I'm making this my Christmas card next year. *Abuelita* is gonna have to light twelve candles for my soul."

"I'm sure that's exactly what she wants for Christmas," I laugh.

We walk back to the party before security throws us out for being inappropriate. Getting banned from *the Met* is not something I have on my bucket list. I don't want to ruin my chances of being invited to all the super elite galas that are definitely in my future.

"So on a scale of one to ten, what do you think are the odds I'm gonna get hired after this internship?" Emanuel asks as we cross into the Great Hall where Winter Wonderland is taking place.

"Ten, definitely," I say. I don't want to tell him Ana already offered me a position. But I can't see Ana not offering Emanuel one too. He works hard, stays late, and always refills his staplers. That's the kind of employee I'd want on my team.

"Well, in the unlikelihood that Bree gets hired, I'm requesting a desk change."

"River seems to like her," I say.

"Yeah, because she's sucking his dick on the regular."

I desperately try to shake that mental image out of my head.

I need to bleach my brain.

Emanuel ditches me for the sushi bar, mumbling something about how he's going to eat enough spicy tuna rolls to turn himself into a fish. I appreciate his dedication, but the thought of eating that much sushi makes me sick. I'd rather take my chances with the make-your-own-crêpe station. All you can eat Nutella? Yes, please.

Before I can put myself in a chocolate-hazelnut coma, my phone buzzes from the home it's made in my bra. I glance around to make sure no one is watching before I reach in to grab it. The last thing I want is to get a notice from HR about fondling myself at a company event.

Asher
I have to run over to the office.
Save me at least ONE Nutella crêpe.

Olivia
That's an awfully big demand.
I might be inclined to follow through if you bring me some of the expensive chocolate from your desk.

Asher
I don't have any in my office.
But I have some at my apartment.

Olivia
Are you trying to get me to come home with you?

Asher
What kind of man bribes a woman with chocolate?

Olivia
A smart one.

Asher
In that case…

"You're blushing."

I look up from my phone to see Willa grinning down at me. She towers over me on a normal day, but when you add in five inch heels, I need a ladder to meet her eyes.

"I was just… adding to my Instacart order."

"Damn, those delivery fees must really get you going," she laughs.

"On the contrary," I say. "It's the *free* delivery promo codes that do it for me."

"Okay, I feel that," she says. "You planned a really amazing party."

I smile. "Thanks, I just played a small part."

"I've been coming to these things for, like, ever and there has never been a cupcake bar," she says. "That was all you."

"I mean, I take dessert pretty seriously."

"As everyone should," Willa laughs.

She talks my ear off about how Ollie is a stage-five clinger and how she not-so-secretly misses him. The only reason she hasn't caught a flight back to London is because she doesn't want to miss Lily's first Christmas.

To be young and in love!

As if I'm not young and kinda in love.

Willa eventually ditches me when she gets a call from Ollie, so I find myself standing at the crêpe station with a group of children, who are all somehow taller than me. I hold an empty plate against my chest as I wait *patiently* for my turn. I take a quick sweep of the room, mostly to make sure Levi isn't anywhere near me.

He's not.

But I do see Bree sneak off, her metallic gold dress reflecting off the Christmas lights. We haven't spoken since she stormed out of the children's hospital. She called in sick yesterday and today.

I'm trying to pretend it doesn't bother me, but it does. All I ever wanted was to be her friend. And I thought we were... for a while. I'm still not sure what happened, but I have a hunch that it runs deeper than my relationship with Asher.

"Olivia," Ana's voice is rushed and distant, like she's not really here. "Have you seen Asher?"

"He ran back to the office."

"Oh, okay," she says. "When you see him, can you let him know I'm looking for him?"

"Of course."

She looks distressed and that's not good for pregnancy, so I take my two Nutella crêpes and head to the exit after begging the caterer for some aluminum foil.

After spending the past few days sulking about my short spout of unemployment, I'm happy to be back in the chaos of last-minute shoppers. I offer smiles to those who bump into me. I stop to admire the storefronts. Maybe, *just maybe*, I'm trying to delay my arrival to the office.

Me and Asher... we're still in a weird place. Are we or aren't we? We haven't had time to have the conversation. We had a chaste kiss yesterday. He saw me in my underwear today. He basically invited me back to his apartment...

And I'd be lying if I said I didn't want to spend the night with him.

God, Olivia, you're so weak.

A guy puts his mouth on your boobs one time and suddenly he's all you can think about?

Even after said guy slammed your heart in his front door?

Start thinking with your head instead of your lady parts!

When I get to the office, the elevator crawls to the fourth floor. Will Asher be more excited to see me or the crêpes?

It better be me.

Because crêpes don't kiss the way I do.

I'm stopped in front of his office when I realize the joke's on me. Because apparently me and my crêpes don't kiss as well as Bree does.

She has Asher pushed against the wall, her lips on his and her hands in his hair. She didn't trip. His lips didn't break her fall. They're kissing.

Bree and Asher.

Kissing.

The plate shatters at my feet. There's Nutella on my shoe. And Asher is raw-lipped when he pushes Bree away.

"Olivia," he says.

Bree can't even look me in the eyes.

It's like she's embarrassed or something.

But the only person who should be embarrassed is me. Because I put Asher on a pedestal when I shouldn't have. And I trusted Bree when I was warned I shouldn't.

"Ana's looking for you," I say and then I leave with what little dignity I have left.

Asher's face is the last thing I see before the elevator closes.

* * *

I'm on the subway, drying my eyes with a napkin from *McDonalds*, when I get the notification from the *New York Post*.

The gasp I make wakes up the homeless man sleeping in the seat in front of me.

WHEN HOLLYWOOD'S TRIPLE THREAT, LEVI BOOKER, BECOMES AN ACTUAL THREAT: NONDISCLOSURE AGREEMENTS, DRUGS, AND SEXUAL ASSAULT

Victim testimonies and how his team of accomplices worked to protect him.

—by Asher McGowan

17

I'M stress-eating stuffed French toast at a Cuban diner with Emanuel. We can't refresh Twitter fast enough. It stalls and freezes, greeting us with an error message with every flick of a finger.

Asher broke the internet.

And my heart.

But that's not really a top priority right now.

Because we can't even get to our office building. Reporters have taken the entire block hostage. It's all flashing cameras and journalists asking questions and demanding answers. It's our PR firm's living, breathing nightmare.

The story went viral in minutes. Joey called from Oslo. Anouk showed up at the apartment with Natasha and Paloma on FaceTime. No one could comprehend that of all the people in the world to expose Levi Booker, it was Asher McGowan.

And now everyone is talking and tweeting and hashtagging. Dozens of victims have come forward, bravely sharing their stories after being silenced for too long. They have control of their lives back, no longer living under the thumb of River McGowan and free from the threats of Levi Booker. I know this isn't the end for them. I know that they have trauma and pain to overcome, but I hope they can find some peace in sharing their truth.

And the fact that Levi got arrested.

At the Winter Wonderland Gala.

Which is the best Christmas present I never had to ask for.

"When I gave that intern from *CNN* my phone number," Manny says, glancing down at his phone, "it wasn't to give him story leads."

"So you mean he *didn't* give Anderson Cooper the inside scoop on *you*?"

"Obviously not," he mutters. "I would have told you if he rolled up to my seventh floor walk up looking for a good time."

"Not sure he'd make it up all the stairs alive," I say. "Would you really want his death on your conscience?"

"Please, he's in better shape than men half his age."

Well.

I can't argue with that.

"*Anyway*," he says, stealing a bite of my French toast. "What's up with you and Asher? You showed up together at the gala before everything turned into an episode of *Cops*."

"Yeah, well," I mumbled into my coffee mug. "Things were going great until I caught him with Bree."

Manny drops his fork with a force that almost cracks the plate. "I'm sorry. *What?*"

"Bree and Asher," I say. "Kissing in his office."

"No." He shakes his head. "Absolutely not."

"I saw it with my own two eyes," I say. "I'm pretty sure Bree wasn't checking for cavities with her tongue."

Not that Asher has any cavities. The jerk flosses after every meal.

"I just don't… *Bree?* Asher hates her more than I do, which is *a lot*. Like, are you sure? What did they say when they saw you?"

"I left before they could say anything," I say. "You know what they say about actions speaking louder than words."

"Ugh, *Liv*." Emanuel's head hits the table with a thump. "Bree is literally Ursula trying to steal your voice. She wants you to hate Asher so you become a miserable toad like her. I can't believe Asher didn't try to come after you. Does he not understand how happy endings work?"

Well.

He *did* call me a dozen times and he *may* have shown up at my apartment, but Anouk told him to go to hell in seven different languages. But whatever. If I meant something to him, he would have stopped Bree before the kissing started.

Or maybe I have it all wrong and Asher was the one that initiated all the kissing.

Maybe I am just another intern to him.

But I can't worry about that now. Because my phone won't stop ringing. And the text messages and emails just keep coming. And I have no idea what to do first.

So I order another round of stuffed French toast, and start fielding calls from all the major media outlets.

* * *

Ana shoves a handful of popcorn into her mouth as we watch the recap of River McGowan walking into court on a sixty-five inch TV. The fire is roaring, the face masks are foaming, and justice is being served.

"I can't believe I ever agreed to work with him," Ana says, grabbing more popcorn from the bowl she has resting on her bump. "What a slime ball. I hope he rots."

I take a break from tickling Lily's toes to look over at Ana. "How's the transition going?"

"Good," she says. "It's a lot of lawyer talk and business garbage. We'll stay in the same offices, make some staffing adjustments, and most importantly—drop the McGowan from our name."

"So just Loveridge International?" I ask.

"I'm thinking WLS International," she says. "Willa. Lily. Scarlett."

"Scarlett?" I ask. "Are you having another girl?"

Ana nods, giving her belly a little tap of love and affection.

"She thinks she's so clever," Willa says.

"She's bloody brilliant," Ollie says from his spot on the floor. He, too, has on a bubble face mask and he's strumming his guitar like a jet-lagged zombie.

He surprised Willa last night. The recap of their reunion was all very romantic. There was hiding in closets and flying elbows and bruised ribs. Screaming profanities and a crying baby. A real *Hallmark* classic. If I wasn't in such a state of distress, I would have written an entire fan fiction about how much I love them together.

"Is my face supposed to feel numb?" Ollie asks.

"Depends," Willa says.

"On what?"

"Does your face feel numb?"

"Yes."

"Then maybe you should go wash your mask off."

I laugh when I see Ollie glaring at Willa. Because even when his face is foamy and he's annoyed, he still looks at her like she's the best thing that has ever happened to him.

I don't let the jealous twinge in my stomach consume me. Instead, I focus on Lily and her determination to fit her entire foot in her mouth. How can I be sad when I have a seven-month-old baby on my lap? I'm pretty sure her laugh is the key to solving world peace.

"Who wants to take one for the team and go get me more popcorn?"

Willa looks over at me, exhausted from a long day of entertaining Lily *and* Ollie. Walking the ten feet to the kitchen would surely be her demise.

"I'll go," I say, passing Lily off to her.

I walk the few steps to the kitchen, passing a wall of family pictures that makes my heart ache more than I care to admit. I almost didn't come when Ana invited me over. I love spending time with her and Willa and Lily, but it's a constant reminder of a relationship I'll never get back.

The doorbell rings as I set the timer on the microwave and I hear a collective groan from the living room.

"Ollie!" Willa shouts. "The delivery guy's at the door. He could be a psycho, so I think you should answer it."

"Pretty sure Postmates doesn't hire psychos," he shouts back.

"Pretty sure Postmates doesn't have an in-depth employee screening process."

"Pretty sure if he is a psycho, he'd give you right back," he says. "I'd be more worried about me. I'm a hot commodity, Willa. Your boyfriend's a rock star."

While I could listen to their back and forth banter all night, the Postmates guy is probably ready to take our dim sum home for himself.

"I got it," I say, already walking down the hall. The apology is on the tip of my tongue when I pull open the door, but it never comes out.

Because it's not the delivery guy standing out on the stoop.

It's Asher. Chapped-lipped and shivering against the Park Slope backdrop. Usually surly and annoyed, tonight he looks tired and defeated.

"I'm not stalking you," he says, his hands tucked into the pockets of his navy blue peacoat. "I didn't know you'd be here."

"Yeah," I say. "Funny how I show up in the most unexpected places."

I turn around, afraid my body would deceive me if I looked at him any longer. But before I can take a step, I feel his hand brush mine.

"O," he says softly. "You have to know—"

"I think it's very obvious that I don't know anything," I say, pulling away from him. "Don't touch me."

"I'm sorry."

It's funny—I don't even know what he's apologizing for.

But what I do know is that I need to leave. Not even the best dim sum in Brooklyn is enough to convince me to stay in the same vicinity as Asher.

"Asher! Mate!" Ollie jogs down the stairs and practically bodyslams Asher into a hug.

"I see you've stopped arguing with Tories on Twitter long enough to catch a flight out of the UK," Asher laughs.

"What can I say? I'm very passionate and they're a bunch of soggy twats."

"How vivid." Asher frowns.

They follow me back into the living room where Ana and Willa are taking turns making Lily laugh. Three minutes ago, I would have joined right in. But now I can't get my coat on fast enough.

"Asher." Ana's face falls when she sees him. "How was your meeting with Vivian?"

"Long," he says. "And expensive. Lawyers don't believe in family discounts."

"What's our next move?"

"Getting all the testimonies in order," he says. "On a more positive note, my father and brothers are never going to speak to me again. It only took twenty-seven long years."

"How are you feeling about everything?"

"I don't know," he says. "I have a lot on my mind. I don't think it's hit me yet."

He's had a lot on his mind? Like Bree? And her lips? And her knock-off Gucci loafers? Bet they kept him up last night.

"At least I have one less stop to make on Christmas," he laughs.

"Are you going out to Connecticut? With your grandparents?" Ana asks.

"No, I'm staying in the city with Morgan and Vivian," he says. "What are you guys doing?"

"We're spending Christmas with Vinny's family, and then we're hopping on a plane to Auckland after New Year's to see my parents. Because flying twenty hours with a seven-month-old is exactly what I wanted for Christmas," she says. "Olivia, what are you doing for the holiday?"

"Oh, y'know, seeing family upstate," I lie, eyeing the front door. This is not a conversation I want to be involved in. "I have to get going, though. I have Christmas presents to wrap. And *Love Actually* is on tonight. And, *oh*, I think I left my curling iron on—"

"Olivia—"

"Thanks for dinner!"

"You didn't eat," Willa says.

"Oh, well, thanks for the popcorn!"

I run out of there faster than I've ever run before. I get halfway to the subway station before I realize I still have my face mask on.

* * *

To: *Loveridge & McGowan Employee Network*
Cc: *Ana Loveridge-Herrera*
From: *Olivia Langley*
Subject: *Secret Santa Swap!*

Secret Santa's making their list and checking it twice! They're gonna find out who keeps replying to all on every global email!

I hope everyone's enjoying working from home for the rest of the year! Our company Christmas party has been moved to the **Roof on Seventh** on December 19th at 7:00 p.m. Come and enjoy the open bar and hors d'oeuvres, and bring your Secret Santa Swap gifts!

Yours truly,
O. Langley
Social Media Intern & Santa's Executive Helper
Loveridge & McGowan International
98 W 52nd St, New York, NY 10019
olivialangley@lmi.com

* * *

I would die for mini grilled cheese sandwiches. Golden-brown bread. Gooey gruyere. Tangy cranberry chutney. And so much butter.

Honestly, I might die *because of* mini grilled cheese sandwiches.

I'm working on my fifth—okay, *sixth*—mini grilled cheese with no signs of stopping. After living off of dry cereal for a week, I've become a ravenous mama bear after a long, *long* winter. Maybe I can shove some into my bra. There are shot glasses of truffle mac and cheese… I bet they'll fit in my purse.

Wow.

All this gruyere is going to my head. I need to pace myself.

And get some wine.

I'm pleasantly surprised by the turnout for the Christmas party. I was half-expecting to be the only one to show up, but my colleagues proved me wrong. Though, I do have a hunch they're here for the open bar. And since we're working remotely, no one has had a chance to gossip around the dairy-free milk cooler. There's a lot to catch up on.

One noticeable absence—not that I *noticed* or anything—is Asher.

Color me sugar-plum fairy shocked.

"Olivia?"

I'm standing in front of my happy place—the mini grilled cheese display—with a glass of mulled wine. I channel whatever zen I have left from the yoga class Paloma dragged me to yesterday. Nothing can ruin this moment.

Not even Bree.

I'm one with the mini grilled cheeses.

"Look," Bree says. "We should talk."

I laugh. Because, well, that's what you do when someone says something completely outrageous.

"If you're looking to compare notes," I say, "I'm not interested."

"I'm not—that's not what I want to talk about," she says. "I want to apologize."

I take a slow sip of my drink, allowing the wine to warm the back of my throat. Bree never apologizes for anything. Not when she bumps into people on the street. Or when she closes a door on someone's face. I'm pretty sure *sorry* isn't in her vocabulary.

"I was upset," she says. "River... there's a lot you don't want to know about that... and I saw Asher going to the office and I... I don't know what I thought."

"You didn't think." I take another sip of wine.

"No, I didn't," she says, her eyes drifting to the floor. She's wearing her knock-off Gucci loafers... or maybe they're vintage. Who knows? Emanuel would have a field day right now. "I saw the way Asher was with you—the way he looked at you. And I guess—I don't know. I figured like father, like son, right? Women are dispensable to men in their circle. I didn't realize that it wasn't like that with you and Asher. I didn't know it was real."

I scoff and down the rest of the wine. "It wasn't real."

We were fake.

Fake.

Fake.

Fake.

"Well, whatever it was, I had no right to kiss him," she says. "I'm the one that blindsided him in his office. He didn't initiate anything, so you shouldn't be upset with him."

"And who should I be upset with, Bree?" I ask. "You? The girl I've worked with for a year? The girl I thought was some weird version of a friend? The girl who kissed the guy that I *may have* had a thing with because she was what? Jealous? Lonely? Because she needed validation from a man? Is that who I should be upset with?"

"Yeah, that's exactly who you should be upset with," she says. "I'm sorry, Olivia."

Bree walks over to the circular table in the center of the room where all the gifts are. She places a box on it that's wrapped in metallic red paper adorned with a gold bow, and then she forces a smile at Alba before she walks over to the elevators.

The jealous twinge I felt when I saw her kissing Asher is replaced with guilt. I always thought Bree was sad, but I've never been able to place why. I've also never understood why I was always her target. What do I have that she doesn't?

"*You're a good person, Olivia,*" Asher told me at the children's hospital. "*Money can't buy that.*"

And sure, I get that. But it still doesn't explain why she resents me so much. All I ever wanted was to be her friend.

"Everything okay?"

Ana's voice cuts through my thoughts, and when I look over at her, she's reaching for the last mini grilled cheese. It's a devastating sight, but it's not like I can wrestle it out of a pregnant woman's hand. I haven't completely lost my mind.

"Did you offer Bree a job?"

"No, I didn't."

"She did good work."

"She did."

"Then why not hire her?"

Ana takes a deep breath. "Because there comes a point when you have to put a person before a business. And as a mother, I couldn't put Bree in the line of fire when I know she has deep-rooted self-worth issues that she needs to address."

"River took advantage of her." I frown.

"There have been a lot of Rivers in Bree's life," Ana says. "But she's taking a timeout for a while, which I think will be good for her. And once she's ready, I told her she'll have a place at WLS."

"That's really nice of you," I tell her.

"What can I say?" She smiles. "I love a good redemption story."

Ana leaves me with a lot to think about, which, after two glasses of wine and a dozen mini grilled cheeses, is not a good combination. I'm so distracted that I miss the entire Secret Santa Swap. I don't know if Eleanor liked her mittens and necklace.

I don't even know who my Secret Santa was.

But I must have been on their Naughty List.

Because I didn't get a gift.

18

"Olivia! Hi, it's Morgan. Chloe wanted me to remind you that her Christmas pageant is this morning. I know that things must be crazy for you right now with the holidays and all, but I just wanted to see if you could make it. You've made quite an impression on her and she would love it if you joined us. It's at City Academy down in Union Square. East 14th and 5th."

I HAVE TWO OPTIONS:

1. I can hide out in *Trash & Treasure* and try on vintage dresses all day.

2. I can woman up and walk down the block to City Academy and watch Chloe Fisher-Walton sing her heart out.

It's an easy choice.

I pay Buzz at the register, wish him a Happy Hanukkah, and brace myself for the harsh wind that has left New York City cold and raw.

I pull my jacket tighter as I cross the street with a herd of tourists, who all stop in the middle of the road to take pictures of a *Reebok* store. I was like them once, so I quickly skirt around them and walk the block to City Academy. Outside of the school, there's a long line of shivering parents. I spot Morgan and Vivian.

And, of course, Asher.

I knew he was going to be here. It's why I was so hesitant to come. Sure, I knew that the kiss was all Bree. And yeah, deep down, I probably knew that all along. But still, it's a lot to take in and I just want to enjoy the last few days of the holiday season without thinking about Asher and the way my heart seems to race whenever I'm around him.

"Olivia!" Morgan waves me over. "You made it!"

"Yeah," I say, avoiding Asher's gaze. "I didn't keep you waiting, did I?"

"Oh, no," Vivian says. "They haven't let us in yet. We pay thirty grand a year for them to keep us outside until *exactly* nine o'clock."

"Well, maybe they'd let us in early if *someone* didn't try to start a filibuster at the Memorial Day assembly over the amount of seats another parent was saving," Morgan says.

"She was saving *two* rows. It was my civic responsibility to say something."

"Right," Morgan laughs.

"Anyway." Vivian turns to me. "I talked to the CEO of the hotel as well as the owner of the restaurant. It turns out that Ivan has a laundry list of complaints no one was doing anything about."

My stomach twists at the mere mention of his name. I never want to think about him again.

"Viv, I thought we agreed no lawyer talk?" Morgan narrows her eyes to her wife.

"I know, I know," Vivian says. "I just want Olivia to know that she's a priority. And not just because Asher calls me about it twelve times a day, but because it's a matter I'm passionate about."

"I appreciate it, Vivian," I say. "I don't know how I can ever repay you."

Literally.

I can't ever repay her.

Her retainer is probably my salary for the next ten years.

They let us in the school a few minutes after nine, and we walk up three flights of stairs until we reach the auditorium, which looks exactly like a lecture hall at a university. In fact, the whole school resembles a college—a privately funded college. Everything is crisp and clean and in tip-top condition. The heat here? It actually works. I remember the days at my elementary school when we had to wear our jackets all day. I bet they have a salad bar here. And a frozen yogurt machine.

"Oh, Olivia! We should switch," Morgan says as she follows Asher into the second row of seats. Before I can put up a fight, she squeezes by me to grab the seat next to Vivian.

And me…

Well, I now have to share an armrest with Asher.

I've shared a car with him. A hotel room. A couch. A bed. And yet nothing has made me as nervous as this. Us in an auditorium. Separated by an armrest. Next to his sister. In front of his niece. I might break out in hives.

"Ash, why are you being so quiet?" Morgan leans over to look Asher in his super broody eyes.

"I'm not," he says.

"You've said all of two words since getting here."

"Some of us don't talk to hear our own voice, Morgan."

"Ugh, you're such a bear," she says, collapsing back into her chair. "I don't know how you work with him, Olivia. You should be sworn into sainthood."

Pretty sure saints don't let their boss touch their butt.

Thank God the rest of the auditorium is making conversation because we're suffocating in silence over here. Asher hasn't complained once about my breathing or my shaking leg, which is a Christmas miracle in and of itself. Asher's favorite thing to do is complain.

Mostly about me.

"Why are you shaking?" he whispers.

Damn. That lasted long.

"I'm not."

"Yes, you are?"

"I'm cold."

"Do you want my jacket?"

"No, I'm fine."

I'm already wearing a jacket. Why would I need his? To drape over my lap? So I can smell like him for the rest of the day? I don't think so. I'm not that much of a glutton for punishment. I might love his choice of Tom Ford cologne, but I love my dignity much, *much* more.

We'll ignore the fact that that's an absolute lie.

Thankfully, the school principal enters from stage left and announces the beginning of the Christmas pageant. We sit through the kindergarteners' adorable rendition of *Frosty the Snowman* before Chloe's first grade class takes their turn on stage. Chloe's enthusiasm puts the rest of the kids to shame. She has Christmas bows in her hair and Christmas tree sunglasses shielding her eyes. She's wearing a string of green tinsel around her neck like a scarf. Is it socially acceptable to raid the closet of a six-year-old?

For the entire performance of *Jingle Bells*, I forget how cosmically bad the past week has been. Because I see the look of pure adoration when I glance over at Morgan and Vivian, and Asher is smiling the way he always does when he sees Chloe. It's been so long since I've felt part of a family. I almost forgot what it's like to belong.

When the show is over, I wait outside with Asher and Morgan while Vivian signs Chloe out of school for the rest of the day.

"Okay, what's going on with you two?" Morgan asks, crossing her arms. She looks between me and Asher like she's about to start an interrogation.

"Nothing," Asher says.

"You've barely spoken a word to each other," she says, looking at him. "What did you do?"

"Morgan, just let it go," Asher sighs, shoving his hands into his pockets.

"I most certainly will not let it go. When have I ever let *anything* go?"

"Never."

"So? What's going on—"

"Olivia!" Chloe shrieks. "Uncle Asher!"

It doesn't take her long to launch herself into Asher's arms with a force that leaves him stumbling into a No Parking sign.

"Jesus," he coughs. "You're gonna break my back."

"Because you're old?" she asks. "Mommy says youth is wasted on you."

"Mommy and her sage wisdom," he scoffs.

"What's that mean?"

"It means that Mommy is the smartest person *ever*," Morgan says.

"Except you're really bad at *Jeopardy*," Chloe says, hugging her arms around Asher's neck. "But you make a really good grilled cheese."

"Thanks for keeping me humble, babe."

"Humble? Isn't that the girlfriend app you told Uncle Asher to use before he met Olivia?"

Asher's eyes flare up and I'm pretty sure he'd be pinching the bridge of his nose if his hands weren't full. Asher on a dating app? Exactly what I want for Christmas.

"Chloe, I have a Christmas gift for you," I say, holding out the paper bag from *Trash & Treasure*.

She smiles. "Do you want me to save it for Christmas morning?"

"That's up to you," I say. "And your moms, of course."

"Will you be at our house with Uncle Asher on Christmas?"

"Oh, no, I won't."

"Why not?" she frowns. "You're Uncle Asher's girl-friend. That means you have to eat pancakes with us on Christmas morning. Then you get to watch me open up all of my presents."

"Chloe," Vivian says, narrowing her eyes. "Olivia probably has plans with her family."

"Oh! Are you going to spend it with your mom? Will you give her the card I made for her?"

My throat goes a little tight, but I force a smile. "Of course."

Asher's eyes catch mine as he sets Chloe on the ground. I don't let him hold my stare for long. It's too unnerving, like he knows something I don't want him to know. Mind reading is a violation of Christmas spirit.

I turn to Chloe and watch her tear into the bag with grabby hands. It takes her .45930248 seconds to rip it apart. She holds up the pink vintage leather jacket for all of 5th Avenue to see.

"This. Is. So. Cool!" she shrieks, throwing herself at me. She's the epitome of *though she be but little, she is fierce.*

"Chloe, what do you say?"

"Thank you, Olivia!" She squeezes me so tightly that I lose my breath. "Are you gonna come to breakfast with us?

I'm getting Nutella stuffed French toast. I'll share with you."

"I appreciate the invite, but—"

"You want another raincheck?" She frowns.

God, how do I say no to that face? No wonder Asher spoils her rotten. Disappointing this child should be a crime.

"You should come," Asher says with the same look of hope Chloe has.

I want to say yes. I want to live in this feeling that I belong. But everything is still so fresh and I don't know how I feel about anything. Just that I'm hurt and confused and definitely in love.

"I'm sorry, I… have an appointment… with my gyne-cologist. Reproductive health is important, y'know? Nothing says holiday cheer quite like a pap smear! Oh, that rhymed. I should pitch it as tagline. Or put it on a card. I should… go. Bye!"

As I run off down the street—ashamed to stick around for their reactions—I contemplate stepping in front of a delivery truck.

For the second time today, I'm sitting in an auditorium. This time, it's not a bunch of first graders entertaining me —it's an entire company of dancers. Francesca flits around the stage like a nimble-legged gazelle. She's all high-kicks and pirouettes. I wonder if spinning so much makes her dizzy.

I'm front row, stage left at this matinee performance. When Francesca prances over to my side, I wave stupidly. She doesn't wave back, obviously, but she must have noticed me because right before the show ends, an usher, *well,* ushers me backstage.

I follow the trail of glitter and bandaid wrappers to a dressing room where two dozen dancers are wrestling off their leotards. Francesca is topless and smiling when she greets me.

"Why didn't you tell me you were coming?" She pulls on a chunky black sweater. "I could have gotten you in for free."

"I didn't know I was coming until I walked by the theater," I say.

The city is the best distraction. Belligerent taxi drivers. Christmas music spilling out of revolving doors. Bells jingling. Phones ringing. Busy chatter and blaring sirens. My track-by-track playlist titled *How to Avoid My Problems.*

Walking.

Three hours. Up and down and all around the city. Never idling long enough to remember what I'm running away from.

My thoughts.

I knew if I went home, I'd just sit and stew until I drove myself crazy. So I walked and walked and walked until I ended up in front of *Radio City Music Hall.*

"You want to grab coffee?" she asks, shoving her bruised feet into a pair of boots. "I have an hour break before I need to get ready for the next performance."

We end up at an over-crowded café across the street from the theater, cramming into two seats at the window bar. Francesca sips green tea. I inhale a triple shot. We split a raw vegan date brownie.

"How's Brent?" I ask. "Did he survive Vegas?"

"Barely," she laughs. "But he's good now. He did a three day juice cleanse and a vitamin drip."

"Sounds expensive."

Francesca laughs. "How's Asher? I read the article. It was intense."

"We... haven't really talked."

"About the article? Or in general?"

"In general," I say. "Remember when I said I wasn't sure if we were going to work out? Yeah, well, we didn't."

"Oh, Liv," she sighs and pushes the weird date bar towards me, like it's the glue for my broken heart. It's more likely to pull out a filling. "Is there anything I can do?"

"No," I say. "It's not like it was serious."

"Liv—"

"Honestly, it wasn't even real."

"What?"

"We weren't together—not really," I say. "When we saw you at the tree lighting and you looked so happy, I wanted you to think Asher was happy too. I kinda forced him into this whole fake dating thing. Why? I'm not even sure. My plans tend to backfire. You turned out to be awesome and Asher ended up being really easy to fall in love with. And now I'm just the fake ex-girlfriend with a broken heart."

She laughs. Breathy and light. Like I've just said the most ridiculous thing she's ever heard.

"Olivia, it was never fake for him. I mean, maybe at the beginning but not at the end."

I replay that the whole walk home.

It was never fake for him.

It was never fake for him.

It was never fake for him.

I'm out of breath after climbing up three flights of stairs. I'm not really sure what a heart attack feels like, but I think I'm having one. I want to fall face-first onto my bed.

There's a package leaning against my door. It's large

and thin. Three feet by two feet wrapped in brown packaging paper with a red satin bow tied around it. Either UPS is stepping up their game, or someone hand-delivered this. I'm curious and creeped out.

Please don't be from Levi.

Please don't be from Levi.

Please don't be from Levi.

I step closer and read the tag.

To: O
From: Your Secret Santa

My Secret Santa? I thought they had forgotten about me.

I fight my keys into all three locks and open my door, dragging the package in with me, which is hard when it's basically as tall as I am. When I rip it free from the paper, my heart drops into my stomach.

It's the Nawaar Qadir photo I saw at the gallery.

Midnight in Roma.

A tear slips down my cheek.

And then another.

And another.

Asher.

19

CHRISTMAS MORNING IS a mess of hairnets and mini chocolate chip muffins. I'm at the women's shelter putting on my bravest face. My problems don't compare to what they're going through, so I smile and laugh with them while they tell me about their past and present and their hopes for the future.

I get home just before noon and change back into my pajamas before falling into the heaping pile of blankets on the couch. *Home Alone* is playing on the TV, but I don't have the energy to pay attention. I want to sleep the day away. Wake me up in 2020.

Christmas Day always makes me sad. Much like all good things, the holiday season must come to an end. And I'm never ready to say goodbye—to let go of the tinsel and the cheer and the peppermint mocha lattes. It's my favorite distraction. Because when I'm not blitzed out on gingerbread cookies and perfectly tied ribbon, I have too much time to think about how sad I am and how empty I feel and how much I miss my mom.

Because I miss her so much.

And sometimes that feeling consumes me.

And I slip into a place that's so dark that I don't know if I'll ever find my way out.

That's what death does to you—it eats you alive until you're a hollow shell of a human who lives in a limbo of grief and guilt and denial.

It's been almost three years and I don't think I've ever said it out loud.

My mom is dead.

Three words. Sharp as a knife. They cut right through me.

Much like the sound of my phone does.

It's Joey. If I don't pick up, she'll keep calling.

"Remember what we talked about before I left?" she says before I can say *hello*.

"I'm not setting the apartment on fire."

"You don't have to *actually* do it," she says. "We're just pretending. I would *never* ask you to commit arson. Unless it involved Levi. But even then, I'd want to do it myself."

My stomach twists at the mention of his name. It's bad enough I have to hear it on the news and read it in the papers. I don't want to listen to Joey go on and on about how she wants to drench him in gasoline and set him on fire.

"Speaking of… how's everything going?"

"It's… going?" I roll onto my back, bringing the fleece blanket up to my chin. "I don't know. It's too hard to get through all the articles. I don't know much more than the rest of the world."

"And how are things with Asher?"

Maybe I should drench myself in gasoline and set the apartment on fire.

I mean, it's what Joey wants.

"He bought me a five thousand dollar photograph."

"*Damn*," she whistles. "The man's got it bad. Have you talked to him?"

"Not really. I went to his niece's Christmas pageant, but we didn't talk much. I'm just... so upset about how the Levi situation went down. Like, he could have told me, y'know? Let me in on it, so I wasn't completely blindsided by it. And then everything with Bree happened—"

"She told you she kissed him," Joey says. "You can't blame him for that. I was under the impression that he never liked her all that much."

"Yeah, well."

"Well what?"

I groan and throw my head back, knocking it against the arm rest. I groan again. A concussion is exactly what I wanted for Christmas.

"I liked it better when you never talked to me," I mumble.

"You have this habit of inserting yourself into someone's life and leaving a lasting impression," she says. "You need to talk to him. So much has happened over such a short period of time and—"

A perfectly timed knock echoes from the door.

"I have to go, Jo," I say, kicking off the blankets. "Someone's here."

"What did you say, Olivia? The fire department is there? The apartment is on fire? Oh my—"

I end the call and toss my phone back onto the couch. It bounces onto the floor.

It's noon on Christmas Day, so I don't know who could possibly be visiting. It's either the kids upstairs securing their place on next year's Naughty List, or it's Mrs. Laghari next door, who always needs to borrow a cup of sugar that we never have.

So when I pull the door open and it's someone else, my heart drops all the way down onto E 17th Street.

"Asher."

His eyes meet mine briefly—hesitantly—before they fall onto his feet, like he's admiring the worn leather of his Saint Laurent boots, which honestly, is a very Asher thing to do. Always so put together, I'm surprised to find him standing in front of me in a pair of black jeans that have been worn one too many times without washing and a wrinkled maroon crewneck. His hair is wrangled underneath a beanie, but a few wisps have broken free.

He's holding a brown paper bag in one hand and a box of donuts in the other.

"They didn't have any strawberry frosted, so I hope chocolate's okay."

For the first time since learning how to talk, I forget how to speak. My brain can't articulate words—just feelings. And I'm feeling everything at once. An ache in my chest. A dizzying sense of grief. Jarring happiness. Paralyzing shock. I'm the human embodiment of someone hitting play on every single Taylor Swift song at once.

He remembered what we talked about when we were on the sleigh ride. Of all the things I've said to him over the last year, this is what he remembers.

I'm all frenzied emotions when I grab his face, cradling his cheeks in my shaking hands. I kiss him because I don't know what else to do—because I want to, because I miss him, because even after everything that happened, the feelings I have for him run deeper than anything I've ever felt.

The kiss is soft and slow and salty from the tears I don't realize are falling. I don't want it to end—I want to stand in the doorway until we ring in the new year—but Asher sighs against my mouth and pulls away.

"O," he whispers, dropping his forehead against mine.

God.

I want to kiss him again.

"Come in."

"You sure?"

"Yeah."

He follows me back to the couch, stepping over the boots, jacket, and pants thrown carelessly on the floor. The apartment isn't a total pit, but it does look like a dryer barfed clothes all over the place. Asher's eyes linger a little too long on a pile of underwear I haven't shoved into a drawer yet.

"I'm surprised Chloe let you out of her sight," I say, sitting down. My mind drifts to the snow day at his house, and how we couldn't sit close enough. Today, there's an entire cushion between us.

"I snuck out when she was distracted by her new puppy."

"They got her a puppy?"

He laughs and leans back into a pillow. "Morgan got her the puppy. It wasn't a mutually agreed upon gift."

"That must have been a fun surprise."

"Yeah, it's kind of terrifying watching them argue."

"*Law & Order* in the flesh?"

"Pretty sure network television would not have let their choice of words fly."

"That's my kind of entertainment."

His lips lift into a soft, shy smile. I smile back, but our eyes barely meet. We're two people who don't know how to act around each other after having gone from one extreme to the next. Sharing a bed. Kissing. Touching. To not speaking at all. We sit in a nervous silence. Just us. The TV. A box of donuts. And Thai takeout.

I want everything to be warm and easy and exciting again.

"Olivia." Asher's lips are pressed together when he looks over at me with the same nervous hesitance that has been flitting around us since he arrived. This is the man who has never hesitated saying anything to me. Ever. "What happened with Bree—"

"I know she came onto you," I say. "I think, deep down, I always knew that. I'm sorry I blew the situation out of proportion."

"You don't need to apologize," he tells me. "I just want you to understand that I'm not my father. Women aren't dispensable to me. I would never take advantage of someone, and I certainly wouldn't abuse my power for some greater personal gain."

"I know you're not your father. Asher, you're nothing like him."

"I've seen the way he treats women my whole life, and I refuse to be like that. I respect your integrity and your dedication to your career too much to jeopardize that with whatever feelings I have for you."

Have.

The feelings he *has* for me.

Present tense.

Meaning he still feels the same way.

"I don't care what people think about me," I say. "And I definitely don't care what they think about us. The only opinion that matters to me is yours."

"And what about your opinion of me?"

I smile at him, and it's the first time in days that it's not forced, fake happiness. Everything I'm feeling is very, very real.

"I think you're wildly cranky and difficult and unreasonable, but underneath all those layers *and layers* of double-toasted-extra-cream-cheese-madness, there is a very passionate and vulnerable man that I'm going to admire for the rest of my life in spite of his terrible taste in bagels and his ridiculous coffee order."

He smiles at me, and I know it's real. Because Asher is as stubborn as he is weird. You have to earn his smiles.

"Not many people have the guts to tell the story you told, Asher."

He twists his body towards me, and sighs. "I'm not the brave one. I was just the one that had the means and the platform. It's the women who are brave."

"You did an amazing thing."

"I'd like to think anyone could have done it."

"I'm sure a lot of people could have," I say. "But not everyone was willing to put their career—or their relationship with their father—on the line."

Asher groans and drops his head to the back of the couch.

"Have you talked to him?"

"Our lawyers have talked," he laughs. "He's suing me for slander, which is hilarious considering the amount of legal documents we have proving what a manipulative prick he is."

"I'm sorry." I close the gap between us. Literally and physically. I place my hand on his knee, and he doesn't miss a beat when he intertwines his fingers with mine.

"I'm not," he says. "Well, I'm sorry I couldn't have done it sooner. I'm not sorry our relationship is over."

"He didn't deserve to have you in his life."

"You sound like my mom."

"Clearly, she's a smart lady," I say. "What's happening with Levi?"

He rolls his eyes. "He's out on bail until his hearing," he says. "But they revoked his passport, so he can't flee the country."

Sometimes our legal system is a complete joke.

"Where do you go from here?" I ask. "Will you keep working for Ana?"

"I have a few meetings after the holidays with some media outlets."

"You want to do more writing?"

"Yeah." He nods. "It's never been my dream to write press releases and moderate interviews. I'd rather be doing something good. Making an impact, y'know?"

"I get it," I say. "Life's too short to not do what you love."

Asher flashes me another one of his smiles, and I have to bite my tongue to avoid making a noise that definitely isn't meant for Jesus' birthday. In fact, someone should throw some holy water in my face.

I'm embarrassed by how gone for him I am.

Watching someone open a box of donuts should not be borderline erotic.

"For the record, the only donuts I'd ever say no to are jelly filled," I tell him.

"I'm offended," he says, pulling out a sugared donut that is very much filled with raspberry jam.

"Ugh, heathen." I grab a chocolate frosted that's covered in red and green sprinkles, and take a bite. This time I can't help the noise I make. Jesus will understand. "These are amazing."

"They came highly recommended by Chloe."

"I'm officially only eating from places that get the Chloe Fisher-Walton Seal of Approval."

"God knows she's more critical than the Board of Health. She keeps trying to get me to make her an Instagram account so she can post pictures of cupcakes."

"Gotta get in on that influencer check before it's all cashed out."

Asher laughs and finishes his donut. When he looks back at me, he rolls his eyes and my stomach flops.

Wow is there anything I haven't missed about him?

"What?" I ask, but he's already swiping his thumb along my bottom lip. He licks off the chocolate.

Wow.

Wow.

Okay.

"You… um, you lied to Ana and Chloe when they asked you what your plans were today," Asher says quietly, almost like he didn't want to say it all.

I knew this question was coming. I'm not shocked that he's curious. I can't expect him to lay everything out on the table and not reciprocate. Relationships aren't one-way streets.

Not that we've defined what we are or aren't or might be.

"It's just easier than explaining the truth," I tell him. "Because if I tell the truth, I bring everyone down. And I don't want people to feel sorry for me, and I don't want to burden anyone. I mean, they're asking a simple question not expecting to get a heavy answer. It's a lot to put on someone."

"You're not a burden."

"Says the man who constantly tells me I drive him crazy."

"You do drive me crazy, but you've never been a burden."

His arm drops around my shoulders, and instinctively my body curls into his. It takes all the self-control I have not to crawl into his lap and live there. I'm not sure how I thought I was going to make it through today alone. I barely made it through last Christmas and the one before that.

"Will you tell me about her?"

My head finds the crook of his neck, and I take a deep breath. He's all vanilla and wood. It's calming.

"She was… everything," I tell him. "My mom and my best friend all rolled into one. She loved Shania Twain and the color green and trashy soap operas. She made the best chocolate chip oatmeal cookies and never went anywhere without a dozen tubes of lip balm.

"She worked so hard to make sure I had everything I needed. Honestly, I'm not sure if she ever slept. She'd pack my lunch everyday and she'd always write a note on the napkin. Some days she'd wake me up and tell me it was a holiday, and I'd skip school and we'd go on an adventure. She was just… the best mom. I was so lucky to have her."

"How long has it been?"

"Three years next month," I say. "She got pneumonia, and there were a lot of complications."

I'm not going to think about that day in the hospital. Not on Christmas. Not when things are just starting to look up. My mom wouldn't want that. She'd tell me to get it together and enjoy this moment, because time is precious and Asher is cute.

She would definitely think Asher is cute.

I bet I'm getting a thumbs up right now.

"Were you by yourself?"

"No," I tell him. "We had a lot of friends and neighbors that made sure I didn't have to go through it alone."

"God, O," he says, kissing the top of my head. "You're so strong."

"She was strong for me my whole life. It's the least I can do to continue to be strong for her."

I feel his lips brush against my hair once more. It's not enough for me. I tilt my head and catch him in a soft kiss.

"Thank you for the photograph," I tell him. "Did you wrap it yourself?"

"I did," he says. "But then Morgan said it looked like crap, so she redid it. I put the bow on, though."

"Did you have to fight Chloe?"

"Yes, and she's a sore loser."

I laugh and laugh and laugh until a few tears stain Asher's sweater. We stay like this for a while, eating our way through half a dozen donuts while all three *Home Alone* movies play in the background. Eventually, I fall asleep on Asher's lap.

Morgan calls at three o'clock, and invites us to the park to walk the newest member of the Fisher-Walton family. I forgo putting jeans back on, and instead find a pair of fleece-lined leggings that don't have a hole in the crotch. I find one boot in the kitchen and another in the living room, and while Asher waits *patiently* by the door, I slip my arms into the jacket he loves so much.

"Ah, electrocuted poodle chic," he says. "You might offend the dog."

"I'm sure the dog appreciates a bargain."

"Yeah, pretty sure this dog only shops at *Bergdorf Goodman*."

He explains during the ride to Washington Square Park that the puppy originally belonged to his godmother, Minerva Tallcot, but was re-homed with Morgan. Apparently, the puppy's queen-bee attitude didn't bode well with Minerva's other diva-ish dogs.

I've heard *rumors*—well, I've read them in tabloids while waiting in line at *Duane Reade*—that each dog has their own personal chef, nanny, and trainer. A tiny puppy who hasn't even had a taste of luxury surely can't be more of a primadonna than the ones drinking water flown in from Switzerland.

I'm proved wrong the second I see this three pound, well-groomed ball of fluff walking Chloe.

Damn. Who knew world domination was at the helm of a purebred Pomeranian?

"Olivia!" Chloe is sprinting to keep up with her potential National Dog Show contender. Behind her, Morgan smiles. Vivian, however, looks like she might use the dog to smother her wife in her sleep.

"Hey, you!" The puppy reaches me first and growls. Either she disapproves of my jacket, or knows that I drink filtered tap water. I definitely don't meet her dignified standards.

"I thought you were spending today with your mom?"

Eventually, I know I'll have to explain the truth to her but not today—not on Christmas.

"What's your puppy's name?" I ask.

Pricilla? Georgina? Madame Cornelia of Greenwich Village?

"Chewbacca."

Well.

Okay.

"Because she already chewed through Mama's favorite pair of shoes."

I glance up in time to see Vivian twitch. "Mama's favorite pair of Louboutins."

"Relax, dear." Morgan nudges her. "I already bought you a new pair. They'll be here on Friday."

"That's. Not. The. Point."

Chewbacca forces my attention back on her by biting my finger.

"*Ow.*"

Chloe giggles. "We're going to call her Miss Chewy for short."

"Miss Chewy certainly likes to chew."

Miss Chewy dismisses me and moves on to Asher, who is wearing Saint Laurent boots and smells like Tom Ford. Clearly *he* meets her high standards.

Same, girl, same.

"Guess what, Olivia?"

"What?"

"We're going to Turks & Hot Cocoa," she says. "Nanny rented us a whole island. Uncle Asher's coming, so that means you have to come too. But even if he wasn't coming, I'd still want you to come."

I look at Asher, who is crouching down next to Miss Chewy. He sighs at his niece's charmingly brash manners. "Turks and *Caicos*."

"That's what I said." Chloe rolls her eyes. "You're gonna come, right? We can get matching bathing suits and drink lemonade all day. You're gonna have to bring lots of sunblock because you're super white like Mommy and Uncle Asher."

"*Chloe*," Morgan laughs.

"I'll talk it over with Asher," I tell Chloe.

"He's right there," she says. "You can talk in front of us. Tell her about the seats in first class, Uncle Asher."

"Chloe," Vivian says. "We've talked about meddling."

Asher laughs. "Maybe you should talk to Olivia about that too."

I don't get a chance to glare at him. Because the moment the first flake of snow touches the tip of Chewbacca's nose, she starts yapping and yapping and yapping. Clearly, she's a lady whose hair must be protected from the natural elements at all costs.

The snow starts falling harder and faster, flurries frozen

on the ground. Morgan wrangles Miss Chewy into her coat and we say quick goodbyes before running in opposite directions.

We end up at Asher's apartment because it's closer. Also, we're freezing and covered in snow, which would have had hypothermic consequences in my apartment.

"I can't feel my toes," Asher whines. "I can't feel my toes."

"You would think those nine hundred dollar boots would come with insulation."

"You would think you wouldn't be so sassy to the man who rescued you from freezing cold hell."

"I have a hunch you have ulterior motives," I say, peeling off my jacket. I hang it in the hall closet along with his.

"And what exactly do you think those ulterior motives are, Ms. Langley?"

"I don't know," I hum. "You tell me, Mr. McGowan."

He doesn't say anything. Instead, he brushes by me and with a gentle graze of his hand, he urges me to follow him upstairs.

"You hungry?" he asks.

"Always."

"We left the food at your place, but I think I have left-over pizza in the fridge."

"Damn, you really know how to make a girl feel special," I laugh. "As long as we pair it with another two hundred dollar bottle of wine."

"You mean you don't want the four dollar bottle from *Trader Joe's*?"

Up in his loft, Asher goes straight for his dresser. He throws a white thermal and a pair of joggers at me. *Sexy.*

I don't bother going into the bathroom to change. Asher doesn't either. I take off my leggings and sweater until I'm standing there in just my lacy, green bra and a pair of panties covered in reindeer. *Super sexy.*

"Do you have a staring problem, Ms. Langley?"

"Maybe." I mean, how can I not? He's standing there in his questionably sized boxer briefs, looking like the whole goddamn Naughty List.

"Are you going to put your clothes on?"

"It seems kind of pointless," I say. "They're just going to come off."

Asher laughs. "I didn't bring you here to have sex, O."

"That's a shame." I frown. "I might die if we don't."

He groans. He feels my pain. He just won't admit it.

"Shouldn't we take things slow?" he asks, leaning against his dresser.

"Why?" I ask and I'm walking over to him before I can stop myself. I slot myself between his legs and slide my hands up his chest. I'm driving him crazy.

"I don't know," he says, quivering when my lips brush over his jaw. "I'd really like to not fuck this up again."

I grin against his skin. "That's sweet, Asher."

"Yeah, well." His hands *subtly* squeeze my ass. "I'm *trying* to be a gentleman."

"Don't," I whisper into his ear.

And that…

That's all it takes.

We're stumbling backwards. All mismatched kisses and groping hands and *pull me closer.* We fall onto his bed and he drags me up until his body is pressing mine into his pillows.

"You have no idea how much I've missed you." He kisses over my neck and jaw before nipping my bottom lip, begging for more. He's desperate. And needy. I love him like this.

He smiles into my lips, and my arms slip around his waist, pulling him closer. God, I need him closer.

"You're all I think about," he tells me, abandoning my lips.

I groan in protest until he kisses down my neck. "What exactly do you think about?"

His lips are dangerously close to my breasts. Ugh, who even invented bras? They should be in prison.

"I think about your smile." He kisses the dip in my chest. "And your laugh…"

"How very wholesome of you."

"I think about how great your ass looks in panties."

"*Excellent.* Tell me more about that," I say as he kisses his way down to the softness of my belly.

"I think about that day I had you sitting on my desk," he whispers into my skin. "I think about how you'd look in my bathtub up to your neck in bubbles."

I giggle.

"Thanks for that, by the way," he says, pulling away from me. "I get hard whenever I look at it now."

"That's rough," I say as he urges me to arch my back. "It's in a very inconvenient location."

"Tell me about it." His lips are back on mine as his clever fingers sneak around my back, unclasping my bra with ease. He throws it somewhere. Out the window, hopefully.

"What about my boobs? Do you think about them?"

"Yeah, once or twice or every second of the day."

"You must really like them."

"They're alright."

I'm giggling with each kiss he peppers along my body, exploring every dip and curve I have. His current trek includes coaxing out sounds that I never knew I could make. And when he licks over the swell of my breast, I realize that I'm so turned on that I might actually combust.

"Can we speed this along?" I ask him. "You can make the next round last all night, but I really think I'm gonna go into a coma if I don't have an orgasm in the next five seconds."

He laughs—laughs!—at me but doesn't change his pace at all. He's just one long, slow kiss after the other. The tease of all teases. Drinking me in like fine wine.

But I am not fine wine!

I'm the four dollar special that you have to drink in five seconds or else it turns into an unbearably horny girl.

"We have all the time in the world, Olivia."

It's slow torture. From the way he kisses down my stomach to the way he nips at the apex of my thigh. For a moment, I forget that it's December. Because right now, I'm mid-July and it's a heatwave and I'm praying and praying for the sun to set and for the humidity to break, but it never does. I'm on edge.

But Asher is not. He's calm and cool and collected, kissing me slow like honey.

It's agony.

But it's the kind of agony that I'd suffer through any time, any day, whenever, and wherever.

"Well," I say after I've been sufficiently ravished. Has it been hours? Days? Weeks? Months? Time is a construct. Orgasms are not. "That wasn't on my Christmas List."

"You mean you didn't ask Santa for multiple orgasms? That's always on my wishlist," Asher laughs after he crawls back into bed. I waste no time gluing myself to his side. He wastes no time putting his hand on my butt.

"You should mention this in my performance review for Ana."

"And what a thorough performance review I conducted."

"It was *very* in depth," I say. "You touched on things I didn't even know existed."

"What can I say? I take my job seriously."

"You're a true professional."

I nuzzle against his chest and we laugh and laugh and laugh because this feels like the most natural thing in the world, like this is where we were always meant to be.

"For what it's worth, I'd really like you to come on vacation with us," he says. "I think it'd be nice to get away from the city for a while."

I hum. "I think you just want to see me in a bikini."

I look up at him and he's still glowing in post-orgasm bliss, his cheeks flushed red. "I mean, yeah, I'm not about to complain about watching you prance around a beach in something tiny."

I hum again. "Will you take Instagram pictures for me?"

"I can't promise they'll be good."

"Don't worry." I lean up and steal his lips, "I'll teach you my angles."

"Does that mean you'll come?"

"Of course," I say. "Who would say no to Turks and Hot Cocoa?"

He kisses me again and again and again, and we get lost in each other for a second time.

Later, I sneak out of bed to go downstairs. From the window, I watch fat flakes of snow blizzard down from the sky. Asher slips behind me, and I lean into the warmth of his chest as he wraps his arms around me. Together, we watch New York City fall asleep beneath a blanket of snow.

EPILOGUE

To: *WLSI Employee Network*
Cc: *Ana Loveridge-Herrera, Asher McGowan*
From: *Olivia Langley*
Subject: *Ring in the New Year*

Get those party hats and noisemakers ready because we're poppin' bottles—on Ana's tab—at the *Gansevoort* rooftop park! Make resolutions! Break resolutions! Kiss your favorite coworker at midnight! Get ready to say goodbye to 2019 and hello to 2020!

On a more serious note, please take advantage of the rideshare gift cards that were emailed to you this morning. We want you to get home safely.

Yours truly,
O. Langley
Social Media Specialist
WLS International
98 W 52ⁿᵈ St, New York, NY 10019

olivialangley@wlsi.com

* * *

Asher

ALBA from human resources has shown me every feature on her new fitness tracker. It's all very thrilling. I might buy one myself. Hell, I might buy the whole company and give it to her. I'd do just about anything to get out of here.

I'm at the *Gansevoort* rooftop park and I've lost the feeling in my toes. New Year's Eve is meant to be enjoyed inside where it's warm and quiet and away from people. My apartment, for example, is a great place to ring in the new year.

And yet here I am.

On a roof.

In the cold.

And where is Olivia?

Not here.

"I swear to God," I hiss into my phone when her voice-mail picks up. "You better be getting murdered."

I tuck my phone into the pocket of my jacket, and white-knuckle my glass of Stella. My girlfriend has a terrible sense of humor. When we go away next month, I hope she gets attacked by a shark.

"Asher!" Ana is glowing as she waddles over to me. "You made it! Where's your better half?"

"I've been asking myself that question for the past hour."

Ana laughs. "This isn't the kind of event I'd imagine she would want to miss."

"Considering she threatened my life if I didn't come, I'm just as surprised as you are."

"I'm sure she has a good reason for not being at a party she planned."

"Oh, of course."

She got distracted by a dog. Or she fell asleep. Or the government got a hold of her conspiracy theory blog and they've taken her to *Area 51* where she belongs.

"We'll have to make plans for dinner when I get back from Auckland," Ana says. "I want to hear how your interviews go."

"Definitely," I tell her. "We'll bring dessert."

"I like the double chocolate cookies from *Levain*."

"I know you do."

Ana excuses herself to mingle. I'm finishing off my beer when my phone buzzes with a new message.

Olivia
Hello

Asher
Have you been abducted by aliens?

Olivia
Yes, they've taken me back to their planet. I'm their queen now.

Asher
Dreams really do come true.
On a more serious, less intergalactic note, where the hell are you?

Olivia
Your place

Asher
Why?

Olivia
Come here and find out

Asher
Can't.
Sorry.
I'm busy trying to find someone to kiss at midnight.

Olivia
How's that working out for you?

Asher
Very well.
I've got a long list of prospects.
I'm a hot commodity.

Olivia
Well then.
Have a Happy New Year, Mr. McGowan.

Asher
I intend to, Ms. Langley.
Hope you're not too lonely.

Olivia
Don't worry about me.
Betsy is keeping me company.

It's practically impossible to find a cab, but I somehow manage to flag one down. I spew off rushed directions and it takes us twenty painful minutes to get to my apartment.

Inside, I mumble a half-hearted hello to the security guard before pushing the elevator button an excessive amount of times.

Why do things take so long?

Humans have evolved enough.

Teleportation should be a thing.

When I finally get upstairs, I fight my key into the lock. Everything is so hard.

And I mean *everything*.

The first thing I see is a pair of black heels that have been carelessly kicked off. I follow their trail to a shimmery gold dress that's thrown over the back of my couch. On the railing of the stairs is a flimsy lace bra, and placed on the fourth step is a pair of barely-there black panties that leave very little to the imagination.

I groan.

And when I step into my loft and see Olivia in the tub, up to her neck in bubbles, sipping a flute of champagne, I think I might die.

I really need to call my realtor and apologize to her. A tub in the bedroom is so not impractical. It's the best thing ever.

"Figured you'd be kissing Harriett from accounting by now," Olivia hums.

"She was a top contender."

Olivia grins slyly at me and it takes all the self restraint I have not to grab her from the tub and throw her on my bed. The honeymoon phase is a very real thing. We've barely left my apartment in a week.

"How was the party?" she asks.

"Over the top," I say. "Ana should really find a new event planner."

"Heard the one she hired was a bit of a flake," she says. "Didn't even show up today."

"So unprofessional."

I'm kneeling beside the tub and I'm living a fantasy I didn't know I had. I'm stupidly in love. It's disgusting.

"I can't believe you've been using this tub as storage when you could have had me in it all this time."

"I'm an idiot."

"The biggest idiot," she says. "You don't deserve to see me so hot and bothered and soapy."

"Surely, I can do something to convince you I'm worthy."

She hums and a smirk toys at her full, red lips. Wrapping her fingers around the collar of my shirt, she pulls me down until our lips meet. The kiss is indulgently slow, her tongue tracing over my bottom lip.

I want to do this for the rest of my life.

"Happy New Year, Asher."

"Happy New Year, Olivia."

THE END

ALSO BY ASHLEY SHEPHERD

The Fine Art of Losing Control

ABOUT THE AUTHOR

Ashley Shepherd lives in Boston where she is a full-time French toast bagel connoisseur. When she's not writing or daydreaming about being in Disney World, she's baking (mostly cupcakes), watching TV reruns (mostly Friends), and shopping (mostly at Target). Her debut novel, The Fine Art of Losing Control, was published on October 7, 2019.

Made in the USA
Las Vegas, NV
30 November 2021

35631431R00185